THE
GUMBALL
EMPRESS

Tennille Jo Mortensen

Dedication

To my niece McKammen – whose ravenous appetite for the written
word prodded me along the journey

Chapter One

No Ordinary Gumball

The fog was so thick I was sure if I stuck my tongue out, I would taste marshmallow fluff. I turned the corner to the bakery shop that I secretly stopped by every morning, knowing full well that my parents would disapprove of any food not containing tofu or edamame. Mr. Martindale, for whom I worked every summer, made the best maple donuts in town. Even after working for him for three summers in a row, I had yet to discover his secret. I wasn't sure if it was the ingredients or Mr. Martindale himself.

His big bald head was shining under the fluorescent glow of the shop lights. His blonde handle bar mustache that extended past his chin was often littered with remnants of his early-morning taste testing, whether it be crumbs or flecks of icing clinging to the bushy mass. His large rounded belly was also evidence that he truly enjoyed his work, right down to the last morsel. At first glimpse, one might mistake Mr. Martindale for a big, scary biker, but I knew better. Despite his rugged appearance, he was the kindest person I had ever met. For some reason, he had taken a liking to me when I was just young, and I truly considered him to be part of my eccentric family.

"Good morning, Elli!" Mr. Martindale greeted me, handing me a sack with my morning indulgence already to go. My given name was actually Ellinnet, but I had revealed that fact to very few people.

"Is it June?" he asked, looking over his small, round reading glasses. It took me a moment to realize he was referring to the strange weather.

"Oh, yeah…the fog. Crazy, isn't it?" I said as I handed him a crumpled dollar bill and collected my donut.

"You ready to start work next week?" he asked.

"If it would get me out of my final exams, I'd be ready right now." He laughed his full-bellied laugh as I turned to leave.

I took a big bite of my donut as I headed toward the door, when something caught my eye. Mr. Martindale had a large gumball machine just to the side of the front door. I'd walked by it a hundred times or more, but this time it was filled with the strangest gumballs I had ever seen. They were black and swirled with a rainbow of colors in the center that almost seemed to leap out at me.

"Are these new?" I asked, turning toward the counter, although I knew the answer. Mr. Martindale, however, had already disappeared into the kitchen. I wasn't much of a gum fan, another forbidden treat in my house, but these were incredible. I shuffled through my backpack for some change. A few paperclips and cracker crumbs later, I finally found two quarters. I dropped them into the slot and turned the knob. Instead of the familiar clink, clink of a turning gear, however, the sound of a rushing river filled my ears. I watched as the gumballs literally rearranged themselves, allowing the gumball sitting on top of the stack to fall through the slot. I hesitated before lifting the cover to retrieve the strange gumball. An eerie feeling crept over me as I touched its spherical shape. I felt warmth spread from my fingertips into my hand and up my arm before permeating my entire body.

I closed my fingers around the mystical gumball as I walked outside. I was still staring at my closed hand when I walked straight into Leo, who was just about to enter the bakery, probably in search of me. Leo was my next-door neighbor and my best friend. His parents were every bit as odd as mine, and we conjectured that they had escaped the same hippie commune before we were born. Even his name, Elleon, was as strange as mine. He had the same dietary restrictions of tofu, soymilk, and homegrown fruits and vegetables only, which forced us both to become experts in the covert acquisition and distribution of banned food items. Though Leo was only seventeen, he was over six feet tall with thick black hair, which invariably boosted his appeal with the female population. We couldn't have been more different, yet I couldn't picture my life without my comrade in arms.

"You okay?" he asked, looking at me with concern etched in his forehead. I shook myself out of my trance, not wanting to try to explain to Leo what had just happened. I was low on sleep as it was and had probably imagined the entire experience.

"Yeah. Great," I lied, an uncomfortable feeling settling over me as I stuffed the gumball into my backpack. "You ready for that history final?"

"As ready as I'll ever be," he said as we started toward the crosswalk. We only had four more days of school before summer break.

"Hey, did you see that fog this morning?" he asked. It was only then that I realized the fog had dissipated. The sky was cloudless, and the sun was already gearing up for a summer scorching. Even without a mirror, I knew my black hair had taken on its notorious purple hue, as it always did in the sun. I assumed the purple tint came from the inordinate number of blueberries I consumed, regards of my mother. She had a soft spot for blueberries and put them in absolutely everything she made from her spinach blueberry morning smoothie to her homemade shampoo.

"Weird, huh?" I muttered, still lost in the strangeness of my morning while trying to keep history facts at the forefront of my mind until I could do a brain dump after the final exam.

"You gonna eat that?" Leo asked, gesturing to my donut.

"Strange, but no," I said as I handed it over to him, suddenly feeling slightly nauseous.

"There's something definitely wrong with you if you're freely relinquishing this little taste treat," he mumbled while stuffing the donut into his mouth.

"Just test day jitters, I guess," I replied with a shrug. I couldn't wait for my exams to finally be over. Unlike Leo, I wasn't a natural at school. In fact, he had become my unofficial tutor during the past year. The guy drove me nuts because he could ace every exam and assignment without even studying. I, on the other hand, could study for hours and hours and barely pull a B grade average, not that my parents cared. I had to beg them to let me attend public school after enduring a childhood of homeschooling, which didn't really include much schooling in the traditional sense of the word. Leo didn't attend school until I did either, but he picked up on things so much quicker than I. Though he was a year younger, we had been placed in the same grade. I was already eighteen and just finishing up my junior year of high school.

Mr. Martindale taught me to read and write and encouraged me to attend school. Of course, my parents didn't know that. He did it on the sly when my parents thought I was selling produce at the farmer's market. I did sell all the produce I ever took to the market because Mr. Martindale himself bought it – all of it. My parents didn't particularly care for Mr. Martindale, which I never really understood. They definitely would have objected if they had known that one of my favorite activities during the summertime was kicking my feet up in Mr. Martindale's backyard while drinking ice cold lemonade. He had the most amazing flower garden, complete with gazing balls, water fountains, and the whole nine yards. That was by far my favorite place aside from the rooftop ledge outside my second story bedroom window. Oh, I couldn't wait for summer to come.

"I had that dream again last night," Leo confessed. For over a year now he had a recurring dream at least twice a month. Lately, he was having it almost once a week, sometimes more. Had I not been so distracted, I probably could have guessed without being told. He had dark circles under his eyes again this morning.

"Anything different this time?" I wondered.

"No," he affirmed. "Same old thing. Everything goes dark, and I can't see anything until two eyes pop up in the sky. Just white balls – no pupils or anything, but somehow, I know they're eyes, and they're watching me." He shuddered before continuing, "It's so creepy, El. I can't shake it even now."

"And the girl?" I prodded.

"Same deal. I can see her hand beckoning for me as if she's in danger, but her face is hidden in the darkness. It's just this arm hovering in mid-air, frantically motioning for me to come, but I can't move. And then it just gets stuck on repeat – the same thing over and over all night. I need to help her. I want to help her. I…" he let his voice trail off, and I saw him try to hide a blush. I waited for him to continue, but he didn't.

"You what?" I urged. He shook his head, indicating he wasn't going to tell me. I punched him in the arm.

"You what, Leo?"

"I feel like I'm supposed to be with her…that I have to be with her…that I love her or something," he stuttered, his face beet red from embarrassment.

"Leo, it's an arm. Better yet, it's an arm in a dream. A dream, Leo," I tried to talk some sense into him.

"I know it sounds stupid, but…never mind. You wouldn't understand," he muttered, almost inaudibly. He was right. I didn't understand. I'd had dreams before, even dreams of guys on whom I'd had a crush, but my dreams didn't give me dark circles under my eyes and leave me in turmoil with a sense of helplessness. I needed to be more empathetic.

"Have you told your mom and dad yet?" I asked.

"Nah. What are they going to do about it?" he shrugged. His parents were off-the-charts worriers when it came to Leo. They'd probably rush him to the hospital for brain scans and the works. I didn't blame him for not divulging every aspect of his life to them, especially this one. His mom would probably sit by his bedside in constant vigil every night.

"Maybe you ought to invest in a dream catcher," I joked, trying to lighten the situation because I knew how these dreams affected him. He hadn't been quite the same since they started happening more frequently. We approached the school grounds and the time to part ways.

"Good luck on your exam," Leo called to me as he walked to his first class.

"Thanks," I called back, "but I'm going to need more than luck." He just shook his head in response. I glanced at my watch: ten minutes before the tardy bell rang. I sat down under a tree near the door. I decided to look over my notes one last time. As I pulled my notebook out of my backpack, the gumball tumbled to the ground. I picked it up, the same warmth spreading through my body. I decided to pop it into my mouth to give me a little sugar shot before my exam.

I had never tasted anything like it before. As the flavor slid down my throat with each chew, I felt as though each of my memories had been used as an ingredient from my mom's tofurkey at Thanksgiving to Mr. Martindale's Christmas morning cinnamon rolls to my dad's homemade toothpaste. And then there was nothing. No taste at all, and the gum had disappeared. I didn't think I'd swallowed it, but then again, I also didn't remember closing my eyes. Maybe for once in my life I should have listened to my parents and chosen not to let my sweet tooth rule my actions. Something was definitely not right with this whole situation.

I opened my eyes just in time to see something whizz by my head. I blinked, turning to face the direction from which that something had come. I half expected to see Leo standing armed with his infamous origami flying birds, but there was no one there. I hadn't taken two steps in that direction when a second something whizzed by my hair, lodging into the tree by my side. I turned to look at the tree, only to find a steel arrow protruding from the deep brown bark. An arrow? I surveyed my surroundings as I realized I had no idea where I was. What was going on? I didn't have time to get my bearings since two more arrows zoomed in my direction. I ducked behind a rather large tree. I was in some kind of forest or grove of trees. My heart started to hammer in my chest. I had no idea where to go. I was quite certain now that the gumball was the culprit of my current hallucination, but why?

I wasn't left with much time to contemplate my crisis because I heard a volley of arrows thud into the tree behind which I was hiding. I had no choice but to get away from wherever I was. I belly crawled to the next tree, my hands shaking. I stumbled to my feet only to find my legs trembling with fear, and then the adrenaline kicked in. I felt the blood coursing through my body at incredible speed – just the shot of energy I needed to steady myself as I began to sprint at full speed, zigzagging and dodging behind trees as I fled. I don't know how long I ran. I never stopped to look behind me, though I found it odd that I never heard anyone following me. I only heard my own clumsy retreat through the thick foliage, my own heavy panting, my own heart pounding, and the occasional whiz of an arrow as it sliced its way through the air seeking its target. Why was someone shooting at me? Where was I? These questions circled in my head as I ran, hungry buzzards waiting to feast on my sanity. My own voice pleaded for the answer as if at one time I had known but had simply forgotten.

It had been some time since the last arrow had cracked through a small sapling just inches away from my arm, and I was too exhausted to run another step. I fell to the ground trying to catch my breath. I saw a thicket of bushes I recognized from one of my dad's drawings he had hung above the door to my bedroom. In my search of something familiar, I crawled to the bushes and huddled up inside of them. I began to shiver, and then I began to sob, trying to stifle the sound so as not to give myself away. I had never been so frightened in my entire life. I was confused and lost. I could hardly believe that just moments ago the most pressing matter in my life was a history final when now it seemed my life was on the line, and I had no idea why.

Oh, what I wouldn't have given for Leo at that moment. Why hadn't I at least told him about the gumball? He would have had a clue as to where I had gone. He probably would have bought one too, and at least he would be here with me. When would anyone even notice I was gone?

Where would my parents begin their search for me when they got the truancy call from the school that I hadn't shown up for my first class? Did Mr. Martindale know about the strange gumballs that had so mysteriously appeared in his machine? Oh, why had I eaten that stupid gumball? I asked a million questions, reprimanded myself a thousand times, but in the end, I was still alone.

I wiped my tears. I had nowhere to go, and I wasn't ready to leave the safety of my bushes. Their sweet smell was comforting, and they reminded me of home

– the one place I wished to be right now more than anywhere else. Home – with all its oddities. I didn't belong here, but I was too tired to move – too tired to try to think of a plan. I did the only thing I could. I closed my eyes and let sleep carry me away from this alternate reality. I only hoped when I awoke, I would be sitting under the tree at school. I didn't even care if I had missed my history exam.

Chapter Two

Transformations

"Ellinnet." "Ellinnet."

"Wake up, Ellinnet."

I could hear the voices of my parents. They seemed distant, but I willed my eyes to open. I had to blink several times before I could focus on anything. I sat up, expecting to be in my bedroom. Instead, a branch poked me in the eye. A branch? I quickly surveyed my surroundings, horrified to find myself still hunched in the thicket of bushes I had hid in earlier. There was still light in the sky, so I had no idea how long I had slept. It was obviously not long enough to release myself from this nightmare. I had heard my parents calling my name though. I was sure of it.

"Ellinnet." There it was again. Maybe this was a trick to lure me from my hiding place.

Funny – I didn't even know from whom I was hiding. I decided to take my chances. If I was captured or killed, well that would be the end of this little delusion, and I could get back to my life, my real life, which seemed so much less bizarre now. If my parents really were here, I had to warn them of the danger they were in. I couldn't risk their lives. I cautiously rose to my feet. I scanned the area, happiness swelling in my chest when I saw them standing side by side in the distance.

Though my legs ached from my morning marathon, and my back was cramped from my stint in the bushes, I urged myself forward as fast as I could. I didn't dare call out, but I kept my eyes focused on my mom and dad. The short jaunt seemed to take an eternity, but at long last I reached them, tears streaming down my face in relief.

"Ellinnet," my mom whispered as I approached, "are you all right?"

"I am now, but how did you find me?" I asked wanting to gather them both in a tight bear hug, but I resisted the urge. My parents weren't the touchy-feely type. Hugging made them especially uncomfortable, even though I was their only child. When I was within a foot of them, I shrieked with horror as their faces began to distort. My mom, or whatever was pretending to be my mom, grabbed my arm, but it wasn't the touch of an enemy. She gently held me in place as she grew to be seven feet tall. Her skin turned a ghastly grayish color, and her face elongated and wrinkled as if she had aged a hundred years in a few short seconds. My father was undergoing the same transformation. He stretched his long skinny arms toward the sky when his alteration was complete.

"At last," he said, his voice now a raspy baritone. He bowed to me reverently.

"What did you do to my parents?" I screamed, twisting my arm to get away from the creature that was now holding me. Steel arrows seemed less ominous than what I had just witnessed.

"Empress Ellinnet," the thing that used to look like my mom said.

"Excuse me?" I had no idea what she was talking about, but I had the sinking suspicion that she wasn't going to release me until I heard her out. She didn't look as if she was intent on hurting me though, so I finally asked, "Who are you?"

"I am Yelnirb, your custodian," the female said. She seemed relieved. At least that made one of us.

"And I, Empress, am Yelnats, your second custodian," the male introduced himself.

"Let us try to explain, Empress Ellinnet," Yelnirb cooed.

"This must be a serious case of mistaken identity. I am NOT who you think I am. I am NOT an empress. I'm just a regular girl who does regular things who apparently ate a not-so-regular gumball – a decision I'm seriously regretting." The two creatures looked at each other, worry drifting into their eyes.

"It must be an after-effect," Yelnirb conjectured.

"Good thinking, Yelnirb. That's the only explanation – an after-effect."

"Stop it! Both of you just stop it! I don't care who or what you are. I don't care who or what you think I am. I just want to go home. I want to go home right now!" I demanded. "What have you done with my parents?"

"We are one in the same, Empress. You saw us in our humanoid form when we were watching over you in the other realm. In this realm, this is the form we assume."

"Prove it," I challenged.

"As you wish. In the other realm, you were partial to the nickname Elli. You were also partial to that baker, Mr. Martindale. Despite our emphatic objections, you enrolled in public school at his insistence. I have made you a spinach blueberry smoothie every morning for breakfast for the past ten years. You have a soft spot for the food of the other realm, particularly anything with unnaturally large quantities of sugar –"

"Okay, okay," I interrupted, convinced that Yelnirb was telling me the truth. It wasn't so much that she could relate basic facts about me. Anyone could have found that stuff out. It was her eyes. I watched her eyes, and those eyes unmistakably belonged to my mother. They were the same eyes I searched for when I needed comfort. They were the same eyes that often filled with tears when she thought no one was looking. I had seen those eyes my entire life. Gray eyes – the iris lined with brilliant green and pupils dilated all the time. Yes, I knew those eyes.

I had to admit that I would have much rather believed a lie – that they had taken my parents hostage, and I had at least a remote chance of my life returning to normalcy. As much as I wanted to believe that, however, I knew that my life would never be the same again. I'm not even sure how I knew it, but I did. The truth was tugging at my conscience as if trying to jog my memory – a memory so deeply buried under layers of time, I wasn't even sure if I could retrieve it. Yet I knew it was there. I felt it. I felt it just as surely as I could feel the bark on a tree. My only choice now was to make the best of this new reality.

"I have so many questions," I said as I ran my fingers through my tangled hair. Yelnirb released her hold on my arm.

"Let's start with a welcome home," Yelnats said happily, bending backwards to stretch.

"If I'm home, then why don't I recognize anything, and why is someone or something trying to kill me?"

"What?" The alarm sounded in Yelnirb's voice.

"Steel arrows seem to be magnetized toward me in these woods." Before I said the last word, Yelnirb bent over me as if she were forming an arch around me. Yelnats did the same in the opposite direction, so I was completely enclosed by their gangly bodies. Then, I felt myself jolt downward into the ground. I didn't see a hole, but suddenly the sunlight was gone, and I could smell the earthy aroma of dirt. I found it difficult to breathe, and before I knew what was happening, I was enveloped in a stream of water that was pulling me along. I was whisked along the twists and turns of the tunnel by the current of water with no sign of Yelnirb or Yelnats. I couldn't call out to them for fear of drowning. As quickly as I had been sucked underground, I sprang out into the sunlight once again next to a very large, odd-looking tree. The bark on the trunk and branches was as smooth as silk and as black as midnight with teardrop-shaped leaves in varying hues of deep violet. Yelnats and Yelnirb appeared beside me out of thin air.

"Ah, now that was a deeply refreshing mode of transportation," Yelnats proclaimed, bending side to side grasping his hands over his head as he moved.

"Sorry we had to do that so suddenly, but you were in serious danger. There's no way they could have known about your return so quickly."

"Who?" I implored, more confused than ever.

"Not here. Not here," Yelnirb ushered me toward the tree. She ran her long, feathery fingers over its soft bark in a strange sequence of finger tapping, almost as if she were playing a piano. The bark glowed a soft purple, and an opening appeared. She motioned for me to enter, but my feet were glued to the ground. She tapped Yelnats, who was taking slow, deep breaths.

"Stop preening, and lead the way. Have you become so casual in your task as custodian that you have forgotten to whom your obligations lay? This is your empress, and she is in danger," Yelnirb chided.

"Of course. Of course," he bowed to me. "A thousand apologies, Empress." This whole empress business was beginning to wear on my nerves. Empress of what? Empress of whom? I didn't feel like an empress any more than I felt like a prom queen. I simply wasn't the type. I preferred my low-profile, unassuming life where I was free to go and do whatever I wanted simply because no one noticed me. I bit my lip — no one that is except for Leo. If he were here, he would know what to do. Aside from Mr. Martindale, Leo was the only person who understood me, and I most likely would never see either of them again. My thoughts were cut short as Yelnirb ushered me inside the opening from behind.

Though it was completely dark in the corridor, I could see as we descended the spiral, stone stairs as if my eyes had themselves become flashlights. The air grew dank the deeper we went, and then the ground finally leveled out. We stopped in a circular area, though the walls were lined with moss and creepy, crawly bugs of all sorts.

"Forgive the appearance of our humble abode, but it appears no one has kept it up in our absence. Perhaps they thought we would never return," Yelnirb's voice vibrated with melancholy as she looked around.

"You live here?" I asked curiously.

"All Treefs live in such places," Yelnats answered as he began scraping moss off the closest wall.

"Treef?" I queried.

"Our species," Yelnats explained. "We are distant cousins to the tree spirits that inhabit these woods, which is why they allow us to use their root systems for quick transportation."

"Root systems? You mean I traveled here in tree roots?" I could hardly believe it, and yet the explanation made perfect sense. This must be the reason behind my *parents'* gardening expertise. They could grow virtually anything, and everyone always complimented them on the superior taste of their fruits and vegetables. Even the local supermarket had begun buying their organic produce when the produce manager had tasted their grapes after a trip to the farmer's market.

"Precisely," Yelnats confirmed. "I suppose our relation to the tree spirits is why your mother chose us – our kind – to be your custodians as did her mother before her." His black, beady eyes beamed with pride.

"Please, sit," Yelnirb offered, pulling out a stone chair with no back. She sniffed as she wiped off the dirt and dust that had accumulated over the years.

"I'm sorry…about your home." I didn't know what else to say to her, but I felt obligated to say something since she seemed so distraught.

"Prittle prattle," she said, just as she had said when she was pretending to be my mother. "This is a great honor to have you as a guest in our home. Never before has an empress graced us with her presence. We are good enough to be custodians, but too far beneath the royalty to be anything but acquaintances."

The comment stung, although I didn't think she meant to offend me. I suddenly felt ashamed of how I had treated them when they were my parents. I had acted as though I knew more than they did – as though I were their superior because of their backwardness and eccentricity and that was when I thought they were my parents. I guess they never said anything to me about my lack of respect because they expected it of me, even though I didn't really know who I was to them. Was it in my nature then to be like that? I certainly didn't want my genetic code to dictate who I was and how I treated others, and I vowed to be more vigilant in the future to guard against such behavior. That is not who I wanted to be. The silence was growing awkward in the room, but it seemed to bother Yelnats most.

"So, I suppose you're wondering about your history?" he finally asked. I nodded my head. "You remember nothing?"

"No," I said quietly.

"I…we…had hoped you would regain your memory when you entered your own realm, but I see that is not to be. Most unfortunate, since we are not historians in the least. We leave that to our cousins, the tree spirits. They are the record bearers. They write our history in their rings, recording it with each passing of the twin suns."

"Twin suns?" I interrupted. I hadn't noticed through the trees.

"Of course, twin suns. Our habitation was formed as the afterbirth of the twin suns who reign in tandem in the sky, and when they bed down at night, the twin moons watch over us," he said matter-of-factly, and I realized I had a lot to learn about my new "home."

"You'll need to understand the history of this place in order to understand your role here. Several centuries ago, a child was born to the royal family – a little girl. After four boys, the ruling family of Annyad was ecstatic. It was soon evident, however, that there was something wrong with the child. Eneli was not like other children. There was something different about her that scared her parents and her brothers. She could do things – unnatural things. She could communicate with all living things, and in fact, discovered a whole new world that only she could see. She could summon the starlight, and using its power, she could do magical things. Her family was tolerant in the beginning, but as she grew older, they could no longer stand to have her in their presence. She was an embarrassment to them, you see. Or so she told the tree spirits that she later awakened. In the end, Eneli was banished from Annyad.

"After wandering by herself for several years, mastering her powers, Eneli came across another group of refugees displaced from Annyad by her parents. She united with them and began *The Awakening*, calling all the living to her, forming her own home, her own kingdom in the Forest of Notxarb – a place supposed to be uninhabitable. There were wars that pitted the clans of Annyad against Eneli's clan. Enelians have long battled to regain the lands that should belong to them – that were taken from them when Eneli was expelled from their presence – and to finally overcome their oppressors who had stripped them of their dignity. So much life has been lost on all sides, and yet the battles have continued from that time forth, and, I suppose, will continue until there is a complete victory – a complete annihilation of one clan or the other. The Annyadians claim the Enelian empresses are all evil sorceresses, and yet the Annyadians generate more evil than I dare recount. Ever since Empress Eneli's death, her gift has been passed to the eldest girl in the line of her descendants. That eldest girl for this generation is you."

"And my mother?" The question slipped out, but I couldn't help but notice her absence. "Murdered at the hand of your older brother, Imperator Einnep. Though not more than a boy himself, he was the military leader of your clan because of your father's ill health – a trusted military leader at that. He was the most brilliant Imperator to have ever been born – your mother used to say. Under his direction, she had made significant progress toward regaining that which was rightfully hers…until your birth. We can only suppose that Einnep grew jealous of you for he knew rule would pass to you once your mother died. His jealousy must have driven him to betrayal. Your parents were awaiting word from Einnep of an Annyadian surrender outside the safety of their hidden lair, but instead he came with their death warrant. They were executed on the spot, all while Einnep watched on. As we all watched on…even you.

"As a mere child, you were about to be executed as well. Your death would have not only have been the ending of your kind, our kind, and the rebellion, but it would have also secured Einnep's favor and position in the Annyadian clan. You see without the power of *The Awakening* possessed by the empress, we, as in the living who have been summoned from the lands of our slumber, we, fall back into our own realm. But just as the executioner's blade was about to come down, something happened. Even now, I don't know exactly what it was or who intervened. One moment Yelnirb and I were hovering over you to protect you, and the next minute we found ourselves in another realm, struggling to continue our vow of protection in a strange world so unlike our own." Given that explanation, I couldn't fault them for being so eccentric.

"This isn't a fairytale then, is it? This is a dark nightmare. Why couldn't I be the beautiful princess awaiting rescue by a handsome prince? Was that too much to ask? Instead, I'm the evil sorceress everyone, including my own brother, wants to kill? So, what am I supposed to do?" I inquired hopelessly.

"Pardon me, Empress Ellinnet," Yelnirb interjected, "but we cannot advise you on such matters."

"If no one knows where I went all those years ago, then why was someone trying to kill me?" I asked.

"Einnep," Yelnats suggested. "If I know him, which I do as I was his custodian as well, he will be ever vigilant until you have endured the same fate as your parents. Well, perhaps not at his own hand, but as he is most assuredly in the good graces of the rulers of Annyad, I would bet that Annyadians patrol these woods regularly." I felt sick to my stomach again at the thought of having a brother. I had always wanted a sibling. Having the knowledge I had now, I would have recanted that wish a thousand times over. My stomach grumbled as I rose to my feet.

"Are you hungry, child?" Yelnirb asked. I nodded, unsure whether I could stomach anything at the moment, no matter how hungry I was. Yelnirb and Yelnats vanished, and I assumed they had gone to gather food from the forest. Alone again, I began looking around their humble home. There wasn't much to it really. One large room with sparse furnishings: a stone table, two stone chairs, a stone grinder, and a stone counter that encircled nearly the entire circumference of the room.

There didn't appear to be anywhere to sleep. With words I had never heard before swarming in my mind, I laid my head down on the stone table. Annyad crashed into Notxarb. Einnep erased Eneli. Yelnats and Yelnirb hovered above my own name. As the words battled each other trying to make sense of the jumbled mess of information, I succumbed to sleep once again.

Chapter Three

The Path of Arrows

A faint glow lit the corner when I awoke. I could hear the rugged breathing of Yelnats and Yelnirb as they cuddled together on the floor on a bed of fresh leaves. My neck was stiff, and my whole body ached. This wasn't the first time I'd fallen asleep with my head on a table, and I was almost surprised not to find a book as my pillow. It took me a moment to get my bearings. I tried to stifle a yawn.

A bowl sat on the edge of the table. My stomach gurgled in anticipation of whatever food my custodians had found. Custodians? It felt odd using the term to describe the two people who had played the role of my parents for as long as I could remember, even if they didn't look the same. I slid the bowl closer and peered inside, unsure of what I'd find. White, spongy chunks lay atop green leaves and yellow and orange berries. I glanced over at Yelnirb and Yelnats, who were sleeping soundly, probably overjoyed to be in their own home again, however humble it appeared to me.

I ventured a taste of the food, unable to stave my hunger off any longer. The food tasted surprisingly like the food to which my palate was already accustomed. The white chunks were similar to tofu, the yellow berries to edamame, and the orange berries to cantaloupe. All this time Yelnats and Yelnirb had been grooming me for my eventual return to this place, so I wouldn't be embroiled in the discomfort of culture shock.

I couldn't help but wonder what else they had done to train me for my eventual return. The weekend hikes in the woods prepared me for the rugged terrain of the Forest of Notxarb. They had tried to live as Treefs in a world where Treefs were nonexistent. They made do with what they had - living off the land, finding food similar to their own. Even the paintings with which Yelnats decorated the house were replicas of the Forest of Notxarb.

The meal seemed meager, but I was amazed by how filling it was. After I finished, I found myself wide awake with nothing to do. There was nothing to be learned from the inside of the tree, so I decided to do a little exploring on my own before Yelnats and Yelnirb woke up. I crept up the stairs quietly, so I wouldn't disturb them. With each step I took, I knew that I should just turn around, but my curiosity urged me forward.

I felt pretty safe since we'd traveled quite a distance from the archer who was hunting me earlier. I leaned against the tree, trying to push the door open. Sensing my presence, the tree scooped me up, somehow depositing me onto the forest floor before the opening disappeared altogether. I stood up and brushed the twigs and dirt from my clothes. I had torn a hole in the knee of my jeans, and I was completely filthy from my afternoon hide-and-seek game in the bushes. I inhaled deeply at the thought to ward off the fear. That had been no ordinary game of hide-and- seek; it had been a matter of life and death, and I'd been drawn in against my will.

I started walking to clear my mind. The darkness of night had draped itself over the forest. I looked toward the sky, but I saw no stars. I began to wonder if there was a cloud cover until the two moons drifted into view. They were marvelous. They looked as if two magical crystal balls had been propped up in the sky to mesmerize spectators. I'm not sure how much time passed as I gazed at the mystical spheres bobbing in the sea of black, although the absence of the stars sent shivers up my spine. The longer I watched, the brighter the moons beamed their light through the Forest of Notxarb.

I noticed a chill in the air as I resumed walking, and I glanced around to get my bearings. I was struck with a sudden jolt of fear because I didn't recognize any landmarks around me. I was sure I hadn't walked but a few feet from the tree, but there wasn't a single dark tree in my midst now. I was surrounded by trees with a pale blue bark save a few charred trees every now and then, blackened by fire perhaps. Since those trees resembled more closely the custodial tree, I decided to investigate.

I wondered what strange power these twin moons possessed over the land. As I neared the closest darkened tree, I saw a thick purple sap oozing from its branches. I put my finger out to touch the sap, but as soon as it touched my skin, my knees buckled, and I fell to the ground. A few minutes passed before I regained my footing. I leaned on an adjacent tree for support. Only then did I notice a shiny steel arrow protruding from the tree's trunk. I recognized the arrow as the same that had been shot at me before, but I knew I hadn't wandered that far. I wasn't where I had begun. The arrows seemed to beckon to me, and for reasons I can't explain, I began to walk in the direction the arrows led. I was sure each blackened tree had been struck by an arrow, yet I had never seen an arrow affect a tree in such a manner. Were the arrows poisoned? Was I not the intended target of the archer after all?

Having nowhere else to go, I pressed forward, following the arrows to which I seemed so drawn. I was shaken by the experience I had when I touched that sap. As I was trying to sort it out in my head, I came to another blackened tree. Careful to avoid the sap this time, I laid my hand on the blackened bark. When nothing happened to me physically, I let out a sigh of relief. I became aware of a faint crying sound needling its way into my consciousness. It was so faint, in fact, that I wasn't sure if I had imagined it. I moved my hand and looked around warily, but the sound was gone. How odd. I touched the tree again, surprised when I heard the same distant sob.

I knew instinctively that the tree was crying. I realized that when my skin had touched the sap, the sensation I felt was one of intense pain, possibly death. These trees were dying, and I could not only hear it, but I could feel it as well. My heart swelled with sorrow as I looked ahead to the next blackened tree trying to figure out what was going on. Was someone killing these trees on purpose or merely having target practice, unaware of the pain the arrows were inflicting? I felt driven to find the perpetrator as intense anger nestled comfortably in my heart, causing me to feel invincible. The feeling scared me, and I turned my thoughts away from its beckoning as my mind traced its way back to Yelnirb's story about Eneli and her ability to talk to all living things. Was this my gift, my power? Was I meant to help these innocent victims – to save them from the steel arrows that were literally stealing their lives away? I reached out to touch the tree one more time, wondering if I possessed some ability to heal it.

"It's the tree spirit's death mark. When the tree was pierced by the arrow's tip, the spirit inside withdrew, thus killing the tree. But then, you already knew that didn't you, Enelian?" The thickly accented voice came from behind me, and I stood frozen with fear. I was sure at that moment, from the spite in his voice as he said the word Enelian that I had just walked into a trap. Stupid, stupid me. Why had I left the safety of the custodial tree? I hadn't even heard the snap of a twig at the approach of the individual, but I was certain the sound of the voice was accompanied by a bow and arrow. Finally, I turned toward the voice, surprised to see a young man only a few years older than me, his arrow cocked and pointed right at my heart. When I turned, his eyes widened with disbelief.

His hand quivered for a moment, and I was sure I was as good as dead.

He kept the arrow pointed at me as he walked slowly toward me, scrutinizing me as he approached. I was studying him as well, very much surprised at how normal he appeared to be. If not for the yellow tunic, he would have fit right in with any other kid in my high school, although he looked to be in his early twenties. His sandy blonde hair was cut short in the back and on the sides, but his bangs hung to his eyebrows. It looked as if he hadn't shaved in a few days from the scruff on his face. He was strong and tall, and I noticed an insignia on his tunic and on his bow. I surmised that he must be a soldier, an Annyadian soldier, which meant I was in serious trouble. If only I could be whisked away in the root system now. That gave me an idea though.

I took a step backward and touched the tree. Again, the sound of crying permeated the silence. I took a mental picture of my surroundings and the hunter coming toward me, begging the tree subconsciously to take the message to Yelnirb and Yelnats. I had no idea if it would work, but I assumed transporting a message was easier than transporting a human. If it was possible, I was sure the tree would do it, if it had any strength left to transmit the message before it died. It was my last-ditch effort, my only hope.

I must have appeared equally as strange to him in my torn jeans and dirty pink t-shirt. I was sure when I spoke, I would sound as though I had a strange accent to him as well. When he got within arm's length of me, he finally lowered his arrow. I supposed that meant I was going to be taken captive rather than killed on the spot. I'm not sure how I felt about that after hearing what my "brother" was capable of. From the anger smoldering out of this soldier's eyes as he looked at me, I knew I couldn't look to him for mercy.

"Put your hands in front of you," he said flatly. I did as he asked. What else could I do? If I ran, he would have shot at me. Besides, I had no idea where I was.

"Where are you taking me?" I asked as he tied my hands up with a cord.

"Back to Annyad, of course," he looked at me curiously as he spoke. He tied the length of cord to his belt buckle and began to walk at a quick pace, pulling me along behind.

"Who are you?" I asked as I tried to avoid tripping over tree roots. He didn't respond. We walked a while longer before I decided that I wasn't going to play this game. I wasn't going to go willingly to my slaughter. I needed to stall him to give Yelnirb and Yelnats a chance to find me. I planted my feet in the ground where I stood, jerking the soldier in front of me to a stop as well. He doubled back toward me.

"What do you think you're doing?" he asked.

"I'm tired. Couldn't we rest for the night?" He seemed to contemplate my request for a moment. I noticed sleep clinging to the edges of his eyes, and his pace had begun to slow over the last mile. I forced a yawn to make my point and nearly chuckled when he yawned too, trying to cover it up with a cough. He scanned the area, seemingly relieved to be stopping for the night. He found a clearing and sat down. I had no choice but to follow since I was still tied to him in an unbelievably complicated knot that I had made zero progress loosening, let alone undoing.

"What are you doing wandering about in these woods all alone anyway?" he asked as he pulled out a glowing stone from the pack on his back. I could immediately feel the heat radiating from the stone, and I inched closer.

"I got lost," I said.

"I'd say you got lost," he retorted. "This forest is a long way from the quarry."

"The quarry?" I whispered in echoed confusion.

"You must have smacked your head on one of those trees," he said spitefully.

"Something like that," I mumbled, edging a little closer to the glowing stone.

"Don't get too close," he commanded, and I knew the comment had nothing to do with me getting burned. He made it clear by the tone of his voice and the scowl on his face that he could hardly stand to be in my presence. I had never before felt so despised. I could hardly bear the smothering hatred he was emitting with every breath.

"Why do you hate me so much?" I finally asked. "You don't even know me." He jerked my hand out from its folded position and forced my palm open roughly.

"That tells me all I need to know," he answered, pushing my hand back toward me in revulsion. I stared at the long purple scar that had branded my right palm since before I could remember. My parents had told me I burned myself on a hot iron just after I learned to walk. I had no reason to think otherwise...until today. Apparently, that story was just another cover-up designed to hide my true identity. I traced my finger over the deep gouge as I'd done a hundred times before, but this time it began to give off a faint purple glow. I quickly closed my palm and drew my hand into my pocket before my captor grew even more suspicious. I had a sinking feeling that the glow meant more than I knew. The boy eyed me warily.

"You can't hide the brand of Eneli," he muttered disdainfully as he ran his fingers through his already tousled hair.

"But you couldn't have seen that from a distance," I prodded, desperate to find out all I could.

"I didn't need too. There were other tell-tale signs. The dark hair. The fact

27

that you are wandering through the Forest of Notxarb all alone when it's been declared off limits to anyone but those issued special warrants. The brand just confirmed what I already knew." As he made the matter-of-fact statement, I felt suddenly defensive. He did not know anything about me. His hasty judgments had been drawn because my appearance resembled his sworn enemy.

"That only confirms that I am an Enelian. That doesn't define who I am as an individual," I reasoned.

"You killed me brothers," he spat the words at me as though they were poison.

"They died in the war?" I surmised.

"Murdered, you mean," he corrected.

"But not by my hand. I'm not even old enough to remember the war," I countered. I didn't add that I had only just this morning learned of the war in the first place.

"That makes no difference. You are who you are. You're all the same."

"You can't truly believe that. Why must I suffer for the wrongs others have committed?" He was starting to perturb me, accusing me of murdering his family when my family too had been murdered because of the war. I knew it was different for him because he had probably known his brothers, and I hadn't even been aware of the existence of my parents. I would not be burdened with the guilt of deaths I could not have prevented had I known about them. I had lived in an alternate reality entirely.

"You pay the price for your potential to become what they were, I suppose."

"That makes no sense. My parents were killed in the war too. Is that not enough of a punishment?"

"For whom? If you weren't supervised in the quarry, you'd only seek revenge.

You've probably already begun your plans of rebellion."

"I'm not the person you were taught to hate. Must all generations of Annyad and Eneli be at war just because our parents were? When does this vicious cycle stop? Does anyone even remember why we're at odds in the first place or are you just carrying on a past grudge?" I had raised my voice unintentionally.

"I hardly call murder a mere grudge," he countered.

"But I'm not responsible for that murder any more than you are responsible for the murder of my parents," I reasoned. To be honest, I wasn't overly comfortable with the story Yelnats had shared with me. Whether exiled or not, Eneli did not have a right to declare war on her family, effectively forcing generation after generation to wage her battle of revenge. As much as I wished it weren't true, I knew that I was on the wrong side of this skirmish. The Enelians had launched the offensive with the sole purpose of annihilating the Annyadians, and if Einnep had not intervened, I felt quite certain the Enelians would have declared victory. I couldn't help but wonder how different my life would have been if that had happened. Maybe I wouldn't have become the person I was today. Maybe I would have embraced my family's ethics and carried on the battle cry.

"You forget that there is no war now. Master Einnep put an end to that affair."

"Yes, Einnep," my stomach turned as I spoke his name. "Why has he not been held responsible for the murder of your brothers? He was the imperator for the empress, was he not?" While I did not know Einnep, I could not hold him in any amount of esteem after slaughtering his own parents. He would have slaughtered me as well had I not been transported elsewhere, and I was an innocent child.

"You would detest him for thwarting the evil plans of the empress. I'm sure you feel betrayed," he laughed, a sickening sort of laugh.

"We'll see who is to be betrayed. You honestly think that someone in his position with his power who willingly planned and carried out acts of war against your people can one day wake up and decide to switch sides with no ulterior motive? You can believe that of him, but you can't believe that someone like me deserves a chance?"

"You spin a treacherous web."

"It is not my web." Einnep wanted only power, I was sure of that, and he would stop at nothing to get it. He didn't seem to care who he had to kill to get what he wanted.

"Just be quiet," the soldier said as he turned away from me. I had hit a nerve. I just hoped that meant that I had at least planted a seed of doubt into Einnep's character. I would never sway anyone to my side if they did not first see Einnep for what he was. It was curious to me how those feelings of animosity toward Einnep were so deeply rooted in me as if I had known him all my life. I wondered if the "after-effect" to which my custodians had referred earlier was wearing off. They seemed to think that when I came back here, I would automatically know everything that had gone on here prior to my departure, regardless of my young age. I assumed that is why they had never told me who I really was or tried to teach me anything about this place.

"You said you were tired, so go to sleep." Sleepiness hung itself snugly on the end of each syllable he spoke. That gave me an idea. I backed as far away from him as I could, stopping when I came to a large tree I could use as a back rest. I remembered whenever I couldn't sleep as a child, Yelnirb would often sing to me a lullaby. The words seemed to be peppered with the sandman's dust, and as much as I resisted, sleep always overtook me. I couldn't help but think there really was something magical about the song, and so I quietly began to sing:

"Rise me moon. Rise me moon,

The dark descends upon us soon.

Light the path upon which dreams walk,

Rise again that we might talk.

Rise me moon. Rise me moon.

The requiem of this day haunts my tune.

Grow me from this seed so small,

Embrace me with your beams that sprawl.

Rise me moon. Rise me moon.

For you shall be my shadowed boon.

While others sleep in weary shadows,

Tonight, our song we shall compose.

Rise me moon. Rise me moon."

It worked like a charm. His head drooped uncomfortably, and I watched as his hands relaxed by his side. I sang the verse again just to ensure he was in a deep sleep. I had noticed that a knife hung from his belt, but I wasn't about to attempt to unloose it from its sheath, especially with my hands tied together. It wasn't until then that I realized the ropes had loosened. I knew they had been tight before I started singing, so I surmised that the singing truly did have some magical power. I was able to slip my hands out of the loops. I didn't know where I was, but I did know that I needed to go in the opposite direction the soldier who had been escorting me to Annyad. I began my journey into the night, picking my way through the trees by the light of the moons.

Chapter Four

Voices

I traveled all through the night rather aimlessly. It didn't take long before I had entirely lost my sense of direction. I could have been walking in circles for hours for all I knew. I half expected Yelnirb and Yelnats to materialize out of nowhere to help me. In fact, I had hinged my hope on their rescue, but now I found that hinge rusting rapidly. I was hearing sounds that tunneled their way through my skin to make the hairs on my arms stand on end. Shadows hovered in every direction as if waiting to pounce on me if I dared cross their path. I was getting frightened, so frightened, I almost wished I hadn't escaped from the soldier. I didn't understand what was going on in this place. It was as if the fog of hatred was so thickly settled across the land that everyone had lost sight of what was truly important. Interesting choice of words – fog of hatred. Had there not been an unusual dense fog in the air the day I ate that gumball? I could hardly believe that was only yesterday. I felt as though I had been trapped here for an eternity.

Lost in my thoughts, I must have gotten careless in my wanderings because the next thing I saw was a man standing poised with an arrow in his bow. I blinked once trying to focus my eyes – trying desperately to convince myself that it was only another shadow, but the speed at which my heart was pounding told me otherwise. He stepped into the moonlight, so I could see him clearly. This man was much older and gruffer than the first soldier I encountered. He wore the same tunic but with a bolder shade of yellow and a bunch of patches, which I assumed signified he held a very high position in the Annyadian army. He had a large red scar running the length of his cheek from the corner of his left eye to the base of his chin. Given the dark gleam in his eye, the sneer on his face, and the white knuckles with which he grasped his bow, I didn't have to ask how he got the scar. I already knew he held me personally responsible.

"I should kill you here and now," he seethed as I stood frozen in place. I simply could not move. This was not how I pictured my ending at all, but I was also amazed to find that I was not afraid anymore. My fear had been seamlessly replaced by a feeling of injustice. I felt anger lick at my heart like the flames of a fire first ignited and rising to inhale the air around it, and I seemed to draw strength from the anger just as a fire draws strength from the air.

"Be my guest," I heard the words echo in own voice, surprising me at their boldness. The man laughed indignantly.

"Yes, you'd like that, wouldn't you? A nice quick death compared to the slow torture your brother has in store for you when I take you back to Annyad."

"So, you know who I am…" I wasn't sure if I was asking a question or making a statement. I wasn't sure about anything at the moment. I wasn't even sure who I was anymore.

"Of course, I know who you are, Empress," he confirmed with a sarcastic bow as he lowered his weapon. "I've been searching these woods all these years, waiting. I knew you'd return, and me diligence was rewarded yesterday when I saw you appear out of nowhere just yards from where I was eating me midday meal." He had moved uncomfortably close to me now, and I could smell the rankness of his breath and the body odor permeating through his unbathed skin. This was the man who had tried to kill me when I first came to the Forest of Notxarb. He was the hunter, and now he had caught his prey.

"A bit out of practice on moving targets, I'd say." I have no idea what possessed me to say such a thing – to provoke this man who already had it in for me. I could not shake the feeling of anger that was emboldening me. In once swift movement ran the sharp tip of his arrow down my cheek. I felt the searing pain the instant it severed through my skin. His breathing had become hard and labored as he stared me in the face, his nose just inches from my own. I stared back at him defiantly, trying not to wince at the pain. Then, he started to laugh raucously as he backed away. I felt a drip of blood fall from my face, but I didn't bother to wipe it away. The anger seemed to be masking the pain now, or maybe it was the adrenaline rush I was experiencing as my heart rate continued to accelerate. The man reached into the bag he had slung around his back and pulled out a dirty burlap sack.

"Where are me manners? I don't believe you've had the pleasure of me introduction – a name you'll not soon forget, I daresay: Sivart. Admiral Sivart to you," he said sappily as he came toward me again.

"Wouldn't want you to get any ideas into the little head of yours," he whispered as he put the bag over my head. I nearly vomited with the smell. He must have kept game he killed in the bag for it reeked of death. He tied me with the same kind of rope and knot the other soldier had used, although he tightened it until the rope dug into my skin. Then he started to pull me along as he ran through the forest.

I have to say being masked was one of the best things that could have happened to me at that moment because I was forced to use my other senses rather than just my eyes – other senses I didn't even know I had. For instance, I could feel when I was approaching a tree, and I could easily maneuver around it. I'm not even sure how I knew; I just did. It was almost as if the trees were guiding me along the path, and then I heard their humming. It was the most beautiful music I had ever heard before – a combination of wind pipes and flutes making magical sounds. I almost felt as if I was being transported into another reality – their reality. I found the anger fading away and a feeling of tranquility being infused into me.

I should have been terrified. I should have been tiring after miles of running the same quick pace. I should have been a lot of things, but I wasn't. I was completely at ease, flowing through the trees like a passing breeze. I listened to their conversations – whisperings of my return. I say that I listened for lack of a better way to describe what was happening. The trees didn't use words as I knew them. They weren't talking as Leo and I used to do for hours on end. Instead, they were sending feelings to and from each other on the passing breezes. It really was inexplicable. I sensed a melancholy in their "voices" as the trees "spoke" to one another, but I also felt a surge of hope at my arrival. I did not know what they wanted from me. I did not know what they hoped I would accomplish, but it was a stark contrast to the hatred that had initially overwhelmed me.

As I focused on their exchanges, a vision of Yelnirb and Yelnats suddenly popped into my head. They were searching for me. Yelnirb seemed distraught because I wasn't where I said I would be. Yelnats was trying to console her. They had received my message after all, and they were looking for me. I could feel their distress as if we were one being. I wished I could say that I was relieved, but I wasn't. I suddenly felt guilty for having left the safety of their tree, for putting them in this situation. As suddenly as the vision came, it was gone again. I forced myself not to dwell on it. I had to come up with a plan to get back to that tree – to get back to Yelnirb and Yelnats so I could figure out how to get out of this place once and for all.

I slammed into the back of Sivart as he abruptly stopped. I quickly backed away from him, but he caught me up with his hand before I got out of reach. He yanked off the bag, and I took a deep breath of fresh air before vomiting on his foot. I quickly regained my composure and scouted the area to find out why we had stopped. It didn't take long to locate the young soldier who had captured me the first time.

"Look what I caught, young Nedys." The young soldier's eyes widened at the sight of me. "Been tracking her for some time now. Completely disappeared she did. Master Einnep will be most interested in meeting her again."

"Again?"

"This, me young sapling, is the long-lost empress," Sivart informed him, and my previous captor looked at me in surprise. It was only at this moment that Sivart actually made eye contact with me, and what he saw must have disturbed him greatly for he swiped his hand gruffly down my cheek where he had earlier cut me.

"What dark magic have you been working behind me back, witch?" he demanded. I didn't know what he was talking about. I brought my hands up to my cheek, but I felt nothing there. I knew I had been cut. The blood stains had dried as evidence on my shirt, but there was no cut on my face. I was just as surprised as he was, but I said nothing.

I glanced at the soldier, Nedys. He seemed anxious, and then I realized that I held his future in my hands. If I told Sivart that he had captured me and I had escaped, he would probably be punished right along with me. What I saw in his eyes was pleading. He wanted my mercy – mercy he was so unwilling to give me just hours before. Who would have known that mercy was such a precious commodity in these parts? I looked at him long and hard, and I was surprised to find that I could not make myself hate him. I had told him that I was not who he was taught to hate, and I wanted to prove that to him now, so I said nothing. I gave him the one thing he had denied me.

"Let's get moving. I want to be in Annyad before nightfall," Sivart said. Nedys quickly took his place behind me. I was grateful that Sivart had apparently forgotten to cover my head with his nasty sack again. He was probably distracted by visions of the praise and glory Einnep would shower on him upon his return. We continued our trek in silence once again, but this time I noticed I could not feel the trees. I wondered what made the difference – certainly not that sack.

We stopped only once more near dinnertime as the suns were beginning their descent in the sky. The place seemed to be a post of some kind that was frequented often by these soldiers. Sivart and Nedys sat on large stone chairs and brought out some sort of rations in sealed packages to eat. Sivart ate greedily and gulped his water in front of me. I was tired and thirsty and so hungry that my stomach had curled itself into a knot in search of nourishment. I wasn't sure I would have the strength to walk another step, and yet something told me Sivart would have no problem dragging his trophy behind him.

"I'm going to scout about for a bit. See if I can find Ile. He's supposed to be posted in this area," Sivart said as he got to his feet after his meal had been devoured. "You keep an eye on the prisoner." He untied my rope from his waist and tied it to a metal spear that was sticking out of the ground, yanking my whole body with the rope when he found it too short to reach. I fell forward in the brush at the unexpected tug. Sivart laughed boorishly and tromped off into the woods, leaving me alone once again with Nedys.

Nedys stood up, stepping toward me until he was hovering over me. He helped me up, set some food in my lap, and then he offered me a drink from a small stone cup.

"Eat quickly before he returns," he directed as he moved back to his chair. I assumed this gesture was his thanks for not ratting him out earlier. I ate as fast as I could chew. He had given me dried animal meat of some kind and dried fruit. I had just swallowed my last bite when Sivart reared his ugly head through the brush. In a matter of seconds, I was running again.

Chapter Five

The Stone City

I knew the minute we had stepped foot out of the Forest of Notxarb. My surroundings suddenly became barren, not a tree in view. A hushed silence seemed to descend over the landscape, and with the silence came a sense of foreboding. I knew then that I had merely grown accustomed to the musical whisperings of the trees in the forest; they had not ceased to speak. Now I heard only the echo of my own heart pounding in my chest and the crunch of gravel with each footstep that disturbed its rest. When I looked up, I was in awe of the great stone city that stood before me. The architecture resembled the ancient Incan city of Machu Picchu with its dry-stone walls and spiraling structures in the mountain-top. Ever since studying Machu Picchu in school, I had dreamed of visiting Peru to see it for myself. But now, as a similar structure rose before me, the great workmanship echoed only death as the inanimate stones covered the treeless citadel of Annyad.

As we drew closer to the city, I heard the rhythmic clanking of pick against stone, each stroke perfectly synchronized as if great stone drums were being beaten. I looked around for the source of the noise, only to draw in my breath to find that it was indeed a symphony of slavery. The quarry. I peered down a ledge as we ascended the mountain to find a host of people excavating rock, surrounded by guards in yellow tunics. This was surely the quarry Nedys had mentioned when he had first captured me, and I was now seeing the fate of the Enelian people after the death of their leaders. How could Einnep have allowed his own people to be enslaved and forced to perform back breaking labor all the day long? Tears accumulated in my eyes as I watched a little girl no more than eight years old carry a stone over half her size – her vacant eyes void of emotion. I must have slowed my pace as my eyes meandered through the quarry because Sivart jerked on the roped, causing me to stumble.

"Don't worry, Empress. Master Einnep has much better things planned for you than the quarry," Sivart laughed as he jerked the rope again. I ventured a look at Nedys, but he averted his eyes. Was this nothing more than a stone city built by those with stone hearts? Is that why Eneli had fled in the first place?

We ascended the steps leading to the entrance of the city. There were no guards blocking our way – no gates to be drawn open for Annyad had no enemies, save me. I supposed if I knew how to harness the fullness of my power, a mere stone gate would not keep me from exacting my revenge. And yet, I still had no idea which side was right and which side was wrong. Generations of hatred and war had blurred the lines so badly that neither side seemed to be fighting for any cause other than revenge. I already found myself struggling not to pit myself against Einnep, since he had clearly pitted himself against me. He had declared himself an enemy to the empress, and I doubt he would believe that I meant him no harm. Or did I? After seeing what he was capable of – enslaving children just because of their lineage – it was easy to view him as an enemy. I felt that familiar anger lap against the shores of my heart, washing away the sands of reconciliation I had been trying to gather over the last hour's march toward Annyad. When we finally arrived at a centrally located building, Sivart stopped before entering the doors.

"You are dismissed, Nedys," Sivart said curtly.

"Sir," Nedys acknowledged the direct command as he clicked his heels together and slightly bowed his head. It was clear that Sivart was going to march me to his master by himself to claim all the credit that was due. I suppose he did deserve all the credit. After all, I escaped from Nedys, and we had just come across him in the forest by happenstance. Or had we? Was there more to this young Nedys than met the eye? He clearly despised me just as he had been taught, but I couldn't help wondering about his kindness in offering me a bite to eat and drink.

As Nedys turned to go, Sivart barked, "Report to the main hall after you've cleaned up." Again, Nedys nodded. I couldn't really figure him out, but he was the least of my worries at this point.

Sivart charged through two elaborately decorated doors as soon as Nedys had disappeared from his sight. A large rectangular table was positioned in the middle of the room. The ornately carved stone tile on the table depicted a repeating pattern of circles that looked much like a grapevine wreath. The walls were decorated with murals depicting forest scenery, which I found odd since there were no trees anywhere near Annyad. At the head of the table sat an older gentleman, who wore a bright yellow tunic and a large necklace with the same symbol that was carved in the tile on the table. In the center was a large, pale-yellow sphere that protruded from the flat surface. The man was clean-shaven with a full head of salt and pepper colored hair. Seated next to him was a handsome man, his short, black hair accented his tanned skin. His eyes were equally as dark. He, too, wore a bright yellow tunic, but instead of a necklace he wore a large ring with the same insignia. Just as I entered the room and both men looked up at the abrupt distraction, the suns peeked through the clouds and shone directly through the window. The purple hue in the black hair of the man with the ring confirmed beyond a doubt that he was in fact my brother, Einnep. As soon as his eyes met mine, he stood, scrutinizing me with such focus, I thought he might have x-ray vision that could see into my bones. I shuttered. He smiled.

"Lord Governor Atrebor. Master Einnep. I have —" Sivart wasn't able to finish his sentence before Einnep cut him off.

"Dear sister! So nice of you to stop by for a long-anticipated visit," Einnep exclaimed, his voice deep and articulate.

"But I…" Sivart began, unhappy that Einnep had not acknowledged his role in my capture. "There, there Sivart. You shall get your credit. Now be gone," Einnep commanded. Sivart curtly bowed and left the room, slamming the doors behind him. If Sivart had been Medusa, Einnep would now be nothing more than a stone statue. I was somewhat surprised that Lord Governor Atrebor said nothing. He looked weary — maybe sick. I directed my attention to him, but he had yet to make eye contact. Einnep leaned in close to my ear.

"He cannot see you, lucky for him. He's been blind these many years — just about the time you put on your little vanishing act," he explained with accusation tainting his words. He was blaming me for the blindness of someone I had never met? Einnep turned to address the blind leader.

"Lord Atrebor," he cooed. "May I introduce you to my sister, Empress Ellinnet?" Lord Atrebor bowed his head in the direction of Einnep's voice.

"Me only wish is that I had the pleasure of seeing you for meself," his voice was raspy, certainly not the voice I had expected to match his face or the steady, confident voice of a leader. I had to wonder what the Annyadian victory had cost him personally, other than his sight.

"We had just been speaking of your return, had we not Lord Atrebor?" Einnep said.

"Indeed," Lord Governor Atrebor affirmed. "But now I take me leave to let you get reacquainted."

My stomach plunged to the bottom of my toes. I wanted to call out to him, plead with him not to leave me alone with this maniac, shared genetic code or not. He couldn't just abandon me to this monster, but I didn't call out. I didn't say anything. I just stood there, tied with my rope, staring at the mural directly in front of me.

"Come now," Einnep said, grabbing my arm and ushering me toward the great stone chair Lord Governor Atrebor had just vacated. "Please sit and have something to eat."

He scooted a plate close to me. As much as I wanted to resist his request in an act of defiance, I was so hungry I hardly had the energy to keep my hands from shaking. I wanted to devour all the strange food in one swallow, but I restrained myself, lifting a bite of food to my mouth with my filthy hands still bound in Sivart's filthy rope. I took a few awkward bites as Einnep studied me closely. Each bite was delicious, thankfully, tasting nothing like the food Nedys had given me. Even the water tasted divine, but then again, I was so parched I would have willingly drunk mud if I had come across any. As I ate, I relished every bite as if it were my last. I was so consumed with eating and the contentment finally settling my knotted stomach that as I finished, I sat back in my chair and sighed, forgetting where I was. I looked up expecting to see Leo, but I found Einnep still staring at me. I was sorely disappointed by the cold, dark eyes that stared back at me. I knew he wasn't one to give without expecting something in return. He had given me food, and now it was time for me to pay up.

"Now that you've had your fill, let's talk," he said.

"I have nothing to tell," I replied. His eyebrows shot up.

"Nothing to tell? Nothing to tell?" He laughed as though in disbelief. "I beg to differ. Let me start you off. Where have you been for the last sixteen years?"

"Away," I answered, not wanting to mention my custodians, whom I still hoped were looking for me, although, I knew the trees would be no help in communicating my whereabouts now, since there were none.

"Away, where? Where did you get that hideous garb you're wearing?" He persisted. I didn't answer, so he proceeded. "Are you alone?" Again, I held my tongue. I didn't want to give him any information that could endanger my custodians, or anyone else for that matter. Unfortunately, I wasn't exactly sure what information could be used against them or me. I knew so little about what was really going on. I had been given the cliff note version of this place rather than the unabridged account I desperately needed. I jumped when Einnep slammed his fist down on the table.

"I'm not in the mood for childish games, Ellinnet!" he yelled. I winced when he said my name. It seemed so foreign coming from his mouth. He had no idea who I was nor did he care. I was just another road block in his scheme for power. I waited to hear myself lash out at him as I had done to Sivart, but no words escaped my lips. At this moment, I felt completely indifferent toward Einnep's anger, and he could tell.

"We'll see what a night in the dungeons will do to jog your memory," he seethed as he stood, clapping his hands together three times. Sivart and Nedys entered the room, both freshly bathed and wearing clean uniforms. I would have loved a bath right now - such a simple thing really. I had gotten myself into such a heap of trouble, and I was thinking about a bath. I chuckled at myself.

"You think this is funny, do you?" Einnep turned to me and pinched my cheeks in between his thumb and pointer finger.

"I think you're a fool," I whispered. He released me roughly. I meant what I had said on more levels than one. He was a fool if he thought anything I knew would help him. I knew absolutely nothing. I hadn't even known my true identity until recently, and I daresay, he could care less about history exams or friends or maple donuts. He was also a fool to think I would help him even if I could. He had nothing on me. I knew my custodians were safe in the Forest of Notxarb. As long as their existence remained a secret, he couldn't touch me. He couldn't threaten me. I didn't know these people. I didn't care about their feud, or maybe I was fooling myself. I hadn't been able to get the image of the child in the quarry out of my mind since I'd seen her. Maybe I didn't know these people personally, but I did know they had a right to be free – free from the likes of Einnep.

"Take her to the dungeons!" Einnep commanded. Sivart stepped forward and grabbed the end of my rope. He yanked on it, and I stood up to follow. The ropes had dug into my skin, rubbing my arms raw. The yank ripped open the newly scabbed wounds again, sending pain shooting through my wrists. I bit my lip to stifle the scream that was climbing up my throat. I would not give Sivart or Einnep the satisfaction of knowing how much I was actually hurting. I couldn't see my feet, but I knew several large blisters had already popped. I could feel puss oozing between my toes as my feet throbbed with each step. I was a little bit puzzled by the fact that Sivart's handiwork on my face had miraculously disappeared, and yet not all of my wounds had been healed.

Sivart led me through several corridors and hallways before he began descending a spiral staircase that seemed to stretch forever downward. The air grew musty and dank the further down we descended. The natural light was swallowed up in darkness, so every few feet were illuminated with what resembled small flashlights. I'm not sure why, but I half expected flickering torches. The flashlights reminded me that I was very much in a part of new convoluted reality, not some storybook nightmare.

We finally reached a rectangular plateau. It looked as though we'd come to a dead-end hallway, but on closer inspection what I had first thought were stone walls, were actually stone doors. There were literally hundreds of them, paneled throughout the room. Nedys, who had been behind me, stayed on the last stair. Sivart stopped at a narrow stone door slightly to the left of where the staircase ended, which to my surprise, opened automatically at the touch of Sivart's thumb. He tossed me inside, and I listened as the large stone door scraped the floor as it closed. It was dark, except for narrow lines of dim light filtering through the crack of a slotted opening. I assumed that was where food would be sent in, if in fact, prisoners got any food.

I rested my head against the hard wall and slid to a sitting position. My body ached as my brain tried to make sense of the new sensations of pain it was experiencing. I tried to focus on my full stomach as I let my eyelids slide to a close. Now surrounded by darkness, I drifted into a comatose sleep where Leo was flying an origami bird in our shared backyard, laughing as it came to rest in a blossoming apple tree.

Chapter Six

Twists and Turns

Golden eyes. I was awakened sometime during the night by a faint light shining through the food drop slot. When my eyes adjusted, I saw two golden eyes staring at me through the slot. They were gone as suddenly as they appeared, but seeing them left me unsettled, and I couldn't get back to sleep. The events of the day ran through my mind over and over again – a marathon of unanswered questions loped a steady pace through the rest of the night.

The food slot opened again several hours later. No golden eyes this time. Instead, a single piece of stale spongy food fell to the floor. Breakfast was served. I picked it up and sniffed. The smell of rotten egg stung my nostrils, souring my appetite. Einnep's food would have to tide me over a little bit longer. I set the food aside, just in case desperation overtook me. I doubted this was a three-meals- a-day type of arrangement. There was no light, and when I got to my feet to stretch, I found the darkness had zapped me of my strength. Interesting. I was beginning to think any power I had was tied to the light. I figured that's why Einnep had stuck me in a dungeon void of light.

The stone room was only large enough for one person. If I could have stretched my arms to full-length from my sides, I would have been able to touch both walls on either side. There really wasn't much exploration I could do – nothing I could learn about this ancient city or my current predicament. I sat in the silence for what seemed like an eternity before the door finally opened, and Sivart towered above me.

"Master Einnep has summoned you," he reported flatly. I got to my feet as quickly as I could so he wouldn't touch me. That didn't stop him from grabbing the rope that was dangling from my hands. I hadn't been able to work the knots free nor had I been able to summon any magical lullaby to assist me. I had grown accustomed to the constant throbbing in my wrists and feet as the night had worn on, but as I was forced into action once again, new surges of pain shot through me. I crumpled to the floor unexpectedly. I could not will my feet to move. Sivart tried to drag me, but that would have expended too much of his energy.

"Yellehs!" he barked at the guard who was still standing by my door. "Pick her up and carry her to the main hall." Yellehs, a large bulky brute, looked frightened. I could see it in his eyes just as clearly as if he had the word chicken tattooed on his forehead. He was afraid of me, even as I lay on the floor, helpless. Who did he think I was? What atrocities had the empresses before me committed? What lies had Einnep spread about me? I didn't know much, but I did know that fear could lead people to do stupid things, even to blindly follow someone as horrible as Einnep.

"That was an order, coward!" shouted Sivart. I wanted to tell Sivart that he was the coward. As I thought back, I couldn't recall a single time he had come in direct contact with my skin, not when he cut my face, not when he tied me up. Never. He had never touched me. Beneath his seemingly hardened exterior, he was afraid of me too. I tucked this revelation away for future use as it would do nothing but deepen his hatred for me, if that was possible. Yellehs temporarily overcame his fear and hefted me over his shoulder roughly. He headed for the stairs faster than a cheetah after its prey. Even Sivart was struggling to keep up with him.

When we arrived at the main hall, I was surprised to find it empty except for

Einnep. The twenty chairs surrounding the large table were empty. Yellehs dropped me onto the nearest chair, not waiting to be excused before exiting the room.

"Who's to be protecting Nalla today, Sivart?" Einnep asked.

"Nedys takes over at the top o' the hour with the change of the guard," he replied. Einnep mulled this information over for a few moments.

"Yes, that will do, I believe," Einnep finally announced. "Escort them both down immediately."

"Sir?"

"It is not for you to question me, Sivart. Have you forgotten the chain of authority of late? I do not like to repeat myself!" Einnep shouted as Sivart's face shaded a deep red before he turned to leave, closing the door behind him.

"Incompetent – the whole lot of them," Einnep muttered, directing his attention at me. "I hope your sleeping accommodations proved adequate." I turned my face away from his smile. The evil emanated from every pore of his face. I couldn't stand to look at him. I felt that familiar warmth of anger creeping through my body – the same feeling I had when I had first met Sivart.

"Still not up for a little chit chat, I see," he moved from around the table, closer to my chair. "I think I can clear that up as well. Tomorrow morning, the just and wise Lord Governor Atrebor of Annyad has scheduled a public execution, and you're to be the guest of honor!"

Einnep's words seemed to release a swarm of angry bees in my stomach that were lurching about trying to get free. I felt the color drain from my face, and my heart began pounding, harder and harder until I thought it would burst. This was it. I was to be killed simply for being born an empress. This wasn't happening to me. This couldn't be happening.

"I have committed no crime," I managed to say without sounding too childish.

"You're breathing, aren't you? Isn't that crime enough?" he snickered as he took a step closer.

"What happened to you?" I implored. "You are the one who should be executed. You had our parents murdered. You have subjected your own people to slavery in a stone quarry that has robbed them of their lives. You couldn't possibly have done all of this, committed so much treachery, merely for the want of power – for a title you have no real claim to." I had found my voice again at last.

"The mighty child empress has spoken," he clapped his hands together in mockery. Before he could say anything more, the door opened and in walked Sivart, Nedys, and a young woman whose face was covered in a bright yellow shroud. I presumed this to be Nalla.

"Ah," Einnep said. "Sivart you may go do whatever it is you do all day." Sivart was not happy at his dismissal, but he was wise enough to leave without provoking Einnep a second time. Einnep turned his full attention once again to me, not bothering to address Nedys or Nalla.

"Let me tell you something. Empress or not, you are nothing to me," Einnep pointed out as I watched the hatred smolder in his eyes. Oddly enough, I felt that same hatred reflected in my own expression.

"You're wrong there," I countered as nonchalantly as I could manage, given the pounding of my heart. He glared, daring me to explain.

"I'm everything to you." He averted his smug stare. "You need me. Whether dead or alive, you need me. Without me, you have no purpose. Whatever you're planning will never come to fruition without me." I watched Einnep as he rubbed his hand over the scruff of a beard that had appeared overnight. He was looking intently at the wall. I assumed his deliberate silence was an attempt to disconcert me, but as I watched I couldn't get a read on his emotions. Einnep leered at me with a haunting smirk on his face that turned the hair on my arms into porcupine quills. Right then and there, I ruled out my hope that Einnep had a good side. He was sinister through and through. My parents would be proud in that at least. I just wished I knew what he was up to and exactly how I factored into that plan.

"You don't know anything," Einnep whispered as he drifted close to me. "And I'm afraid you don't have the time figure it all out, dear sister." He placed his hand on my shoulder and squeezed hard enough to leave a bruise. I did not let my fear or my uncertainty show. Instead, I focused on my anger at his unprovoked malice toward me. I felt a surge of something electric in my blood. The surge shocked Einnep's hand, and he quickly released me, staring down at his trembling hand. His fingernails had been blackened by the jolt. He looked up at me, his left eye twitching. While I had no idea what had just happened, I wasn't about to let him know that. I wanted him to shake in his boots. I was sure he would have retaliated against me then and there if not for the two witnesses that had backed themselves into the corner.

"Nalla!" Einnep yelled callously. She stepped forward and curtsied while Nedys held his ground. Einnep walked toward her, and I was afraid he might take his anger out on her. Thankfully, he seemed to collect himself at the last moment.

"Sorry, my sweet," he said as he traced his fingers down the side of the shroud where her cheek was. "I must ask a favor of you." She curtsied again, this time bowing her head slightly.

"Please make my sister more presentable, if you will. She has a very important day tomorrow, and I want her to be at her very best. Spare nothing. I will have some Enelian fineries sent to your chambers at once," he instructed. Again, she said nothing, but curtsied and bowed. "Do take your morning meal with me first. I shall escort you back myself. Nedys, take Ellinnet to Nalla's chambers. Mind that nothing happens to her while she's under your watch, won't you? You have the makings of a great soldier. Let this be another patch on your tunic."

Einnep took Nalla by the arm and left the room. I bit my lower lip to stop the tears. Just two days ago, I had been a fairly normal teenager. Now, I had a death sentence on my head and some insane power to hurt people that I had no idea how to control. Despite these new anomalies in my life, I was still just a teenager who didn't belong in this place. I was lost, alone, and scared. I couldn't stop the tear from sliding down my face, and I wiped at it quickly with my fist as Nedys approached. I searched his face for empathy as I looked at him, but it was stone cold. He was a good soldier for this stone city. I had seen a glimmer of humanity in him earlier; however, I dared not hope to find an ally in him.

Nedys untied the rope from the leg of the table where Sivart had secured it earlier. I tried to stand up, but my legs collapsed again. I attempted to lift myself to my feet as I gripped onto the chair and winced with the pain of the weight. Without a word, Nedys picked me up and hoisted me over his shoulder just as Yellehs had done that morning. Nedys's touch, however, was gentler. I was surprised by his strength. He carried me as easily as Yellehs had, but he was half the size of the older soldier. Not even a grunt escaped his mouth with the exertion of burdening the extra weight. As he began navigating the twists and turns of castle, I silently wished I could navigate the twists and turns that my life had taken with as much ease.

Chapter Seven

Change of Guard

"Thank you," I said as he sat me down on a cushioned couch in an elaborately decorated room.

"For what?" he asked, turning his back to me.

"For carrying me gently."

"I thought you could heal yourself," he blurted out. He doubted me. He thought I was trying to trick him, and yet he had still treated me with respect and kindness – quite the shift from our first encounter.

"If I could, don't you think I would have done it by now?" I posed another question instead of answering directly because it seemed I could heal myself or something had healed me. I'm sure Sivart had related the story to his young apprentice.

"But the cut, me…" he didn't finish his sentence. I could do no more than shrug my shoulders. I had no answer as to why the cut was healed, yet my feet and wrists were not.

"I guess none of that really matters now anyway," I finally said to break the awkward silence that had ensued. I had tried to forget the unexpected turn my life had taken this morning, but it hovered over me like a guillotine.

"I don't think he'll really follow through with your sentence," Nedys surprised me with his conciliatory remark.

"And why is that?"

"You're the bait," he answered flatly.

"The bait?" I didn't quite understand. I knew Einnep needed me, but as bait?

"He's trying to lure whoever saved you out from hiding," he explained.

"The person who saved me?" I queried.

"He fears the Guardian," he answered matter-of-factly.

"The Guardian?" I echoed yet again, seeking more explanation.

"How is it you know none of this?" He was perplexed. I could tell by his furrowed brow and the look of exasperation on his face that he had expected more from the long-awaited empress.

"I was only a small child – not old enough to remember. I was taken far away from this place, from this life, and I was told nothing about its existence. I've only just recently discovered my identity, and I'm just trying to piece together the little bits I'm gathering along my way." I felt a flood of relief at not bearing that secret alone anymore, but now in my stupidity I had left myself vulnerable. If Nedys told Einnep…

"Don't worry," Nedys reassured me as if he had just read my thoughts. "I'll keep your confidence."

"You're not like the others," I said aloud, not really meaning too.

"Funny. That's what Master Einnep says to me as well. I remind him of himself at this age. And then I think to meself – I'm not sure I want to be like Master Einnep. I don't agree with his cruelty…and there's Lordess Nalla –" he stopped himself mid-thought as if he had said too much.

"The girl with the shroud?" I asserted. She must be the Lord Governor's daughter. No wonder Einnep kept a good eye on her.

"I've said too much," Nedys stepped back. I sensed he would say no more about Einnep or Nalla as he would be marked a traitor if anyone else heard him say such things.

"Would you tell me more about this Guardian?" I ventured onto safer ground.

"I suppose. It's common knowledge, though I would have expected you to be the expert on that subject. the Guardian watches over our lands from the skies. He is powerful and mystical. No one has seen him or heard his voice for centuries, but our Histories clearly tell us of his presence, and we sense his watchful eyes. Some conjecture that he removed himself from us when we starting warring against each other – sister against brother. That's when he withdrew to the skies. We cannot know for sure. It has been said, and your brother believes this to be so, that the Guardian himself saved you and took the orb from its place of imprisonment when the last empress…was killed."

"My mother," I filled in the blank, and he nodded in the affirmative. "What is –?"

"The orb," he interrupted, shaking his head. "You've not heard of the orb?" He was clearly flabbergasted.

"I told you. This place, my identity, were kept hidden from me. I explained that when you first captured me, but you wouldn't listen to what I was trying to say. Your hatred of me was deafening you to the truth. Have you ever heard of the United States of America, the Beatles, cotton candy, maple donuts, 9/11, Osama Bin Laden, Abraham Lincoln, the Gettysburg Address?" I lashed out somewhat unexpectedly. Was no one listening to me? I was pretending to be someone or something that I knew nothing about – all for the sake of preserving my own life and possibly helping those who could not help themselves – those who had been enslaved because of me. Now it seemed I would not do either of those things. If this mystical Guardian didn't show up before my execution, and I had no idea whether he would, I may be dead in twenty-four hours. I felt a knot in my throat.

"I know nothing," the last three words came out as a whisper as I tried to choke back fresh tears. I had been strong. I had tried, but this…this was too much. Nedys studied me as I blinked away the tears before they could begin their cascading waterfall.

I was not what he had expected at all. Empress. The very word depicted a woman who was regal, powerful, and commanding. I was none of those things. I was just a girl on the brink of adulthood, scared, confused, and flailing. His opinion of me must have descended to the nth degree. Instead of guarding a dangerous, formidable enemy he had hated all his life, he found himself babysitting a blubbering child. There was little reward or egotism to find in that task.

When I looked up, however, he was not looking at me with the disgust I had pictured. His face bore the expression of empathy. I'm not sure that made me feel any better. I needed an ally, not someone who pitied me because I was weak. I needed someone to believe in me – to give me the missing pieces of my personal puzzle that would allow me to find my strength. I needed Yelnats and Yelnirb. I needed Leo. I needed this Guardian. Instead, I had a young soldier who had to spoon feed me information as if I were a baby. Nedys shifted on his feet, looking uncomfortable at my vulnerability.

"The orb," he stated, and then reconsidered. "We might as well start at the beginning while we're waiting for Lordess Nalla. What do you know?" I related to him everything that Yelnirb had told me.

"You're kidding me, right?" Nedys responded unexpectedly.

"Is something wrong?" I asked, confused by his agitated reaction.

"Is something wrong?" Nedys repeated. He ran his fingers through his hair in frustration. "Is something wrong?" he repeated more emphatically. "Of course, there's something wrong. The whole story is wrong! Is that what you believe? Is that what the Enelians believe?" he asked as he paced back and forth in front of the door, where he had been standing the entire time.

"Kicked out of Annyad for being different?" he asked, shaking his head in disbelief.

"Just calm down, okay?" I finally interrupted his rant. I wanted to hear his side of the story before Einnep returned with Nalla. "Why don't you tell me what happened?"

"I certainly will!" he exclaimed, eager to set the record straight. "Lordess Eneli was indeed endowed with magical gifts. She was not shunned for it though. She was admired and revered, even as a young child. As she grew older, her powers increased as she learned how to harness them. Unfortunately, wielding such power went to her head."

"Wait just a second," I interjected. "I've heard a lot about this power she had – the power I'm supposed to have – what exactly is it?"

"Well…" he cleared his throat and shook his head. "I'm sorry. I just never imagined meself explaining this to the empress herself."

"Yeah, well, I never imagined myself in this position either," I agreed.

"She could communicate with all living things, animals, trees, and plants. The Histories tell of her magnificent gardens. She also had a way with people. Everyone listened to her, flocked to her. She was able to easily manipulate them to do as she wished. She was also blessed with the ability to draw the strength from the Guardian through the twin moons. She made stars dance in the sky and summoned the starlight from their midnight waltzes to create new plants with healing properties," he explained as if reciting a childhood fairytale.

"I think I can see where this is going. She began to misuse her power to control all the living things around her," I said, mentally noting that I clearly didn't possess this power. I was a pariah when it came to people, particularly people my own age. Although Leo had a big circle of friends aside from me, he was my only friend.

"Yes, but it wasn't only that. As her strength increased, she lost the ability to completely control herself. Her parents sequestered her, hoping that isolation from living things would help her gain control over herself, but she saw their intervention as betrayal. She ran away, taking the orb with her. Let me circle back to the Histories to tell you about the orb. The orb was sent as a gift from the Guardian. It was the essence of all life in Annyad. You may have noticed the spherical insignia that hangs about the Lord Governor's neck. That is a depiction of the orb. The orb maintained balance between all things, but when Eneli left, she stole the orb. She used it to awaken the forest and call forth other life forms never before seen. Treefs, squirdles, and the like. She then convinced the tree spirits to withdraw from Annyad proper, and she also drew away a fourth of the people to resettle in the newly created forest.

"Did you notice that Annyad has no trees? It's because they all left with her. Annyad was left desolate. Many people died as food was scarce and plants would not grow. We were forced to find alternate ways of building and obtaining food, but we survived. Eneli and her people did not make it easy. They were constantly warring with us, trying to overtake Annyad, which Eneli believed she should have ruled because of her special gifts. If Annyadians ventured into the Forest of Notxarb to forage for food or plants, she killed them. She also convinced the tree spirits to withdraw if they were touched by Annyadian articles, such as arrows or axes. The death mark you saw on that tree – she somehow convinced the trees to kill themselves to prevent us from using them. Once a tree has a death mark, not even the wood is usable anymore. It disintegrates as soon as it's cut. That is the story according to the Histories," he concluded.

I knew there were always two sides to a story such as this. I just never pictured myself on the villainous side of the story, but it made sense to me. I knew Nedys was telling the truth or a closer version of the truth than the one Yelnirb had been told. How else does a person convince tree spirits to sacrifice their lives if not for some perceived injustice?

"That's why Einnep needs me. He doesn't know where the orb is," I deduced, still unsure of what he intended to do with the orb once it was in his possession.

"Precisely," Nedys confirmed. "He needs to find the orb, and he thinks the Guardian has taken it."

"And the only way to get to the Guardian is through me," I added. While Nedys had shed light on the subject, I still felt like I needed to know all the major players in the game. Nedys seemed more relaxed now, so I decided to return to the subject of the mysteriously veiled girl.

"So…" I hesitated, "what can you tell me about Nalla?"

"Lordess Nalla," Nedys corrected. "That depends on what you want to know."

"For starters, why the shroud? Do all women in Annyad cover their faces?" I had been envisioning a strict Muslim-type dress code. I figured that was a pretty reasonable assumption since she had been the only female I had seen, but Nedys shook his head no.

"Nice try, but way off," he said.

"Of course, I am," I rolled my eyes. "Why don't you enlighten me then?"

"It is said that the same fire that robbed Lord Governor Atrebor of his sight, also stole Lordess Nalla's beauty. Her face and body were badly scarred. In fact, no one has ever seen her under order of Master Einnep."

"Einnep?" I prodded.

"She is betrothed to Master Einnep as part of his recompense for helping to end the war."

"Betrothed to Einnep?" I could hardly believe what I was hearing.

"They should be here anytime now," Nedys warned. "I shall speak no more." He stepped backwards toward the door, a fair distance away from me. His face became stone cold, and his eyes stared straight ahead. We sat there in silence for nearly half an hour before the door opened. Nedys stepped aside as Einnep entered, escorting Lordess Nalla on his arm.

"She was no trouble, I trust," Einnep directed his comment toward Nedys, who tipped his head forward in reply without any facial expression whatsoever.

"I shall leave you to your work, Nalla," Einnep said. "I'll be back to collect the traitor for public viewing. You have until then to make her presentable. Nedys, you may take your post outside the door. You'll be relieved at the twelfth hour." He left with Nedys at his heels.

Chapter Eight

The Veiled Face

I was left alone with Lordess Nalla, who came to sit by my side on the couch. I was at a loss for words, and we sat in silence for a few moments before she said anything. When she spoke, her voice was an audible fragrance of sorts — strong yet sweet, urging the listener to inhale her words. The rhythmic sound of her words in their strange accent made me feel at peace, safe even.

"I am deeply sorry that you have been treated so unkindly," she said quietly. She bent down and reached for my right foot, but I tucked it under my left foot. I did not want to be healed by her for the sake of Einnep's show.

"Please," she urged, "let me see your feet."

"No," I refused flatly. "I will not be a pawn in his game."

"Empress Ellinnet," she said with a small bow. "I am not your enemy."

"And why is that?" I asked, trying to get a better understanding of her. "After the atrocities my people have been accused of committing against your people, why would you not consider me an enemy?"

"You did not commit those atrocities. You were a mere child," she answered. I found myself relaxing in her presence under the cover of her reassurance.

"But you would see me executed tomorrow in all my Enelian finery?" I asked, mocking Einnep's instructions.

"No, I would not," she assured me, and much more softly, she added, "I will not."

"But..." I began, but she interrupted me.

"Right now, I must help you. You cannot do much in your current condition," she advised as she reached for my foot again. This time I did not protest because I knew she was right. I could not dream of escaping if I could not walk. I tried to muffle a scream as she removed my shoes and socks, sending searing pain exploding through my heels and toes. She left the room for a moment, returning with several stone bowls and glass tubes on a silver tray. She began rubbing a gritty paste all over my feet, which soothed the pain immensely.

"What are putting on my feet?" I gave way to my curiosity. I knew most healing balms and medicines were derived from plants, but I had seen so few plants in borders of Annyad, and I couldn't imagine Lordess Nalla foraging in the forest.

"It is my own remedy," she explained as she poured a thick, pink liquid over the first layer of paste. "You see, there are still some plants that grow in the crags of the North. Pale pink buds emerge through solid rock but never find the strength to bloom. Spikeball thistles tumble out of the caverns of the South during the season of the wild winds. Poison rippleweed can be fetched from the East underneath the blue stones of the Trickling Streams. I have searched far and wide to find them. And the forest is wealth of resources in its own right." I raised my eyebrow. How could she search far and wide or dare enter the forest when she was seemed to be under lock and key, guarded all day and all night long?

"Ah, you wonder how. I have found my ways and means," she answered, perceiving my thoughts.

She leaned forward to apply another layer of a different paste, and a lock of her hair peeked out from under the veil. I found myself drawn to the color of it. It was a golden blonde, a color I had only seen once before. The connection was instant. The eyes that peered through my door last night were the exact same hue as Nalla's hair.

"It was you," I whispered. She stopped applying the paste and quickly tucked the hair back into her veil. She offered no explanation, nor could I seem to find the words to ask her for one. She resumed applying the paste.

"Unfortunately for you, my remedies are made from dried flowers and herbs. I daresay you know that your healing powers come from the living, so your healing will be much slower than you are used to."

"Than I'm used to?"

"Yes. Admiral Sivart related the story of your miraculous healing to Master Einnep." I didn't want to admit that I had no idea why I had been healed. "Although, I doubt very much that you inflicted the wound on yourself as he explained in his version of the chain of events leading to your capture."

"Of course, I didn't. He did that all by himself," I said defensively.

"Yes, I figured as much. It was a test to make sure you were in fact the empress."

"I…" I stammered, wanting so much to trust her.

"You do not know your powers. There must have been a seed in Sivart's bag, probably from the gizzard of an animal he had killed. The seed, while dormant, was yet alive. It sacrificed its existence to heal you," she explained. I must have looked confused because she added, "Anything that lives in the Forest of Notxarb, will give its life for its master – that is the power Eneli unleashed with *The Awakening*. You may not know who or what those life forms are, but they know you."

"How do you know all of this?" I queried, grateful that someone could help me.

"Are you hungry?" she asked instead of replying to my question. I nodded my head. "I shall have Nedys send for some food." She went to the door, and I heard her whispering to Nedys, who was still stationed outside the door. I watched him gave her a slip of paper, which she tucked into the folds of her robe without reading it.

"Where are your custodians?" she inquired when she returned. My face burned red with shame as I thought about Yelnirb and Yelnats.

"I suppose they are still looking for me," I muttered. "I didn't mean to…" I let my voice trail off, not wanting to explain my foolishness.

"They cannot enter the city. Their life force is tied to the forest, and if they leave its protective borders, they will die." I looked up at her in shock.

"They have been very much alive all of my life, and we have been outside of the forest, far beyond its borders," I clarified, surprised that she didn't seem disconcerted by the revelation of my whereabouts.

"The only way they could have lived outside of the forest is if the orb or the Guardian were in close proximity to them, protecting them." Although I could not see her eyes through the veil, I knew she was staring at me, intently.

"There was no orb," I said, sensing her desire. "There was no Guardian. It was just us." I could tell she didn't believe me.

"You must go to them in the forest," she said, changing the subject.

"You're going to help me escape? But what about Einnep?"

"Einnep is not your concern right now, nor am I."

"I don't understand. What good is my escape? He'll catch me again just as he did before. I don't know my way in the forest."

"You may not know the forest, but the forest knows you. It will help you find your way to your custodians." She spoke as if she were much older than she appeared to be.

"And then what?" I prodded.

"I know you have not been among us in this realm these many years. I know that you do not understand all that is happening to you right now, but you will. When you find your custodians, you must ask them to lead you to Idnim, the ancient tree spirit. She will be able to direct you best."

"But how?" How could she have known where I have been all these years?

"Do not ask any more questions of me, Empress. You will know when the time comes what must be done. We must speak no more of this." There was a knock at the door. Lordess Nalla opened it and brought in a tray of food.

"Eat this and rest," Lordess Nalla directed before leaving me alone. I stared at the odd-looking food before me, but I didn't hesitate to eat it. Experience had taught me that the taste was more than amenable to my palate, and I was starving. I ate slowly, savoring each bite and each drink of the cool, crisp water. Could this possibly be my last meal? I tried to push the thought from my mind, anchoring my hope on Lordess Nalla's words. It was a difficult task given how cryptic she was, but then again, I also knew she was putting her life on the line giving me the little information she had. If she truly was going to help me escape, I shuddered at what might happen to her if she got caught. Then, the thought struck me: Why should she sacrifice herself for me? What more did she know that she wasn't telling me? I pondered the questions, but no enlightenment came. I tried to rest my eyes, but I could not get my brain to stop its gears from turning. Sometime later, Lordess Nalla returned.

"You must be in need of a cleansing," she said as she checked the hardened paste on my feet. "It is time to wash your feet." I felt my face flush with embarrassment. I knew I smelled and looked atrocious.

"Please follow me," she encouraged as she walked to a door in the far corner of the room. I hesitated, not wanting to put any weight on my feet. I was surprised when I stood up, however, because my feet felt just fine. I walked through the door, unprepared for what I saw. A waterfall cascaded down a stone wall, which I assumed was my shower.

Lordess Nalla placed a towel on a table near the waterfall and gestured to some containers that I assumed to be soap. She excused herself without a word. I was preparing myself for a cold splash of icy water when I ducked under the waterfall, but I was pleasantly surprised. I let the warm water wash over me, breathing in its clean, pure scent. I never knew how good a warm shower could be – rejuvenating, refreshing. The water seemed to carry away my bleariness as it cascaded over me and resumed its plummet down the drain.

I poured some soap into my hand, which smelled faintly of vanilla, and lathered it through my hair and over my body. I watched as the dark, dirty suds swirled around my feet before disappearing. I was still amazed at how wonderful my feet felt compared to just hours before. They hadn't been completely healed, but the improvement was significant.

Realizing I had taken much longer than I had initially planned, I reluctantly stepped out of the warm embrace of the waterfall and back into my grave reality. I slipped into the clothing Lordess Nalla had also placed on the table. The bottoms resembled yoga pants, and they were paired with a yellow tunic of sorts, similar to the one the soldiers wore. I put on the strange moccasin-like shoes, again surprised by their comfort. I quickly pulled my wet hair into a thick French braid.

When I returned to the main area in which I had eaten, I saw that Lordess Nalla had placed some blankets on the couch. I would have thought that I would be wide awake after my shower, but I found the thought of sleep too tempting to resist. Although I could still see the twin suns lighting the sky from the window, I laid down, wrapping myself in a light blanket. I was immediately consumed by sleep.

Chapter Nine

The Traveler

I felt someone shaking me.

"Just a minute, Mom," I mumbled. "I just need another minute." I rolled over, only to be forced wide awake by the sudden jolt of hitting a stone floor. I had forgotten where I was until I opened my eyes and focused on the familiar green eyes of a young soldier.

"Nedys?" I asked in confusion.

He shook his head, signaling me to be quiet by pressing his finger against my lips, and then he motioned for me to follow him. I followed him to a door opposite the one that was being guarded. We entered a long corridor and crept quickly across the passageway until we reached another door. He motioned for me to stop as he opened the door to peek inside. He slipped inside, and I instinctively followed. I bumped right into the back of him, not realizing he had paused just inside the door. Our surroundings were pitch black – so black that I couldn't see my hand in front of my face.

"You'll have to get on me back," he instructed in such a quiet voice I had to strain to hear. "This is a steep stairwell, and I cannot afford to risk the use of any light, nor can I have you stumbling into me every five seconds." I hesitated, but only for a moment. There was no point in arguing with him. I had no idea where he was taking me or why he appeared to be helping me. I knew, however, that his actions did not come by command of Einnep. I tentatively jumped on his back. Leo had often given me piggy back rides as we were growing up, but I had never felt the burning that was flushing my cheeks as I wrapped my arms around

Nedys's neck. I was grateful for the black cover of night that shielded the unexpected display of emotion painting itself on my face as he touched my arms to loosen my grip so I didn't choke him.

We descended several flights of stairs in complete darkness. Nedys was going so quickly, I struggled to hold on as we curved this way and that. I could feel his heart racing, and I wondered if he was as afraid as I was. He was risking his life for me when just a day before he had claimed me to be his sworn enemy, the murderer of his brothers. The thought did not settle well with me. When we reached what must have been the end of the staircase, Nedys opened another door. He did not pause to make sure the coast was clear this time; he simply made a mad dash to a side building.

"Off," he whispered. I quickly released my grip and slid down his back until my feet touched the ground. He pulled the cover from what looked like an odd motorcycle. It had the body of a motorcycle, but large metal balls took the place of tires. He patted the contraption with admiration before mounting it.

"Get behind me, and whatever you do, hold on tight," he directed. I stared at him in response. The closest I had ever come to motorized vehicles was the public bus, and I wasn't too keen on getting on a contraption that would require me to hold on that tight. Nedys looked at me with growing agitation.

"We've no time to spare. We must go now," he said urgently. I mustered my courage and climbed up behind him. I timidly put my arms around his waist, suddenly blushing with discomfort for a second time in only a few moments. I had never been this close to a boy before (Leo didn't count), and I was suddenly very self-conscious despite the dire nature of our circumstances.

"I said tight," Nedys repeated sternly. He pulled on my arms, smashing me flat against his back. "Hold tight." I did as I was told, perhaps, gripping a little too tightly because Nedys turned his head slightly to say, "But let me breathe."

When he was satisfied with my position, he pushed a button. I did not hear a sound, but I felt the machine shutter to life as the metal balls began to rotate. In another second, the machine was hovering above the ground by at least a foot. A garage type door in front of us opened to reveal the twin moons perched in the sky. Nedys flicked his wrist, and I nearly lost my meal down the back of his shirt.

We were traveling so fast, I had to keep my eyes closed. I don't know how Nedys managed without goggles or a helmet, or some type of protection. I buried my head in his tunic to shield myself from the force of the wind. We had traveled some distance before he finally stopped. My arms felt like jelly from holding on so tightly, but I couldn't seem to unlock them despite the fatigue. Nedys sat on the vehicle for a few moments before I finally unmolded my head from his back to sneak a peek at where we were. Nedys was surveying our surroundings with a pair of binoculars.

"There," he pointed to the horizon. "I believe that will do." He put the binoculars in a small, concealed storage box in front of him and flicked his wrist again. I didn't have to be reminded to hold on tightly this time. Thankfully, it didn't take much longer to get "there."

"You can let go now," he announced as we stopped in a lush valley, dotted with flowering bushes. I slid off the machine weakly and could do nothing but watch in disbelief as Nedys flicked his wrist again and disappeared in the blink of an eye.

This was the plan? I found myself once again alone in a strange place unsure of what to do. I couldn't help feeling a sense of déjà vu. I was more than grateful for the assistance, but I wasn't expecting to be dropped off and left alone without a word. I knew what I had to do; I just wasn't sure how to do it. I looked around the darkened valley, but there was nothing at all familiar about it. I scanned my memory of my father's paintings and sketches, but I didn't remember this scene. This area bore no resemblance whatsoever to the Forest of Notxarb. As far as I could discern, there were few trees to be seen, although the bushes and shrubbery were tall enough to obscure me from view, and my yellow tunic seemed to blend in well with the yellow flowers, by the moonlight anyway.

I shivered. I didn't have anything but the clothes on my back, and the night air was chilly. I was at least thankful that the moonlight was bright as I surveyed my surroundings. I ran my fingers across the leaves of the nearest bush. I held my breath and waited, but to no avail. I felt nothing. I heard no whispers. I knew I would not be able to communicate with Yelnirb or Yelnats from this place. That luxury must have been reserved for trees only. I let a long breath escape my lips as I fought back the urge to cry. My situation seemed hopeless, and I couldn't understand why Lordess Nalla would risk her life for me if I didn't have some chance at succeeding. But succeeding in what? What was I supposed to do? Certainly not save myself. Did she want me to save her from marrying Einnep? Was I to free the Enelian slaves? Was I to overthrow Einnep? I began to walk, hoping some instinct would kick in to guide me to wherever it was I was supposed to be going. Naturally, I went in the opposite direction of Nedys, crunching foliage under my feet as I went.

I stopped when I heard a faint snuffling noise behind me. I tried to ignore it, not wanting to give my imagination a jump start about what types of animals might inhabit this valley. Unfortunately, I heard the noise again, only this time much nearer. I flung around just in time to see what looked like an orange baby elephant with glowing yellow eyes and a Venus fly-trap for a trunk. It jumped toward me with cat-like agility despite its bulky frame. I tried to back away, but I tripped over my own feet. I fell backward and cringed as I saw the creature's bared teeth hovering right above me. I let out a blood-curdling scream as it landed on top of me, stifling my ability to breathe.

I waited for the pain of its bite to announce my premature death, but nothing happened. I had involuntarily closed my eyes, but when I felt nothing except the creature's weight crashing down upon me, I ventured a look. The beast was on top of me, but it was not moving. In fact, I could feel something wet soaking into my tunic top as I lay there struggling to breathe. I mustered all my strength to push the creature off me. As I rolled it over, I saw the glint of a steel arrow in the moonlight. I realized the wetness was the creature's blood, and fear gripped me as my thoughts turned to the archer.

I couldn't see anyone, but I knew whoever shot that arrow was soon to show his face. I scrambled to my feet and turned to run, but I felt a vice grip tighten around my arm. I struggled to get free, kicking and swinging my free hand.

"Watch it! A bit harsh for someone who just saved your life…a second time," the voice belonged to Nedys. I immediately relaxed and turned to face him. He must have seen the confusion in my expression because he said, "You thought I left you, didn't you?"

"Why wouldn't I think that?" I retorted hotly.

"Why would I risk me neck to get you out of the castle, only to leave you stranded as a late-night snack for that reprah there?" He nodded in the direction of the dead animal.

"I…I…" I searched for an explanation, but came up short, so I simply stammered, "Thank you…for saving me…and…and…for coming back." He did not know how happy I was to see him, but I resisted the urge to hug him.

"I had to hide me traveler," he offered. "There's a cave a ways off. I should've said as much, but I saw a pack of reprah headed in our direction. I wanted to lead them off, since I can only shoot one arrow at a time."

"Why couldn't you have at least taken me with you?" I jerked my arm from his grip, anger flaring in my chest.

"I didn't have time to disarm all me traps, and you couldn't have navigated them without injury," he explained softly.

"Traps? Do you come here often?" I wondered, but he didn't answer. Instead, he started walking forward, and I was quick to follow him, rather too closely for my own liking. I didn't want to have another run in with a reprah tonight. The closer I was to Nedys and his bow, the safer I felt.

"Where are we, anyway?" I asked after a few minutes of awkward silence.

"The outskirts of the Forest of Notxarb," he answered. "We'll stop for the night in a mile or so…when we've reached the edge of the forest. There's a place well hidden, and in the morning, we'll venture into the forest to find your custodians." I was suddenly very sorry I had been upset with Nedys just moments before.

"Nedys," my voice quavered, "why are you helping me?"

"I'm not sure that I am," he answered after some thought. I stopped walking.

"What?" I gasped. He turned to look at me, although his face was nothing but shadows as cloud cover had temporarily obscured the twin moons.

"I wouldn't consider it much help if you came to harm in the end," he replied gravely.

"And you think I might?" I asked, shaken by his somberness.

"I don't know what I think," he mumbled and started walking again, but that answer wasn't good enough. I grabbed for his arm to stop his retreat. I had to know the answer before I continued.

"Nedys." He didn't turn around this time when I spoke. "You are risking your life for me, when just yesterday you wanted nothing more than to be rid of me. I have to know why you are helping me now. What changed?" I heard a staggered breath escape his lips as he ran his fingers through his hair. I released his arm and waited.

"You're not the person I was taught to hate," he finally said, using the same words I had spoken to him when we first met. He didn't move, but stood staring at the sky, deep in thought. "I was only a small boy when the war ended. I don't remember me brothers very well at all, but me parents couldn't forget. Me father especially had this rage about him when he came back from the war. The news of me brothers' deaths and the marked transformation of me father broke me mother's spirit. She couldn't bear to be alive, and well...she died. Me father...well, me father only had one thing on his mind after he came home, and especially after mother was gone: revenge. He taught me to hate the Enelians, or tried too, anyway. I wasn't a very willing pupil, I'm afraid. The Enelians had never been anything more to me than quarry workers – slaves. It was hard for a lad to imagine that they were once fierce soldiers trying to overtake Annyad.

"I listened to me father's words and did as I was told so as not to vex him, but I didn't necessarily accede to them. He described a different world than I saw around me. When I was of age, he got a position for me at the palace as a guard and a soldier. That's all he spoke of most of the time – me being his protégé – a great soldier who would one day avenge me brothers' and me mother's deaths.

"When I got me placement, I began to see the workings of the palace, the cruelty of Master Einnep, even to me own father who was a devoted and highly ranked soldier. I didn't exactly feel comfortable in Master Einnep's presence either. There was a darkness about him that I didn't quite like, and I was angry with me father for forcing me into military service. The military had marred me entire life as I saw it, and I wanted nothing to do with it. The seed of doubt and misgiving had been planted, but I didn't have the courage to leave…until I met you.

"You see, I've heard talk of the empress me whole life, and in the last few months, by Master Einnep himself. While I may have doubted much, I did not doubt her evilness. To turn someone as vile as Master Einnep against her, I had no qualms in believing that she was far worse than her brother. But you…well…you're not that person. To be honest with you, the day we met, I was angry with me father for making me patrol the forest. I'm not too keen on the place. I took me anger out on you because I'd finally stumbled upon a reason for the endless patrols – an Enelian reason – a reason for me being a soldier – a reason for me unhappiness.

"But you didn't turn out to be what or who I thought you were. You could've had me skinned by telling the Admiral you'd escaped from me, and I could tell you knew it. But you didn't say a word, did you? And you never tried to exact any favor in return. The stones just weren't falling on flat ground, if you know what I mean. I don't believe it was mere chance that I came across your path as I did. I'm convinced of that. It was time to take me stand, so when I approached Lordess Nalla –"

"You approached Lordess Nalla?" I interrupted, my eyes wide with surprise. I had supposed Lordess Nalla to be my benefactress, but a sudden realization struck me. "That note you slipped her when she requested my food was your offer of help, wasn't it?"

"Be assured, she meant to help you at any rate, no matter the personal cost to her," Nedys recounted. "She never said as much, but it's a funny thing with Lordess Nalla, I knew without her saying anything at all." With Nedys's offer of assistance, Lordess Nalla's hand in the tyranny could be kept secret a while longer and her life preserved.

"Nedys," I started, but he interrupted before I could continue. I was somewhat relieved because I wasn't sure what to say to him. He had turned against his own father to help me. I wondered if things had turned out differently and Einnep had not betrayed my own parents, if I would have had the courage to stand against them. Would I have instinctively known that the things they taught me were wrong? I was grateful that I would never know the answer to that question.

But as I mulled that over, I realized that Einnep had done just that. Why did I automatically assume the worst of his intentions if he was merely turning against the evil? I guess it was the way he did it. He murdered them. He wanted to murder me, and I was just a child. He imprisoned the rest of his people instead of leaving them to live their lives freely in the forest. And there was a darkness about him as Nedys had said. There was certainly something not right about the whole situation.

"We must be going. This place is not safe," Nedys whispered, as he set a brisk pace in the direction of our destination. I took this as a sign that he felt he had said too much — that he hadn't meant to tell me his story. He was just as vulnerable as I was. I would have thought that knowledge would have been disconcerting, but instead, it made me feel safe and comforted in a strange sort of way. We were both in way over our heads.

We walked the rest of the way in silence until we reached a cave opening near a cliff that overlooked the Forest of Notxarb. Nedys took the pack off his back and started rummaging through it. I walked to the edge of cliff and sat down. Despite my earlier nap, I was utterly exhausted from the events of the past two days, and yet I could not close my eyes. They were transfixed by the twin moons, floating so effortlessly in the sky. I'm not sure how much time passed. My back was to Nedys, so I had no idea what he had been doing while I was lost in my sleepless dream. I heard him step closer to me and hesitantly sit down beside me. He was quiet for a few minutes. Then, quite unexpectedly, he started to softly sing in his deep, male tenor:

"Rise me moon, Rise me moon,

The dark descends upon us soon.

Light the path upon which dreams walk,

Rise again that we might talk.

Rise me moon. Rise me moon.

The requiem of this day haunts my tune.

Grow me from this seed so small,

Embrace me with your beams that sprawl.

Rise me moon. Rise me moon.

For you shall be my shadowed boon.

While others sleep in weary shadows,

Tonight, our song we shall compose.

Rise me moon. Rise me moon."

I looked over at him, and I saw him smile for the first time. I couldn't help but smile back. He continued singing, and I felt the weariness overtake me at last. I laid my head on his shoulder, absorbing every note, every word he sang of the haunting lullaby I knew so well. It wasn't long before I finally fell asleep.

Chapter Ten

Pathways

The suns' rays pried my eyes open early the next morning. I was surprised to find Nedys still at my side. I think he had been watching me as I slept because he quickly averted his gaze when my eyes fluttered opened. I had forgotten I had used his shoulder for a pillow, and I quickly lifted my head. He hadn't moved all night, and I could tell by his eyes that he hadn't gotten much sleep himself. I wanted to apologize, but I couldn't seem to formulate the words in my head, let alone speak them. The sunlight appeared to have robbed me of my courage, and I suddenly felt self-conscious in Nedys's presence. I felt an unfamiliar flutter in my chest, and I promptly rose to my feet.

"What's the plan now?" he asked, thankfully ignorant of my thoughts.

"I guess I need to find a tree," I said, thinking of the last place I had seen Yelnirb and Yelnats.

He laughed as he looked down upon the forest, full of trees.

"Is there a particular tree you're interested in because it looks like you've got your pick? We will be in a forest after all," he quipped.

"Of course, it's a particular tree," I rolled my eyes. "It has black bark and purple leaves."

"The Siol Tree?" he queried with a raised eyebrow.

"The what?" Again, I was clueless. It could have been the Octopus Tree for all I knew.

"The Siol Tree. In the ancient tongue, it's interpreted Soul Tree," he explained. Seeing my lack of comprehension, he continued, "It was created by

Eneli herself as the entrance to her underground kingdom."

"That certainly sounds like the right place. How do we get there?"

"Well, that is a good question. The Siol Tree is never in the same place. The forest rearranges itself to conceal the tree's whereabouts."

"Of course, it does," I said sarcastically, but this made perfect sense to me. Now I understood how I had gotten lost so quickly when I left for my little exploration adventure.

"And there's another thing," he added. "I can't go near the Siol Tree."

"Why? Does it shoot daggers at Annyadians as well?" I wouldn't have been surprised at anything at this point. He half-smiled at my sarcasm as he shook his head.

"It's poisonous to anyone without the mark."

"What mark?" I asked in confusion. Would anything ever make sense to me? He walked toward and reached for my right hand.

"This mark," he said as he gently traced the purple scar with his finger. The hairs on my arm stood on end at his touch, and I quickly pulled my hand away as he told me, "The brand of Eneli actually results from the immunization process that protects Enelians against the tree's venom."

"I see," I said, pondering our predicament as Nedys turned to get his pack from the entrance of the cave. "Well, I suppose we don't necessarily have to find the Siol Tree. I really just need to find my mom and dad...um...I mean my custodians, and I very much doubt they are sitting around waiting for me in the tree." He crinkled his eyebrows when I slipped by calling my custodians my mom and dad, but he didn't press me for any information.

"To the forest then," he said as he walked into the dark cave. Nedys had a glowing stone in his hand that dimly lit the dark cave. I had to admit that I was more than a little skeptical of his chosen route – deep, dark caves really weren't my thing. I stumbled several times over the rocks as I tried to follow in Nedys's footsteps. His feet were more adept at maneuvering over the uneven surface. After my fifth near-fall, Nedys reached for my hand to lead me along. I pushed aside a wave of emotion that swept through me at the touch of his hand. For the first time, I was glad the cave was dark because I was sure the color of my face would betray me yet again.

"Sorry about the cave," Nedys apologized, apparently sensing my apprehension. "It's the safest and quickest way to get to the forest. The dangerous animals, like the reprah, don't stray too far from natural light."

"I'll be fine," I assured him as we weaved our way through the rocky terrain. "I'm pretty confident in my guide, and I hear he's an expert archer." I'm not sure what possessed me to add that last comment, but I was fairly certain that Nedys squeezed my hand in response.

"So, what are maple donuts?" he asked out of the blue. An unexpected smile broke across my face, though I was slightly embarrassed. If my memory served me correctly, I had mentioned maple donuts to Nedys in a fit of anger at his exasperation over my lack of understanding the history of this place. Of the many things I listed that were unknown to him, I was amazed that he asked about maple donuts in particular. Mr. Martindale's maple donuts were my personal favorite, and a sudden longing for home overtook me at the thought of them.

"Hmm. That's a tough one," I responded. "A maple donut is a type of food, that's sweet and delicious. Unfortunately, it's hard to explain unless you've had bread or tasted maple."

"Bread?" It was Nedys's turn to be confused. My explanation only led to another question, just as his explanations so often had.

"It's made from a plant – wheat – that's ground up and mixed with yeast, water, and some other ingredients and then fried in grease. The maple comes from trees," I tried to explain, but I knew he wouldn't understand. I had tasted nothing that came anywhere near what I was trying to describe, which is probably why my custodians were so anti-donut. "That doesn't make any sense, does it?"

"Not really," he admitted.

"I guess you're better at explaining the unexplainable than I am," I offered.

"Maybe you're just a better learner," he countered, before asking, "What was your life before you came to be here?" I was so happy to be asked a question to which I knew the answer that I launched into descriptions of my house, school, Leo, Mr. Martindale and his shop, computers, telephones, the city bus, and everything else I could think of that removed me from my current predicament. Nedys seemed to drink everything in. He was particularly interested in modern technology and motorized vehicles. He asked far too complicated questions for the likes of me to answer, so he had to suffice with a description of every mode of transportation and electronic device I could think of. We had walked for at least a couple of hours, only stopping a few times for a snack and a drink of water.

"No wonder this place seems so foreign to you," he said when I'd finished telling him about television. My parents didn't have a television – no surprise there, but Mr. Martindale did, and Leo had somehow contrived a way to get his parents to buy one. "Sounds like a fascinating place – not as … primitive as this one."

"You can't really compare the two. Everything is so different here. I will admit that I definitely liked the fact that no one was trying to kill me there. In fact, no one ever really noticed me. I doubt anyone knows I'm missing, except Leo and Mr. Martindale."

"How could anyone not notice you?" he asked with a puzzled expression on his face.

"There are so many people that I guess I just blend into the background," I answered.

"I doubt that," he muttered more to himself than to me. I wasn't sure what he meant or why he seemed to be so perplexed by it. After all, I wasn't an empress there. I wasn't anyone of importance at all. I had already tried to explain that to him though, so I didn't press the issue. The more I thought about it, the less I felt like an empress here either.

At last, we emerged from the cave, and I had to shield my eyes from the brightness of the suns. The familiar trees and bushes that I saw just ahead of me announced our arrival in the Forest of Notxarb.

"You can take the lead now," Nedys invited, motioning me forward. "The forest doesn't much like me, or any other Annyadian for that matter."

I had no idea where I was going, but somehow, I knew I would be able to navigate through the forest much better than I did before I knew the history of the place and the role I now occupied as the empress of all things living in the forest. I started forward, noticing that Nedys kept close – another role reversal for the two of us.

I paused to touch the first tree I encountered. I closed my eyes and inhaled deeply, focusing on the feel of the rough bark beneath my fingers. I projected an image of my surroundings, and the tree sang in understanding. As I waited, however, an image came into my mind. The picture wasn't clear because tree spirits don't see as humans do, but there were three new people in the forest.

The unexpected presence of the three new beings did not alarm the tree spirits, but it certainly piqued their curiosity.

I projected an image of Yelnirb and Yelnats, but the tree spirits were too busy conjecturing about their new guests to give me any information. I suspected there was a way to get their attention, but I didn't know how. I decided to ask for directions to the three beings since that is where the interest of the tree spirits was presently engaged. The tree spirits were more than happy to accommodate that request to appease their curiosity. At that moment, I realized that I had been touching the tree with my left hand, and I decided to see what would happen if I touched the tree with the hand the bore the brand of Eneli. I switched hands and pressed my palm into the bark. Immediately, I felt a burst of energy that knocked me to ground.

"Empress Ellinnet?" Nedys was by my side in an instant, helping me to my feet. That was the first time he had ever addressed me, let alone used my title.

"It's Elli," I corrected him. "Please call me, Elli, and I'm fine. I'm just trying to figure out how to communicate in the forest. I'm sure I'll have to take a few bumps and bruises here and there."

Nedys didn't exactly look convinced on either count. I could tell he didn't want to call me Elli, and he was more than a little leery about me learning to use my power in the forest. I, however, didn't have a choice. I pressed my palm to the tree again, this time bracing myself for the jolt. It hadn't been painful, just unexpected. I felt the energy rush through me. The weariness from the days travel was instantly gone. I felt rejuvenated, and I was able to ask for the directions to the three strangers more forcefully. I think my question came out more as a demand, which I immediately regretted. I did not want to be that kind of empress. The demand, however, was answered straight away, and I watched in utter disbelief as the trees rearranged themselves to form a path that led through the forest.

"I take it you figured everything out then," Nedys observed, astonished by the scene he had just witnessed. "I've heard that the forest could do things like that, but I've never actually seen it with me own eyes."

"Let's go," I urged, as I started down the dirt path.

"Where, exactly, are we going?" Nedys asked warily.

"I'm not exactly sure, but we're going to meet three strangers that have come to the forest."

"Is that wise? I thought you were trying to find your custodians or the Siol Tree."

"We're taking a short detour. At least, I hope it's short. The tree spirits were too distracted by the presence of these three beings to be of much assistance in finding my parents…um…my custodians," I told him.

"That's the second time you've corrected yourself when speaking of your custodians," Nedys observed.

"Yes, well, I've only ever known them as my parents. In my world, they looked human just like me. They were a little eccentric by earth's standards, but they were my parents. They raised me as their own child."

"Why did they never tell you about this place? About who you really are?"

"I'm not sure to tell you the truth. I think they were scared. They didn't know what had happened. One minute they were witnessing the savage murder of my parents, hovering over me to protect me from the same fate, and the next moment they were in a different world. They wanted me to fit in with my surroundings, so they tried to make my life as normal as possible while still preparing me for my role here, if we were to return. I don't even think they knew if we'd ever come back. I believe they thought that if I did return, my memories would come back to me on their own. Yelnats, my dad, was so happy to return to his true form. You should have seen him stretching, but Yelnirb, my mom, was much more reserved, a little sad maybe. I think she'd grown accustomed to our life as it was."

We didn't talk anymore as we meandered through the forest on our perfect little path. With each step I took, I was feeling more and more nervous to see the three beings that had come. Would they be Treefs, or some other fantastical creature I had never before seen? Would it perhaps be the Guardian himself? Had Lordess Nalla conjured up same way to help us? My mind was abuzz with so many questions that I wasn't expecting to see a clearing in the trees. When my eyes finally focused on the faces before me, I let out a shriek, and Nedys drew an arrow in the bow he had been carrying.

Chapter Eleven

The Unexpected

I recognized that face. I ran as fast as I could and leaped into Leo's arms, engulfing him in a giant hug. Nedys hung back, awkwardly, his bow slightly lowered.

"Leo!" I exclaimed, hardly able to believe he was actually here. He pried me off him with a smile.

"Good to see you too, El," he said.

"What are you doing here? Did you eat that gumball at Mr. Martindale's? How long have you been here?" I started firing off questions in rapid succession, not waiting for any answers. "Are you real?" I asked as I pinched his arm. He jerked away.

"Of course, I'm real. Would you stop that? Take a deep breath and calm down," he advised. It wasn't until that moment that my gaze fell upon his two companions. They were Treefs. I gasped in surprise, not quite grasping the situation. My mind was turning somersaults as it tried to process the scene before me. Leo. Here in the Forest of Notxarb. Treefs. Treefs with Leo. Custodians. Custodians in the Forest of Notxarb with Leo. The light bulb clicked on, and I had to steady myself against Leo's solid frame.

"Elleon," I whispered, my eyes wide with understanding and surprise.

"Elleon," I repeated a little louder than before, smacking myself in the head at my ignorance. How could I have not known before? Our parents were so alike…too alike. We were so alike…too alike.

"You're my little brother," I announced my conclusion aloud as I hugged him once again.

"Well…not so little," he quipped, straightening his back and touching the stubble on his chin. I laughed. It felt so good to laugh with Leo by my side again. Everything would be okay now.

"Let me introduce my mom and dad, otherwise known as Nitsud and Necap," Leo said.

"Empress!" The Treefs bowed so low their heads touched the ground.

"Wait a minute," I said, suddenly suspicious of my lifelong friend. "You're okay with…with all of this?"

"Well, I always knew there was something special about me," he responded smugly with a gleam in his eye.

"Be serious, will you? I've had a rough couple of days in this place," I chided, even as I smiled. I was so glad that someone replaced my somberness with some joviality. "How did you get here, anyway?"

"Funny thing that," he began his explanation. "When you never came home from school, Mom…I mean Nitsud, was in a panic because your parents had vanished as well. She blurted out the whole nonsensical story to me. I didn't believe her at first – thought she'd lost her marbles – but dad or Necap corroborated the story, and well…It sounds crazy but…I just knew somehow it was true. The more I thought about everything…our lives, and our parents, and how we never really seemed to fit in, and I just knew. The only problem was we didn't know where you'd gone. We figured that you had come back here, but we didn't know how.

"When I finally fell asleep that night, the dream came again, but this time it was different. I saw this place. What I thought were eyes, were actually the twin moons. It's strange, but I still get the sense that someone watches this place through them as if they were eyes. Then I saw the girl again, but this time more clearly. I realized that she wasn't hidden in the darkness; she was wearing a shroud. This time though, she wasn't motioning for me to follow her. She reached her hand out to me. She touched me. The crazy thing was that I felt her hand. It was so real. She placed a weird gumball in the palm of my hand before closing my fingers around it.

"And then she vanished. I sat there with the gumball in my hand, not sure what to do. I just stared at the moons and looked at all the trees. Then the dream was over. I woke up in a sweat, and I was in my room. I was thinking about the dream and realized my hand was still closed. When I opened my palm, the gumball was sitting there. I couldn't believe it. Then it dawned on me that I saw you stuff a gumball in your backpack the morning before you disappeared. And you were acting funny – not quite yourself. I ran to mom and dad and told them what had happened. Then, I popped the gumball in my mouth, and we showed up here."

"A girl with a shroud?" I wondered. There was surely something strange about this dream and the gumball winding up in Leo's hand, but the girl with the shroud? I knew that had to be Lordess Nalla, but I didn't understand how she could pass between both worlds. She seemed to have known that I had been in a different place. Why visit Leo in dreams? Why hadn't she come to me? Was she the one behind me finding that gumball in the machine at Mr. Martindale's shop?

There were too many questions to which I did not know the answers. Every time I thought I was getting a step closer, I found I was even more confused at how the pieces fit together.

"Do you know her?" Leo asked expectantly.

"I might. Well, at least I think I do. Lordess Nalla wears a veil to cover her face," I answered.

"Lordess Nalla?" he queried.

"I'll explain later. What happened when you got here?" I pressed him.

"Mom and Dad summoned your mom and dad; I forget their names...They were in a state of panic looking for you. We split up, and we've been scouring the forest ever since. How dunder-brained can you be to wonder off in a strange forest?" Leo asked, a bit disdainfully. I could tell that he had been worried about me too, more than he cared to admit.

"How was I supposed to know the forest would rearrange itself on me?" I had already rebuked myself about my mistake a thousand times, and little good it had done me.

"Elli, what are you wearing? Is that blood?" Leo asked, pointing to my tunic. "Are you okay?" I saw worry cloud his dark eyes.

"I'm fine, Leo. It's not my blood...thanks to..." I turned around in search of Nedys. In my excitement, I had completely forgotten about him. Leo and his parents followed my gaze with their own. As soon as they caught sight of Nedys, Nitsud and Necap jumped in front of Leo, pushing him to the ground. They began to snarl and hiss.

"What the..." I could hear Leo's muffled words as he fought his way to his knees.

"It's okay. He's with me," I tried to quell their alarm as I went to stand by Nedys's side. He had, thankfully, dropped the bow to his side after determining that I was in no danger, but he was looking at me with a strange, unreadable expression on his face.

"He's Annyadian, Empress," Nitsud observed angrily.

"I know who he is, and I said that he is with me," I reiterated, more sternly. Leo finally rose to his feet and brushed himself off. He pushed between Nitsud and Necap and strode toward Nedys, sizing Nedys up and down as he walked. Leo was only slightly taller than Nedys, but Nedys had a more muscular physique, which Leo clearly noticed. Nedys stared defiantly at Leo. I rolled my eyes at this show of testosterone.

"Knock it off, Leo," I said as he came to a full stop, face to face with Nedys.

"Why are you cavorting with the enemy, Elli?" Leo asked, rather haughtily while staring Nedys in the eyes. I could tell he had been told the same story that my custodians had told me.

"Because he's not our enemy, Leo," I replied. "There's another side to this story that you or our custodians don't know about. I want you to listen to what Nedys has to say."

"Why should I believe him over my own parents?" Leo asked condescendingly. I was shocked by his reproachful attitude, and for a moment, the dark shadow of Einnep's face settled over Leo's. I suppressed the urge to punch him as hard as I could in the stomach. I knew anger somehow increased my powers, and I didn't want to hurt him, although I knew he'd balk at the very idea of that.

"Leo," I said as calmly as I could, "I'm not asking you to believe him. I'm asking you to believe me. Do you have any idea why Nedys is here with me, risking his life in this forest?"

"Well…uh no. I hadn't thought…" Leo muttered as he came to stand by my side. I then launched into the story of my last few days, of being captured, of meeting Einnep, of his execution order, of Lordess Nalla's aid, and of Nedys's rescue. Leo's countenance immediately changed, and he became uncharacteristically penitent.

"My apologies," he held out his hand toward Nedys for a reconciliatory handshake. Nedys looked at me in confusion.

"Where we come from, shaking someone's hand is a sign of friendship," I explained.

"In that case, friend, it is," Nedys replied, awkwardly shaking Leo's hand.

"Now for proper introductions: Nedys, this is my brother, Elleon, whom I call Leo. Leo this is Nedys." Nedys seem surprised by the fact that I had a brother, and I wondered why.

I turned to Leo's custodians, "Nitsud and Necap, this is Nedys. Nedys, these are Leo's custodians Nitsud and Necap." The Treefs eyed Nedys warily, but gave a polite bow in his direction at their introduction. I could tell Nedys was uncomfortable in their presence as well.

"Now Nedys, would you mind enlightening my brother on the rest of the story?" I asked. Nedys nodded his head and recounted his history lesson, beginning with the birth of Eneli. He added the pertinent facts that we had discovered together about Einnep's quest to use me as bait to get the orb. I watched closely to Leo's reaction as he listened to the story, and I could tell that he knew, just as I had known, that this version of the story was much closer to the truth than the version he had been told. He seemed especially interested in Lordess Nalla. I didn't blame him for that. I could tell that he was trying to piece together why she had come to him in his dreams for so long. I couldn't get a reading on Nitsud and Necap, and I wondered how Yelnirb and Yelnats would react when they saw me in the presence of an Annyadian soldier.

"So?" I asked Leo as Nedys concluded.

"It seems logical," he surmised. "We do appear to be on the wrong side of the fence on this, Elli."

"Nitsud? Necap?" Leo turned to his custodians for their opinion.

"Absurd! Preposterous!" Nitsud exclaimed under her breath. Nedys sucked in a deep breath. I put my hand on his arm and squeezed it to let him know it would be okay. Some of the worry lines disappeared from his forehead. I didn't want him to lash out at the Treefs as he had done with me when I had told him the story according to Enelian history, but he seemed to be forbearing for the moment.

"Nitsud," Necap admonished. "You must not speak so. You and I had heard the whispers of the tree spirits that the Enelian histories had been tainted with dark lies long before now."

"Traitors! That's what those tree spirits were, and they got what they deserved!" Nitsud began to sob.

"Now, now dear. You have tried to console yourself with that justification for all these years past. Retsil was your friend, and she did not have to die in that way. But you remember...she gave her life that the truth would be free. We are safe now. We can choose now. We can choose to believe Retsil. Elli is our Empress, dear. She will not harm us," he consoled her.

"The death mark," Nedys whispered to me. "The tree spirits don't die willingly as I first supposed. They have been cursed – forced to die because they tried to tell the true story of Eneli. That's how the rumors were stopped. The curse was tied to Annyadians to foster hatred toward us and cover the true reason. That's why the real story does not circulate among the forest. The other forest beings were afraid the same fate would befall them, so they did not pass the story on."

"It is as you say, Nedyssss," Nitsud spoke through her tears, holding the 's' as she stifled a sneeze. Leo leaned over to pat his mother on the shoulder, which only caused her to burst into fresh throes of weeping.

"I'll…uh…leave her to you, dad," he said uncomfortably.

I got up to give them some space and walked to the nearest tree. I put my palm to the bark, and immediately felt excitement and elation rushing through the musical melodies of the tree spirits. I tried to locate Yelnirb and Yelnats, but there was so much chatter clogging the communication lines from the events that the tree spirits had just witnessed that I couldn't get through. I was starting to get angry. I needed help, and I needed it now. It would only be a matter of time before Einnep sent in more soldiers to find me, and I did not know how to undo the curse that killed the tree spirits with the prick of an arrow. I pressed my palm further into the tree bark, focusing on communicating that message through the chaos. I suddenly felt nothing but silence. I opened my eyes.

"What's this? Tree telepathy?" Leo asked, amused.

"She can communicate through the tree spirits. That's how we found you," Nedys defended me, unimpressed with Leo's attempt at humor.

"Oh," Leo muttered.

"Leo, no one is having a harder time coming to grips with this than me," I said, sympathetically. There was no more time for idle chit chat because in the next moment, the trees once again rearranged themselves, and a new path opened before us.

"I think this is the way to my custodians," I surmised, "and we'd better go quickly. Nedys, how long before Einnep sends in soldiers after us?"

"He would have discovered that you were missing this morning and sent out the first and second ranks immediately. They won't reach the forest until nightfall, and they won't dare enter until first light tomorrow," he proclaimed somberly.

"In other words," Leo interjected, "we don't have much time."

Chapter Twelve

Free Fall

The time for walking was far passed, so we started jogging, not sure how long this new path was. I was surprised that I didn't seem too winded, though I wasn't much of a runner. Maybe it was adrenaline. Maybe it was me drawing power from the forest. I couldn't be sure. I noticed the pace slowing the longer we ran, and I could see Leo was heaving from the exertion of the unexpected sprint. Even Nedys, who I sensed was in prime condition, had broken into a sweat. I slowed down before finally stopping.

"How about we rest?" I suggested.

"Rest?" Leo panted. "Rest was half an hour back. Collapsing from exhaustion is more in line with how I'm feeling."

Nedys pulled an animal skin water jug out of his pack. He offered me the first drink, and I gladly accepted the refreshment. I passed it back and was surprised when he offered it next to Leo, who gulped greedily.

"Thanks, man," he said as he handed back the half empty jug, water dribbling off his chin. It was only then that Nedys allowed his own thirst to be quenched.

"Interesting scenery?" Leo whispered in my ear, and I realized I had been staring at Nedys indiscreetly.

"Uh…just deep in thought," I deflected, but I already knew a deep blush was creeping across my cheeks.

"Oh – is that what you call it?" Leo asked with a wink. I gave him a little shove, and he fell off the large rock he had been sitting on. I didn't want to pursue this line of questioning, and I was afraid of what I might find if I tried to unravel my own feelings. They were best left in a knotted ball for now.

"Time to be off," I announced as I got to my feet with that knot of emotions secured in the pit of stomach. Leo grumbled, but he got up and brushed himself off. Nitsud and Necap led the way, followed by Leo, then me with Nedys at my side. We had been running for only a few short minutes, when I felt something approaching from behind. I flipped my head around to see what it was, but there was nothing there. I tried to focus on the path ahead, but I sensed a presence approaching.

Again, I turned my head to look behind me, but there was nothing there. I wasn't sure exactly what happened next. All I know is that I found myself face down in the path with a mouthful of dirt. I lifted my head just in time to see a green blur rush passed me toward Nedys. Nedys must have turned around when I fell because he was facing me, and then he was gone. The green blur barreled right into him, knocking him into a tree and pinning him against it. I got to my feet as fast as I could and ran toward Nedys, spitting debris out of my mouth as I went.

"Empress!" Yelnats exclaimed as I approached.

"Yelnats! What are you doing?" I demanded.

"Saving you, of course. I might have expected a better reaction!" he said with exasperation. I raced to Nedys's side, only to find him unconscious.

"Let him go right now," I insisted. Yelnats's expression turned from pride to injury. "I'm sorry, Yelnats. Thank you. Thank you for trying to save me, but this is a friend."

"Friend? This is no friend, Empress. This is the little cretin who took you – who tried to kill you. I saw his face in your message!"

"Yes, well, he's my friend now," I tried to explain. "He rescued me from

Annyad – from Einnep." Yelnats was bewildered, but he released Nedys, whose limp body slumped to the base of the tree.

"What's the meaning of this?" I heard Yelnirb's voice before I saw her face. She must have been separated from Yelnats because she was coming from the opposite direction with Leo and his custodians trailing behind her. I was so overwhelmed with emotion when I saw those familiar eyes that I rushed forward and embraced her. I heard gasps from Necap, Nitsud, and Yelnats at my impulsive display of affection toward my mother.

The next moments were a whirlwind of confusion in my head. The embrace seemed to allow me to link to Yelnirb telepathically. Somehow, I knew how she was feeling and what she was thinking. In a flash, I could see everything that had transpired in her life over the past few days. I saw her life in rewind as time reversed itself, allowing me a glimpse into her memories. I could see clearly how much she loved me and how she had been torn whether or not to tell me about my life before. I knew why Leo and I had not been raised as brother and sister. I was the empress. The empresses-in-waiting were always kept separate from their siblings so that familial relationships did not interfere with their ability to harness their powers.

There was no knowledge transfer in the connection, but I could see and feel bits of her life from her perspective. I knew now why she had never hugged me before. Though she had longed to do so, she was forbidden at the behest of my mother and her mother before her and on up the line of empresses. This link could weaken the power of the empress as it allowed the custodians to see and potentially exploit vulnerabilities. Treefs who accepted the charge of a custodianship pledged upon their lives that they would have no physical contact with their charges. I had always held the fact that she never showed love in a tangible, touchy-feely sort of way against her, but now I knew how hard it had been for her to withhold that love, and she had done it out of loyalty to me. She had done it to protect me.

I looked up into Yelnirb's face and saw tears streaming from her eyes. I knew they were tears of relief that I was safe and tears of relief that I now knew the things she could not say. I had no doubt that Yelnirb also knew what had transpired in the last few days of my life. I would have no need of re-telling the story to her, and I also knew that she understood Nedys's version of our history and fully accepted it.

"I release you from your oath," I whispered to her, but she shook her head in refusal.

"Too dangerous," she managed to say through her tears. I wanted to argue, but I knew it was true. I knew she thought it was too dangerous for me, but I also knew that she would be much safer if she didn't have that sort of link with me.

"I think he's coming around," Yelnats called out to us as Nedys started to move. I hurried over to him. Yelnats rose to comfort Yelnirb, who was struggling to control herself. As he wrapped his gangly arms around her, I saw his eyes widen for a moment. I knew that she had just told him my story, Nedys's story. I diverted my attention back to Nedys, who moaned. I smoothed his hair out of his face and waited as he squinted his eyes several times before finally opening them. He brought his hand to the back of his head, and I was horrified when I saw his fingers coated with blood.

"Help me," I pleaded. "He's bleeding." Leo was at my side and helped me to roll Nedys over, so we could inspect the wound.

"Head wounds bleed a lot, don't they? Doesn't necessarily mean they're serious," Leo tried to comfort me as we saw the puddle of blood beneath Nedys's head. I ripped the sleeve off my tunic and placed it against the wound, applying as much pressure as I could. Suddenly, Yelnirb was gone.

"She's gone to get a poultice," Yelnats said as he noted the concern in my face.

"Shouldn't I be able to heal him?" I asked in desperation as Nedys groaned in pain.

"You're not a healer. You're an empress," Yelnats retorted.

"But…I…. I healed myself when Sivart cut me," I told him.

"No, you didn't," Yelnats countered. "The seed healed you – it was drawn to the power inside you."

"El, it'll be okay," Leo tried to reassure me, but it was too much. I started to cry, and Leo put his hand over my trembling hand to keep pressure on the wound. I leaned against the tree for support, my free hand resting against its rough bark. What good was all this power I supposedly had if I couldn't help anyone? Nedys moaned and then went still and silent.

"Leo, he's unconscious again," I observed, my voice wavering as I spoke. "We've got to do something – we've got to help him." I heard the desperation in my own voice. I needed Nedys. I needed Nedys to be alive. I noticed blood seeping through the torn piece of tunic and felt its wetness as I pressed my hand on Nedys's wound. I was helpless.

My hand that was against the tree began to tingle – an odd sensation I had never felt before. Only then did I realize that I had my right palm pressed against the tree – the palm with the mark. The next thing I knew I felt as though I was falling off a cliff as I was plunged into darkness with a great swooshing sound echoing in my head. The sound swallowed up Leo's shout as we continued our free fall. The sleeve of my tunic that I had been using on Nedys whipped into my face, plastering itself on the side of my cheek. I swiped it away, groping in the darkness for Nedys. My fingers brushed against a head of hair, and I grabbed on thinking that it must be Nedys.

Leo shouted loud enough for me to understand that he was in fact the owner of the pile of hair I was holding onto for dear life. He reached up and untangled my hand from his hair, gripping my hand in his and pulling me toward him.

"I've got him," he yelled amidst the noise. I'm not sure if it's possible to feel completely terrified and safe at the same time, but that's how I felt with Leo by my side. At least I wasn't alone. We landed with a thud, and the noise immediately ceased, although we were still engulfed in a thick darkness that made it hard to breathe.

"You okay?" Leo whispered.

"Yeah. You?" I asked, still holding onto his hand. He didn't have time to respond because we were both blinded by a brilliant flash of light. I covered my eyes with my free hand, waiting a minute before blinking them open. As they adjusted to the bright light, I couldn't believe what I was seeing.

Chapter Thirteen

Sanctuary

We were sitting in the most unusual meadow I had ever seen. Everything seemed to have been painted in white with only certain objects highlighted in hues of colors I could hardly describe. There was a Great White Tree in the background that was larger than I ever imagined a tree could be. Its white bark was notched with bits of color, and its leaves looked as if they were made from crystal. The bushes and flowers were also a brilliant white with dabs of color here and there – in the center of a flower, on a leaf, filtering in through a branch. The grass that had cushioned our fall was the palest of deep greens and remarkably soft. This place was breathtaking and dreamlike.

As I surveyed my surroundings, a shimmering, silvery shape emerged from the tops of the Great White Tree, floating gracefully to the ground before it began to glide noiselessly toward us. The being took on a more human form the closer it came, but its essence never solidified. I felt as though I was watching a cloud drift toward me – a cloud covered in a sheer skin infused with diamonds. I was mesmerized. When the being was within six feet of us, it stopped and bowed before me. I looked at Leo, whose eyes were practically popping out of his head with his mouth agape. He looked the way I felt.

I shakily got to my feet and bowed before this mystical being. I could make out faint facial features, depicting serenity, although I got the feeling those clear, glassy eyes were staring right into my soul, perceiving my thoughts and feelings. I closed my eyes and deeply inhaled the fragrant scent of vanilla.

"Welcome to my domain, Empress – my sanctuary, if you will," a wispy, melodic voice chimed. "I heard you had returned to my forest, and I hoped to make your acquaintance."

"Thank you," I managed to say. "Forgive me. I should probably know who you are, but I don't."

"As expected for someone who has not been nurtured to adulthood here in my forest. I am Idnim – the ancient among ancients, keeper and protector of the tree spirits and Forest of Notxarb." There was a hint of sadness in her tone as she introduced herself, which evoked such a strong emotional response in me that I couldn't stop a tear from escaping my eye.

"Lordess Nalla told me to find you, but I was supposed to ask my custodians to escort me," I explained.

"Yes, well I could not ignore your plea. After all, I am still under oath to the empress – an oath I cannot break."

"My plea?"

"A-hem," Leo interrupted by clearing his throat, or pretending to. I looked over at him, remembering Nedys. I had somehow summoned Idnim with my hand on the tree bark, although I hadn't spoken a word.

"Please help me," I entreated her.

"You no longer control me. Your powers are weak, and the orb is gone. I can sense it," she said, her voice sounding as if she had struck a sharp on a piano.

"I don't wish to control you. I don't wish to be here at all."

"Why have you returned then?" she demanded spitefully. I felt a swell of anger rise within at her rudeness. I had thought she would be an ally. Why else would Lordess Nalla have sent me to her? Before I could answer, Nedys began thrashing around, drawing everyone's attention to him.

I dropped to my knees at his side, while Leo pinned his arms. Nedys was sweating profusely and mumbling incoherently. As he shifted his head to the side, I saw that his wound was still bleeding. I looked at Leo in desperation.

"Hold his arms," he instructed. At first, I struggled. Nedys was strong, a lot stronger than me, but I had felt a surge of energy in the few moments I had been in Idnim's presence. I focused my mind on that energy and felt a jolt of strength rush through my body. Leo pulled off his outer t- shirt, leaving him in his white undershirt, and wound it into a long stretch of fabric. He then tied it firmly around Nedys's head, which was easier said than done since Nedys wouldn't hold still.

"Ease up, sis," Leo said with a shocked look on his face. "You're bruising his arms." I immediately loosened my grip, slightly amused at Leo's reaction.

"I'll take over," he said, pushing me aside. I moved to kneel above Nedys's head. I took his head in both hands to stabilize him. His skin was on fire. I glanced at Leo, whose expression wasn't hopeful. I had to calm Nedys down, so we could figure out how to help him. I sat down and cradled his head in my lap. I began to hum the lullaby.

Nedys almost immediately relaxed, and I began to smooth his hair around Leo's makeshift tourniquet. I found the haunting words to the lullaby escaping my mouth in song, and Leo, tentatively at first, joined in. Nedys's jagged breathing steadied into deep, slow breaths, and I felt him drift off to sleep. I knew he must be exhausted after exchanging his good night's sleep to stand in as my pillow last night. I also had a sneaking suspicion that he had stood watch all night to protect me. I had to help him. He had risked his life for me. I wanted to try to return the favor, but the knot that still twisted in my stomach when I thought of him told me that mere obligation wasn't the only reason I wanted to save Nedys.

"Please," I pleaded as I directed my attention back to Idnim, who stood staring at me with curious but hard eyes. "Please, help him."

"You request my aid on behalf of another – an Annyadian soldier at that. Curious. Very curious indeed," Idnim responded.

"Will you please help him?" I was at the point of groveling.

"Why have you returned to the forest?" she repeated her earlier inquiry.

"I brought her back here," a voice said from behind me. All eyes turned to the sound of the familiar voice. I was shocked when my eyes focused on the figure because I did not see the veiled face of Lordess Nalla. In its place stood a beautiful young woman with long golden hair that curled in perfect ringlets and cascaded down her shoulders to the middle of her back. Her golden eyes matched the hue of her hair, and her face and complexion were nothing short of perfection. If I had to describe my idea of the goddess of beauty, she would have been it. Her face was not marred by scars of any kind as Nedys had suggested as the reason behind the veil.

"I brought her back," she repeated when no one said anything.

"You?" Idnim sounded displeased.

"She was hoping we could help," Leo answered for Nalla, never breaking eye contact with her.

"How would you know?" I blurted out.

"My dreams. She needed my help," he explained, almost as if he were somewhere else. He had never seen her face, and yet he had somehow pieced together that the beautiful young woman who now stood before him was, in fact, the same girl he had seen in his dreams. He took a few steps toward Nalla, and I watched a slow smile spread across her face. Were they somehow communicating without talking? I became suddenly uncomfortable. Something wasn't right with this situation. Lordess Nalla should not be here. I picked up a rock that was lying by my side. I threw it at Leo, hitting him in the arm and stopping him in his tracks.

"Hey," he yelped, his eyebrows knit with disdain. He only made that face when he was mad – really mad, which didn't happen very often.

"What did you do that for?" he asked as he rubbed his arm.

"I do not want her help. She is the reason I'm in this predicament at all," Idnim broke into the confusion, her eyes focused intently on Lordess Nalla.

"You do not have a choice, Idnim," Lordess Nalla's statement surprised me.

"Why do you need me? What can I possibly do to help you?" I queried.

"The forest is dying," Lordess Nalla said.

"From the curse?"

"The curse is only part of the problem. The orb sustains life on this planet – in this forest. Its long absence is beginning to take its toll. The forest is not strong enough to support itself as you drain its power with your presence," she explained.

"If I'm killing the forest just by being here, why did you bring me here?" Confusion tainted my voice.

"I thought you would have the orb," Lordess Nalla admitted.

"I want the orb returned to its rightful place," Idnim interjected. "Where is it, and why did you not bring it with you?"

"I didn't even know about the orb until Nedys told me after I came here. And even if I did know where it was, Einnep would only use it to gain power."

"You're mistaken about your brother. He does not seek for power," Lordess Nalla countered.

"You expect me to believe that? Why else would he want the orb? Certainly not to protect the forest!"

"You're right. Einnep does not care for the forest. His reasons are his reasons, but I can assure you it is not for want of power." Melancholy cast its shadow over her facial expressions.

"That's why he enslaved his own people? Because he didn't want power?"

"He offered them their freedom, but they would not denounce their loyalty to the empress. He knew they would continue the war if he let them go without a blood oath. He had no choice but to keep close watch on them."

"In the quarry?"

"I'm not saying I agree with that. He was angry and grieving, and in their defiance, they became the object of his wrath."

"Grieving what? Certainly not the loss of the parents he led to their own execution or the disappearance of his younger siblings."

"Watch it there, Elli," Leo interjected. "He has no grudge against me. I was just a baby and aside from my obvious good looks, I have no unnatural powers." I glared at Leo. His smile quickly faded. I knew he was trying to diffuse the situation, sensing the building tension, but now was not the time for his nonchalant persona.

"Sorry," he mumbled, avoiding eye contact. I couldn't stay annoyed at Leo for the one reason I loved him most – his easy, going nature. I knew I had a tendency toward being a little too intense, which was probably why Leo had always been my only friend.

"Leo is correct," Nalla intervened.

"About which part?" Leo asked. "My good looks or my lack of unnatural powers?"

"He is not after you," Nalla evaded the question, though there was a gleam in her eye and an amused tone to her voice I had never heard before. "He does not know you exist."

"What?" Leo and I both said in unison.

"You must have been born just hours before your mother was executed. Einnep does not know the empress gave birth before her death. She must have still looked as if she were with child when she was executed, and you must have been safely stowed away with your custodians inside the Siol Tree," Nalla explained.

"Oh," Leo said, dropping his eyes to his feet. "He thinks I'm already dead."

Leo's downcast expression yanked at my heart. He didn't need to be dragged into all of this, but I had to ask myself why he cared what Einnep thought of him.

"Why did you bring him here? He doesn't need to be a part of this mess. He was fine where he was," I retorted angrily. Nalla returned her gaze to Leo, and he looked up at her instinctively. There was certainly some sort of weird bond between the two of them.

"Elleon," Lordess Nalla addressed her answer to Leo, and the way she said his name made him sound regal and majestic. There was also a hint of longing in her voice.

"Elleon," she repeated. "Your help is needed here as well."

"What can I do?" he asked quietly.

"You must rally the Enelians in the quarry. It is time they had their freedom, and it is you who will lead them to it...peacefully. They will listen to you as you have been with the empress these many years and have not been tainted by the dark shadow your brother has cast over their lives."

"Me? I can't lead anyone. Isn't that Elli's job?" He asked, his facial expressions revealing his confusion and lack of confidence. It was the first time Leo seemed vulnerable.

"I am afraid to say that the empress's presence would only spark a violent and bloody rebellion, which I will not allow to happen. I need you," as she said that last phrase, she walked to Leo's side and took both of his hands in hers. That was enough to snap the last strand of my patience. I was not evil. Why was everyone always assuming I would bring out the worst in every situation, in every person? I was not the evil one here, and I would not allow her to draw Leo into her little web of lies!

"Leave him alone," I shouted, rather more loudly than I had intended. "What are you trying to do? Cast a spell on him or something? Is this why you have been haunting his dreams? What are you anyway – a witch, a sorceress? And what are you doing here? I thought Annyadians weren't allowed in the forest?"

"I come here often to see Idnim. She's my tutor," Nalla answered, not revealing the slightest spite at my accusations. She released one of Leo's hands as she turned to look at me, but I noticed that she still held tightly to the other.

"Tutor?" I asked more confused than ever. Then, it donned on me – the rare herbs she used came from Idnim. "Idnim has been teaching me the arts of apothecary. I wish to become a healer for my people…and for your people."

"But from the rather mysterious appearance of the empress and her underling, I would say you have been dabbling in more than I have been teaching," Idnim joined the conversation at last.

"Please forgive me, Ancient One. I came upon the Pools of Many Waters quite by accident," Nalla tried to justify herself.

"By accident?" Idnim countered.

"Well, I found the Ancient Book of Passageways in the Twisted Silver Tree of the Narrow Path while I was searching for the coral root that you had sent me to find. I couldn't help but read from its pages. I was drawn to them in a way I cannot explain. It was there I found the map to the Pools of Many Waters. I spent many months decrypting the codes in the map until I found the pools at last, well-hidden and protected, but still in existence. The book also revealed the incantations that allowed me sight into other worlds, the worlds where the forest beings migrated and settled in the ancient days. Because you taught me the tongue of the Ancient Ones, I was able to unlock the waters of sight. Although I knew I was forbidden from entering the waters to the passageways, I began my search. I was sure the Guardian had taken the empress to one of these worlds. I searched in the waters through the great expanses of space until I found a world shadowed by the aura of the forest. I recognized it immediately and followed its trail to Elleon. I did not know he had survived the execution until I found him there. One look into his eyes, and I knew who he was. It was he who led me to the empress.

"I watched for twelve cycles of the moons until I knew our situation was becoming most desperate. I studied the book, hoping to find a way to bring them home, but I found nothing. Until the day I returned to the pools and found two small black balls sitting beside the pool leading to their world. The balls were streaked with bolts of color that thrashed about inside of them as though they were alive. I felt drawn to them, and I knew I couldn't leave until I had dropped one into the pool. I supposed the Guardian had sent them to me, choosing once again to intervene on behalf of the forest. As soon as I had dropped one ball into the pool, it clouded over, obscuring the empress. I pulled myself away from the other ball as quickly as I could and left, unsure of what I had done. When I heard the empress had been captured, and I knew the black ball had brought her back.

"After Nedys helped the empress escape, I returned to the pool to bring Elleon home. Only this time, I did not drop the ball into the pool. I reached through the pool with my own hand and gave the ball to Elleon, hoping he would know what to do with it. And apparently, he did," she finished as she looked back to Elleon and squeezed his hand.

"Foolish child," Idnim scolded. "You should not have done such things!"

"I had no choice. I could not sit by and watch the forest die. Without the forest, we will all die. You were foolish to take no action. You are supposed to be the protector," Nalla censured the Ancient One. I was surprised that Idnim made no retort. Her eyes seemed to drift toward the sky, and the Great White Tree shivered although there was no breeze.

"I ceased being a protector when I allowed Empress Eneli to take refuge in my forest and wield her magic here," Idnim admitted sadly.

"You could not have known what she would do here, and you only made the oath to the empress under threat of extermination of all forest kind. You saved the forest, Idnim. You have done all you can, but there is nothing more you can do. There is nothing more I can do. We must allow Empress Ellinnet to help the forest now," Nalla reasoned.

"I do not trust this empress," Idnim responded.

"She is not like the empresses before her. You have seen her heart, Idnim," Nalla clarified.

"She's right," I affirmed. "I don't want to hurt anyone. I want to make things right for the forest, for the Enelians, and even for the Annyadians. I hold no antiquated grudge against anyone here. I wish you would believe me. I'll do what you want if you'll tell me what I'm supposed to do and how I'm supposed to do it."

"I can vouch for her. I've known her all my life – not as a sister but as a friend. She wouldn't hurt anyone." Leo offered. He let go of Nalla's hand and rubbed the spot on his arm where I had thrown the rock at him. "Well, at least she wouldn't seriously injure anyone."

"Until the power takes hold," Idnim countered. "The power will strengthen, and it will change her as it has done every empress before. It has been polluted with eons of darkness. Having not been properly nurtured by the Ancients, she will not have the strength to combat it." I had to admit that I had felt the strength of the power within me. After all, I zapped Einnep when he made me angry. I didn't know how it had happened, and I didn't know how to control it.

"How much time do I have?" I asked, suddenly nauseated. I didn't want to turn into a monster, but everyone spoke as if it were inevitable.

"I cannot say. This is new phenomenon," came Idnim's hopeless reply.

"Well, we better get to it then, hadn't we? I will do what you want me to do, but only if you help Nedys," I bargained.

Idnim bowed her head and slowly approached. She bent down, close to Nedys and blew on his face. I could feel a cool mist envelope Nedys, and it appeared as though his body were wrapped in a cloud. Although I was holding his head in my hands, I could not see his face. Idnim floated back toward the Great White Tree. The thick fog covered Nedys's body for several minutes before finally dissipating just as Idnim reappeared from within the hollow of the tree. She nodded at Lordess Nalla.

Lordess Nalla stepped forward and slowly unwrapped Leo's shirt from around Nedys's head. Idnim handed her a brilliant yellow flower that had a gob of a blue pasty substance at its center. Nalla gently turned Nedys's head and pressed the flower and its paste to the wound. Nedys let out a moan as he slept. We were all silent as Lordess Nalla began to hum an unfamiliar tune as she carefully massaged the blue paste into the wound.

"Is that some sort of spell or incantation?" Leo whispered to her.

"No, Elleon," she answered with a chuckle. "I just like to sing while I work. I find it soothing to both me and the patient."

Nedys began to stir. Lordess Nalla pulled the flower away and stepped back as Nedys suddenly leaped to his feet, his eyes darting about wildly. His gaze settled on Idnim, who was standing right next to him. He jumped away, startled. Then he looked at Lordess Nalla, his eyebrows furrowing in confusion.

"Wh-who? Wh-what?" He stuttered, blinking wildly as if he could clear the scene from his vision.

"Nedys," I said, standing up next to him and grabbing his arm to turn him toward me.

"Empress?"

"Sit back down, Nedys. We have a lot of explaining to do," I encouraged him as I tugged him to a seated position.

Chapter Fourteen

Instructions

I told Nedys everything that had transpired since Yelnats knocked his head against the tree, with a few interjections by Leo and Lordess Nalla. Idnim had begun floating back and forth impatiently not long after I started my retelling.

"No scars," Nedys observed, as he stared at Lordess Nalla, obviously overtaken by her beauty. "Then, why the veil?"

"Oh, there are scars dear Nedys, but they aren't visible, and they aren't mine. Nor is that story mine to tell," Lordess Nalla responded, a look of sadness crossing her face.

"You truly found the ancient passageways?" he asked.

"What do you know of the passageways?" Idnim interrupted.

"Me mum spoke of them in stories when I was a boy," he answered.

"The time for storytelling has come to an end, and now Empress Ellinnet, you should be about your business. The soldier is healed, and you must do as promised," Idnim demanded.

"What promise?" Nedys asked. I hadn't told him that part of the story.

"It doesn't matter," I tried to blow him off, suddenly embarrassed by the implications of my actions. What if he thought there were more to my actions than repayment for his kindness? What if there were more to my actions than that?

"It matters to me," he said.

"She promised to find the orb for Idnim in exchange for your healing," Leo answered for me.

"You know where the orb is then?" Nedys asked me, distrust brewing in his eyes.

"No, I don't," I affirmed.

"We can attest to that," I heard a rustle of bushes behind me as Yelnirb, Yelnats, and Leo's custodians came into view.

"Are you well, Empress?" Yelnats asked as they rushed toward me.

"I'm fine," I reassured him. I hadn't realized I had been clenching my jaw, until I suddenly relaxed at the unexpected appearance of my custodians.

"Idnim," Yelnirb said, with a bow, "she tells the truth. We have not seen the orb in these many years. This is an impossible quest, for surely, the Guardian has taken it from us as punishment for years of war and separation."

"She has made an oath, and she will not break it," Idnim stood firm.

"But the orb is not here in the forest or in Annyad, so how is she to find it?" Yelnirb questioned protectively.

"I believe the orb to be within the realm you have been dwelling. How else would you explain your continued existence outside of the forest? She will return there and bring it back." Idnim instructed.

"We surely cannot travel to the other realm again," Yelnats chimed in.

"In that you are correct, Treef," she said the latter word with as much scorn as she could muster. "There is a way that she can return. This portal of which I speak can be used once and once only – there and back again. The empress can pass through the gateway into a world she has before inhabited, but she must take with her one who has been born of her kind in our world in order for the return gateway to unlock when the time comes."

"I will go," Lordess Nalla volunteered.

"And what of Master Einnep? You will be missed," Nedys noted. "If you are to liberate the quarry workers without bloodshed, you must remain with Elleon. I will go." My heart started to pound in my chest. Nedys was volunteering?

"Yes, it must be the Annyadian," Idnim agreed.

"We cannot allow the empress to go without her custodians," Yelnirb insisted.

"If she does not go, the forest will die. Would that be your choice?" Idnim asked.

"Of course not, but what of the empress's safety? And how is she to find the orb without our help? She doesn't even know what she is looking for," Yelnirb inquired.

Idnim held out her hand, and two thick silver bracelets floated from the Great White Tree into her palm on a breeze she had conjured. She motioned for Nedys and me to come forward.

"You will wear these at all times. They are not only the keys to opening the portals, but also the way in which you will locate the orb. Note the flat circle in the middle, amidst the filigree of silver foliage. When the orb is near, this spot will glow a bright yellow," she told us as she fastened the bracelets on the wrists of our right arms.

"There is one problem, however," Idnim paused. "The portal is within the Siol Tree." I looked up at Nedys, knowing what that meant.

"But it's poisonous. Nedys can't go in there. No one here can except for me or some other Enelian who bears the mark," I said for the benefit of Leo, who didn't understand the problem.

Although Leo was an Enelian, he did not bear the mark either, probably because he had been too young, and there hadn't been enough time to perform the ceremony.

"This is true," Idnim admitted, "but it can be remedied. He must undergo the ceremony and receive the mark, and you, Empress, must perform it."

"I don't –" I began to protest before being interrupted by Idnim.

"You don't have a choice, Empress. You will perform the ceremony, and the Annyadian must comply. Your custodians are well aware of all the procedures and can serve as your guides," Idnim finished coldly.

"I'm sorry," I said finally turning to face Nedys, but I was surprised that he did not bear an expression of anger.

"For what, saving my life? I hope you're not sorry about that," he said with a smile. No, I certainly wouldn't regret ever doing that, no matter what the consequences.

"For what I'm about to do. Although I have no idea what that is exactly, from the looks of my scar, I'm pretty sure it's going to be painful," I explained.

"I volunteered, remember?" he offered.

"You didn't know what you were in for though," I countered.

"You don't see me backing out now, do you? The way I see it I've only got two choices anyway. Go under the blade at your hand, or go under the blade at the hand of me father and Einnep. I choose you," he said very seriously. I didn't argue, knowing full well he was probably right, and I knew I wasn't planning to kill him.

"On the seventh night after the ceremony, he will be well enough to travel," Idnim said. I saw Nedys's face pale as he mouthed "seven days?" to me. I bit my lip. It seemed it would be quite the procedure after all.

"You will wear the Cuff of Creation on the wrist of the hand that bears the mark. Do not remove it. And now for the instructions to the portal. You must leave when the twin suns are in the height of the sky. No sooner. No later. There is a portal that exists within the Siol Tree. Behind the Fountain of Glowing Waters, you will find a plant – the Flowers of Eternal Bloom. You will pluck the dark purple flower with the white center. While both of you hold onto the flower with the hand the bears the mark and the Cuff of Creation, the empress will repeat the words, 'Carry me plus one to the land apart, the land where I dwelt – the land of my heart.' Repeat the words twice, once for each traveler, but only you will say the words. Make sure you keep hold of the flower. It will be the means by which you return after you have found the orb. You have only until the last petal falls from the flower to find the orb, or there will be no return and the forest will die along with all those who are living here," Idnim explained pointedly, looking straight at Leo as if to tell me that she was holding Leo prisoner to ensure my return. "When you are ready to come back with the orb, both of you hold onto the flower with the marked hand, while the Annyadian repeats these words: 'Carry me plus one back again – the land of my birth – to the ancient den.' Understood?"

"How do you know of this flower?" I asked, wondering how Idnim would know of its location.

"That is none of your concern," she snapped, her tone icier than ever. I saw Yelnirb shake her head ever so slightly as a warning to me not to pursue the topic any further.

"Do you understand my instructions?" she repeated, glaring at me.

"Yes," Nedys and I answered in unison.

"Very well," she raised her hand and a small vile came floating from The Great White Tree.

It stopped as it hovered in the air in front of me, so I opened my palm.

"If the Annyadian's body begins to reject the immunization, give him a drop of this every hour on the hour until he has recovered," she instructed as she placed the vial of liquid in my hand.

"But how will I know?" I asked somewhat panicked. I hadn't thought the process was going to be life-threatening.

"Oh, you'll know," Idnim said without offering further explanation. I hoped for Nedys's sake that it wouldn't come to that.

"Now be off, and remember, once you've picked the Flower of the Eternal Blossom, your time is limited," she reminded us.

"Are you sure about this, Elli?" Leo approached me as Idnim drifted back to the Great White Tree.

"I have no choice, Leo," I said. "What about you?"

"Likewise," he echoed my sentiment. Then, he reached over and hugged me unexpectedly. "You can do it," he whispered in my ear.

"And so can you," I whispered back. He pulled away and looked long into my eyes.

"I should have known you were my sister – and an empress at that," he smiled as he spoke.

"Now's not the time to get all sentimental on me, Leo," I cautioned as I gave him a light jab in the arm.

"Take care of my little brother," I said, emphasizing the word little, as I turned toward Lordess Nalla. "I'd like to see him in one piece when I get back." She nodded in response as she pulled Leo away through a path that had been concealed by shrubbery. I noticed that he didn't look back.

"We better be off as well," Yelnirb advised as she moved toward a different path. I looked at Nedys, who gestured for me to go first.

Chapter Fifteen

Encounter

We walked in silence for a while until we were quite a distance away from Idnim's sanctuary. I was lost in my own thoughts trying to make sense of the new pieces of my puzzle that had just fallen into place.

"We shall summon the tree here," Yelnirb stopped suddenly. I looked around, but there didn't seem to be anything unusual about this particular spot of the forest.

"Summon the tree? Last time it just appeared," I remembered.

"Last time we traveled in the root systems to its location. We cannot do that with the young fellow here, now can we?" Yelnats explained. "He is not permitted to travel that way, and the tree is still a fair distance away. At least another day's walk from here."

"How are we supposed to get to the tree then?" I asked.

"You wait here with the young fellow," Yelnirb instructed. "We will go through the root system to the tree and bring it back with us. We need to gather the necessary supplies and equipment from the tree as well. It may take a while, though. We did not have time to check out the condition of the main quarters of the Siol Tree."

"Main quarters?"

"Empress, you saw only our own humble abode when you first entered. That is not your home. In fact, you should never have been subjected to those cramped quarters. The Siol Tree is merely the entrance to an underground palace

119

of sorts. The doors open to whatever area is tapped out into the bark. I don't know whether the palace proper came out unscathed after the death of your parents. Surely, the Siol Tree would have detected Einnep's treachery at once and hidden itself, but if he was already inside before the tree recognized the circumstances surrounding the empress's death, he may have been allotted a period of time to wreak havoc on the palace. We will go now and return as soon as we can. Please do not leave this spot," Yelnirb requested.

"I promise I won't go anywhere, but how will you summon the tree to this spot without hurting Nedys if it's poisonous to him?"

"As long as he does not touch any part of the tree, bark or leaf, he will remain unharmed. It is only through prolonged exposure to the shade of the Siol Tree or direct contact with the tree itself that one suffers permanent damage from the poison," Yelnats answered. I didn't want to ask what the permanent damage was. There were some things I would rather not know.

"Where is the ceremony performed then?"

"The initial steps are performed in the shade of the Siol Tree. Then, the young pledge is moved to the inner walls to allow the inoculation to take effect."

"How is it that Leo hasn't been branded?" I wondered aloud.

"The poison isn't harmful to infants, Elli," Yelnats said. "It only affects those older than two, which is the age the ceremony is typically performed on forest-born children. But enough talk. We must leave if we're to get back." With that they were gone, leaving Nedys and I alone once again.

I leaned up against a tree, concentrating on the astonished whispers spreading through the forest. There was excitement at the prospect of the orb being returned and a certain tone of hopefulness that it was in fact the Guardian who had it in his possession. It had been centuries since anyone had seen or heard from the Guardian, and the thought that he was still out there somewhere watching over them was a comfort.

I glanced in Nedys's direction. He was standing in a little clearing off to the side of the path a few feet away from me. He appeared to be lost in his own thoughts as he traced patterns in the dirt with the toe of his boot. I looked down at my hand, running my fingers over my own scar – the brand of Eneli – the brand that would soon sever Nedys from his Annyadian roots forever.

"Nedys," I called to him. He looked up from his dirt drawing, his eyebrows raised in expectation of what I might say. Too bad I wasn't sure myself. I wanted to let him off the hook and send him back to Annyad, but I couldn't. Without him, I couldn't save the forest.

"Never mind," I mumbled.

"What is it, Empress?" he asked.

"Nothing…well…I just…oh, I didn't mean for you to get caught up in this mess. That's all," I stammered.

"I made me own decisions, Empress," he said matter-of-factly.

"But if I hadn't shown up here, you wouldn't have had to make those decisions," I countered.

"And that wasn't your choice either, was it?" he pointed out.

If I were to be honest with myself, I really wanted to know that he wasn't just doing this because he had no other choice than be stuck with me or punished by my brother. I didn't want to be the better of two bad options, although I knew I was probably was. I couldn't force the words out of my mouth. Besides, I was pretty sure I didn't want to hear his answer.

"Nedys?" a voice called out from somewhere behind Nedys. My heart started to race, and I hid behind the tree I had been leaning against. Nedys quickly closed the gap between him and me, surprise registering on his face, but not alarm. He didn't reach for his bow, which was propped up against a nearby tree. He turned his head toward the direction of the voice, so I could only see the back of his head. His hair was matted with blood and dirt and stuck up in every direction.

"Nedys, me boy!" The voice exclaimed as a figure emerged from the trees.

"Hairam," Nedys stepped toward the approaching young man. The young man appeared to be in his late teens with hair so blonde it was almost white, worn in the same style as Nedys's. His Annyadian tunic revealed his position as a soldier. He stepped gingerly toward Nedys, engulfing him in a quick embrace and patting him hard on the back.

"I didn't think I'd find you," he said, as he stepped back to survey the area. "What have you been about? The city is practically on fire with the news that the empress has escaped." I felt my already racing heart jump at the remark.

"Escaped, has she?" Nedys asked, although he didn't sound surprised. He was going to have to be more convincing than that if his fellow soldier was going to believe him.

"Funny thing that you went missing about the same time. Quite a coincidence, eh?" Hairam said, a smile pressing on his lips. A smile? I wasn't sure what was going on.

"How'd the traveler do, then?" he asked, seemingly unconcerned with Nedys's apparent involvement in my escape.

"You'd have been proud. She's a dream, that she is," Nedys replied.

"I found her anchored in the cave and figured I'd try me luck in the forest, though I'm surprised I happened across you so close to the border. Are you returning then?" Hairam asked. "I'll vouch for you. We can come up with some scheme, just like always."

"You know I can't do that," Nedys said. Hairam didn't press him for details.

"And what of the empress? You can come to your senses now that you're not bewitched by her beauty, eh?" Hairam laughed.

I felt a blush rise to my cheeks. What did he mean by that? I knew he couldn't be referring to me. I was no beauty under the best of conditions, and Nedys had only seen me at my worst. But then Hairam couldn't have been talking about Lordess Nalla either, since everyone thought her to be badly scarred. Nedys cleared his throat.

"What's this now? You can't fool me, Nedys. We've known each other for far too long, me friend. She lurks about, doesn't she?" Hairam began scanning the area in search of me. I cowered behind the tree. I saw Nedys raise his arm and motion for me to come out without even bothering to turn his head in my direction. I didn't move a muscle. There was no way I was going to reveal myself to a perfect stranger.

"Empress," Nedys finally turned in my direction. "I'd like to introduce you to me good friend, Hairam." After all, Nedys had done for me and was about to do for me, I decided to appease him. Besides that, I also had a rising need to meet such a longtime acquaintance of Nedys who could so easily dismiss his treachery in aiding and abetting the enemy. I came out from behind the tree, squaring my soldiers and walking as confidently as I supposed an empress should walk. I only wished it were more than a pretense. I felt my confidence shrivel as I became incredibly self-conscious, just as I always did when I was in the presence of Leo's friends.

"Empress," Hairam gave a little bow as he spoke, and I was sure he was mocking me, "a pleasure to make your acquaintance." He surveyed me with a look of displeasure. I glanced down at my tunic, stained with reprah blood and missing a sleeve. It looked as though I had rolled around in a slaughterhouse.

"Pardon my appearance," I said, flushing. Hairam gave Nedys an amused smile.

"Well, I must say you're not exactly what I was expecting from the…description I received," he was interrupted by a jab in the ribs from Nedys's elbow. Nedys sent a glare in his direction, an unspoken threat that silenced Hairam. It appeared that Nedys had told Hairam about me, leaving Hairam with a favorable impression at least – until he met me in person anyway.

"From the looks of both of you, you've had a rough go of it since the escape. It was an escape, wasn't it? I hope Nedys didn't kidnap you for his own personal gain."

"If you know him as well as you say you do, you would know that such an accusation is not in Nedys's character," I refuted, impressed that I had managed to sound somewhat regal in my reply. Hairam looked at me with interest.

"Well, Nedys did have one thing right about you. You're nothing like I expected you to be."

"I should hope not. Though I fear few people would actually believe that given the long, dark Histories that tell much different tales of the empresses of the past."

"The past is always a formidable enemy, Empress. You're lucky, me boy Nedys prefers to live in the present."

"I consider myself more than lucky. He's already saved my life twice and is about to try for a third time."

"To be sure? My, my, such gallantry you show, dear Nedys. It's a wonder you were Einnep's pet. But what's this about a third time?" Hairam looked around as if in search of an unseen enemy.

"He's about to help me recover the orb at great personal cost to himself," I explained, wondering if I should have been so presumptuous. Nedys trusted Hairam, didn't he? Doubt shimmied its way into my thoughts. Nedys didn't give me any reassurance since he kept his eyes fixed on a tree.

"Nedys?" The amusement left Hairam's tone completely as he turned to his friend, his eyebrows furrowed in concern.

"What news can you give us from Annyad?" Nedys deflected the question, and I knew I must have made a mistake in telling Hairam.

"Nedys, that's not going to work with me, and you know it."

"I don't want you entangled in this, Hairam."

"Too late for that, I'd say. We've never held any secrets between us, so out with it," Hairam urged.

"The orb must be returned, but not on Einnep's terms or using his methods. The empress has come to an agreement with Idnim, the last Ancient who still resides here in the forest. She has promised to go back to the world she came from and bring the orb back. She needs someone from our world to accompany her, so she can return to the forest through a portal."

"A noble quest, indeed. And dangerous to be sure," Hairam commented.

"There is a catch," Nedys interjected. "I have to be branded before we go."

"Tell me your joking, me boy," Hairam said as the color drained from his face.

"It's no joke," Nedys affirmed.

"Do you know what you've gotten yourself into? The branding ceremony isn't to be taken lightly. I've heard tales of the pain..." he let his words trail off as he studied the resolute look on his friend's face. "I know that look, me boy – you'll not be persuaded out of it by the likes of me. I'll petition the moons on your behalf." He clapped his hand on Nedys's shoulder.

"Now, what news of Annyad?"

"Need you even ask that question, me boy?"

"Has Einnep sent out the troops? First ranks, maybe second?"

"Surprisingly, no. Lord Atrebor forbade him to act."

"Lord Atrebor? He never intervenes."

"Strange times these are. Strange times."

"What is he waiting for? I was sure Einnep would hunt her down like the animal he is," Nedys inquired.

"Lordess Nalla has taken ill," Hairam answered. I had to stifle a laugh. Lordess Nalla looked to be the picture of health the last time we saw her. It was not Lord Atrebor who intervened, but Nalla through her father. I exchanged looks with Nedys.

"What's this?" Hairam pointed his finger back and forth between Nedys and me. Nothing escaped his notice it seemed. "Lordess Nalla is not ill, I take it."

"Lordess Nalla is the one who brought me here," I told him. "She's been sneaking out of Annyad for quite some time, studying apothecary under Idnim. We just saw her this morning."

"Treachery runs deep. Einnep's made some powerful enemies if even Lordess Nalla is in league with his lifelong opponent," Hairam surmised.

"It's not what it seems. Lordess Nalla would never betray Einnep in the way you might be thinking. Her motives are pure – she wishes only to save the forest, which is dying in the long absence of the orb. That and the fact that she seems to have taken an interest in my brother," I said.

"Brother? She's already betrothed to your brother," Hairam stated.

"Not that brother," Nedys clarified. "The empress has a younger brother who was taken away with her. He is on his way to unify the Enelian quarry workers with Lordess Nalla, so war doesn't break out."

"They'll be freed then?"

"I'll have it no other way. Einnep has been cruel to imprison his own people, and there will be no more war on my account," I stated.

"Change is coming then. What would you have me do?" Hairam asked.

"Go on as before," Nedys answered. "Pretend you know nothing, but keep a sharp eye out for Lordess Nalla. Einnep will not view her actions as anything short of betrayal."

"Certainly. She has a friend in me, but I'm none too sure I'll be assigned to guard her anymore because of me close association to you."

"For that, me friend, I am sorry. I had hoped he would not take me actions out on you," Nedys apologized.

"Your father is a hard man. Border patrol isn't the worst he could have done to me. I can handle a little reprah here and there. Speaking of border patrol, it's about time for me to check in. I best be off. Good luck to you, me boy!"

"Take care of yourself, Hairam," Nedys cautioned. "I'm glad I got to see you again. Your friendship has meant more than you can imagine these past years. Whatever happens, know that at least...and the traveler, she's as good as yours." I felt as if I were witnessing their last goodbye, and the feeling didn't settle well with me. Hairam clapped his hand on Nedys's shoulder one last time before disappearing into the forest once again. I guess I hadn't really considered Nedys's life outside of being a soldier. I suppose he did have friends and pastimes just like any other person might, and he was giving all of that up.

"Hairam's the best sort," Nedys told me as he continued to stare off into the trees where he had last seen his friend. I retreated to my tree, not wanting to intrude on Nedys's solitary moment. Besides, I didn't really know what to say to him.

Chapter Sixteen

Branded

There was a whirring sound just before the tree appeared in front of me. It was more hauntingly beautiful than I remembered it. The smooth black bark glistened in the waning light of the day, and the brilliant hues of the leaves were mesmerizing. I looked at Nedys to find that he, too, seemed taken back by the Siol Tree.

"It's real," he whispered as he gazed on its splendor. "I mean, I knew it was real, but seeing it with me own eyes…" Nedys took a step forward, hand outstretched as if to touch a deep purple leaf that hung close to him. I rushed toward him, putting myself between him and the tree.

"Stop," I shouted, more forcefully than I intended. Nedys blinked as if he could not see me clearly. He did not drop his hand but kept reaching for the leaf that would surely maim, if not kill him. I raised my hands to his chest and began pushing him away from the tree. He resisted, but I continued to push him away, grateful the forest lent me its strength. Finally, Yelnats emerged from the tree. Seeing my predicament, he reached my side in two long strides. He pulled something out of his pocket and threw it into Nedys's eyes. His trance broken, Nedys's hands went to eyes, scratching at them furiously.

"Forgot to warn you about that," Yelnats said. "The tree draws the unprotected to it – a lure if you will."

"What did you do to him?" I asked.

"I threw a bit of sand in his eyes," Yelnats stated.

"Sand? What on earth did you do that for?" I asked incredulously.

"To break eye contact with the tree, of course," Yelnats seemed exasperated.

"But you've hurt his eyes," I explained.

"He's not hurt as badly now as he would have been if he'd touched that leaf, now, is he?" Yelnats demanded. Unfortunately, I couldn't disagree. I bent down to see if I could help Nedys just as Yelnirb emerged from the tree. She cast a disapproving look at Yelnats and bent down next to me.

"Sand, Yelnats? Honestly. There are other means you could have used that would not have caused as much discomfort," Yelnirb chided as she grabbed Nedys's face with the long, gangly fingers of one of her hands. With the other hand, she pried his eye open and spit, repeating the process with the other eye. I wrinkled my nose in disgust, but Nedys immediately quit clawing at her.

"Ah," he said with relief, "That is much better. Thanks. I don't know what came over me."

"Nothing a little sand couldn't fix," Yelnats muttered. I don't think he'd forgiven Nedys for capturing me that first night in the forest.

"Now keep your eyes fixed on the ground," Yelnirb instructed as she helped Nedys to his feet. "Under no circumstances are you to look at the Siol Tree. Understood?"

"Not even tempted to look," Nedys admitted as he fixed his stare to the ground and wiped sand and spit remnants off his face.

"Very well," Yelnirb acknowledged before turning to address me. "Empress, it is as we feared. The Siol tree was ransacked by Einnep before he left, and we haven't the time to prepare the palace for your arrival. The suns are now setting, and we must prepare for the ceremony as it is done in the moonlight."

"Just tell me what I need to do," I said.

Yelnirb turned toward Yelnats, who was now holding a black velvet bag.

Yelnirb reached inside the bag, withdrawing a knife, its silver blade reflecting the last rays of sunlight. She placed the black handle inlaid with purple gems in my hand. It was lighter than I expected, and an odd feeling crept through my body as I held it. A hundred images danced through my mind: faces, moonlight, blood, screaming. I seemed to draw power and strength from them. I dropped the knife with a start, shaking my head as I backed away. I did not like the dark feeling that had come upon me. I would never be able to get those images out of my head. Nedys looked up at the sound of the knife clattering to the forest floor. He must have seen the fear in my eyes, the dread. He bent down and retrieved the knife and placed it once again in my hand.

"You must," he urged, looking deeply into my eyes. I forced the images to the back of my mind as I tried to focus on Nedys. I focused on the green of his eyes rather than the blackness connected to the knife. And suddenly, I knew what I had to do. I reached for Nedys's hand and led him into the shade of the Siol Tree to a large stump that was knee-high. Its surface was flat and smooth and bore the dark stains of blood – blood from humans and blood from the Siol Tree. This stump always accompanied the Siol Tree in her journeys through the forest for this very purpose. Without being told, I knew that the stump was the remnant of the first tree spirit who sacrificed her life to increase Eneli's power as she started *The Awakening*. I knew all this just because I was holding the very same knife Empress Eneli had wielded.

"You don't have to do this. It's not too late to back out now. If you could have seen–" I was pleading with Nedys not to make me go through with this dark ritual, but he cut me off mid- sentence.

"What do I need to do?" he asked the question in a tone that didn't allow for further argument. I would have to lean on his courage to carry this out.

"Kneel here," I told Nedys. I walked to the other side of the stump, which was about three feet wide, and knelt across from him. He placed his right hand at the center of the stump without being asked. I placed my left hand underneath his to hold it in place as I brought the knife above his hand. I was surprised to find that my hand was not shaking because inside I was trembling at the thought of what I was about to do. Yelnirb placed a glass cup filled with violet liquid on the stump next to me. The liquid was the blood of the Siol tree – the sap that oozed from the small hole Yelnats had bored just moments before. I brought the knife point to Nedys's skin and hesitated.

I looked up only to find him still staring intently at me. He nodded his head as if to tell me he was ready, and I looked away from his face as I pressed the knife point into his palm, cutting a two-inch line into his flesh. I could tell that he was holding his breath. I saw his muscles tense as he struggled to prevent the reflexive action of drawing his hand away from the pain, but other than that, he did not flinch. As I sliced through his skin, I chanted the words that came unbidden to my mind:

"With this blade I thee wound, with this tree become attuned."

The wound was bleeding all over the rock, and I lifted his hand up, sliding the glass cup underneath to catch the blood. His blood ran into the cup, fizzing and steaming when it came into contact with the violet liquid. I lowered Nedys's hand back to the rock and poured the now boiling liquid into the open wound as I chanted:

"Blood and poison, mix and blend,

With your allegiance, me defend.

Find safety in this home of mine,

Sealed by the moons' powerful shine.

This brand protect you, firm and true,

Your life must now begin anew."

Nedys was biting his lower lip as he clenched his hand into a tight fist to quell the searing pain. The hot liquid cauterized the wound, so the bleeding immediately ceased. I knew the poison would race through his veins, carrying that same intense pain throughout his entire body. The pain would be so severe, he would lose consciousness briefly as his body tried to defend itself against the unwelcome and potentially deadly invasion. I cupped his fist in both my hands, knowing I could not bring him any relief. I heard his labored breathing as I raised my eyes to his just as the moonlight wound its way to the stump. I saw the anguish in his face before his body slumped forward onto the stump. As his body gave way to the immunization, I felt a surge of power spark within me. I was growing stronger even as he grew weaker, and as much as I tried to resist, there was nothing I could do about it. Yelnirb and Yelnats were at my side, lifting Nedys so they each carried one of his arms over their shoulders. His head lolled forward as they took him to the tree and disappeared inside.

I remained outside for a few minutes, staring at the leaves of the Siol Tree, glimmering in the moonlight. I looked down at the blood-stained knife that rested on the stump, the images once again cascading through my mind. I was grateful I had been spared a childhood in this place, but I couldn't help but weep for those who had not been so fortunate. The empress was much like the lure of the Siol Tree – ensnaring innocent people with her lies, enticing them to give up their very lives for her. In bearing the title of empress, I was now that villain. No, I would not be that villain. I was the key to introducing a new kind of empress to the people of Eneli and Annyad.

I picked up the knife and wiped the blade clean with the inside of my tunic.

That would be the last drop of blood that would be shed on my account. I would make sure of it. I placed the knife back inside the black velvet bag and walked toward the Siol Tree for the second time since I had arrived in the forest. I hesitated at the entrance. My fingers almost automatically rose to a certain place on the bark that was slightly raised and glided over several bumps in a sequential pattern.

Déjà-vu. I had been here before, standing at this exact spot watching my fingers glide across the bark to open the door. I had been almost three years old. I felt a sudden flurry of childish excitement at the thought of returning home – a place I felt safe and secure. The memory faded as the opening appeared, as did my sense of security. With trepidation, I slipped quietly inside.

Unfortunately, I felt a dark shadow attach itself quite securely to me. The dark magic had found me at last; or rather I had found it. I had unleashed it when I touched the knife and inflicted pain on someone I cared about. I felt a heaviness in my chest that weighed me down as I struggled against the power surging through me. The war had begun, only it wasn't as I imagined it would be: me against Einnep and his Annyadian forces. The war would be raged within me: good versus evil.

As I descended the steps slowly, I found myself in a large room unlike anything I had seen before. I suppose in my head I had pictured marble floors and staircases, but this resembled an indoor botanical garden with ivy-like vines climbing the walls and ceilings. This place was the opposite of what it should be. It was green, beautiful, and brimming with life. The lighting in the room was as bright as if daylight were streaming through nonexistent windows, though I couldn't find a light source anywhere. The sweet smell of the forest after a rainstorm wafted through the air, reminding me of summer camping trips with my parents, Leo, and his parents. A sudden longing for my real home nestled beside my uncertainty of the future.

I could hear some scuffling to my right, so I followed the noise through a veil of low hanging flowers until I emerged in yet another room not unlike the first. It was bursting with color and life. On the far wall, Nedys was writhing on four-poster bed as Yelnats tried to restrain him.

I approached quickly, curious to see how Nedys was fairing and hoping he wasn't as bad as my visions had foretold. I was disappointed in that wish, however. Nedys was tossing and turning on the bed, his hair wet from sweat. A purple web-like rash was climbing up his neck and onto his face. Yelnats was struggling to take his tunic off, and Yelnirb was nowhere in sight. As Yelnats tried to take Nedys's arm out of the tunic, Nedys thrashed at him, shouting in his delirium, "Get away! Don't touch me!" I hurried to help.

"You hold his arms, and I'll pull," I offered. Yelnats didn't object. I worked to free one arm and then the other, slowly lifting the tunic over Nedys's twisting head. As I worked, I hummed the tune to the lullaby I knew so well, hoping it would soothe him as it had done in Idnim's sanctuary. Here inside the Siol Tree with its poison coursing through his veins, the melody did just the opposite. It seemed to agitate him more as he began writhing about with renewed vigor. Yelnats was practically laying on him so he wouldn't fall off the bed.

"Best not sing that one," Yelnats cautioned. "It'll cause the poison to react faster than he can fight it off. The poison is alive you see. It responds to its master."

"Sorry...I didn't know," I mumbled, chiding myself for causing Nedys even more pain.

"Now for the undershirt," Yelnats instructed.

"Where's Yelnirb?" I asked as my face flushed red at the thought of taking off Nedys's undershirt.

"She's preparing the tonic to help him survive this. This is no time to be shy, child. We must remove the clothing before it melts to his flesh," Yelnats advised as Nedys struggled to free himself from Yelnats's confining embrace.

"Hurry now!" Yelnats requested urgently. I did as I was told. The undershirt was dripping wet with sweat. I quickly pulled his arms out of the sopping fabric, but it got tangled at his neck. Nedys broke free for a moment, grabbing at me, but Yelnats quickly re-pinned his arms to his sides. I probably could have held Nedys down better than Yelnats given the infusion of strength I had just received from using my dark power, and that wasn't saying anything against Nedys's own strength.

His tunic didn't do his muscular build any justice as I was now observing. I couldn't force myself to use that tainted strength though. I had a strong feeling the more I used the power I had been given, the stronger the hold it would have on me and the less time I would have before it absorbed my will to fight it.

The undershirt was twisted around a black cord that hung from Nedys's neck. I somehow managed to untangle everything as I slipped the undershirt over Nedys's head. My eyes fixed on the smooth, blue stone that dangled from the end of the black cord – the culprit of the entanglement. I wondered why Nedys wore it under his clothing. It must have been important to him, so I didn't bother removing it. I gasped as my eyes were next drawn to the purple rash winding its way across Nedys's muscled chest. This was no ordinary rash though. With every beat of Nedys's heart, it surged with a bright purple light like a strobe light. I could feel the heat emanating from his body as if I were standing too close to a campfire in full blaze. Thankfully, Yelnirb came rushing into the room, holding a tray of assorted bottles and bowls.

"Elli, you shouldn't be in here," she said, glancing down at the undershirt I still held in my hand.

"Yelnats needed some help," I responded. "And besides, I'm not leaving him." Yelnirb exchanged a wary look with Yelnats.

"Listen, he wouldn't be in this mess if it weren't for me," I tried to explain away their worry.

"Very well," Yelnirb relented. "We must immobilize him." She reached for a bottle of red liquid as she set the tray down.

"Elli, you hold his head," Yelnirb said. I grabbed Nedys's head and held tight while Yelnirb pried his lips open and poured the liquid into the back of his throat. Nedys coughed and sputtered as droplets of the red liquid splattered on my face. Yelnirb kept forcing him to drink until the bottle was empty. I felt Nedys's body slacken, and Yelnats finally let go of his arms.

"Is that a sedative?" I asked.

"I bet he wishes it were, but no. It simply paralyzes his muscles so he can't move, but he can still hear and feel everything."

"Can't we just put him to sleep for a few days?" I asked.

"Elli, my child. This is a pledge of pain. If we put him to sleep, he will never wake up."

"This is crazy. The empress put small children through this?" I had no memory of such trauma.

"No. The hardest part for a child is the cut and maybe a slight fever. Their bodies are growing at such a rapid rate that the inoculation is designed to merge and alter their genetic structure rather seamlessly. For a grown man, it's much more difficult, and his body must be fully awake and aware as the poison tears down the old and makes the new."

"Has anyone died from this?"

"Several spies sent in to infiltrate our stronghold — at least that's what the empress said. Few adults from Annyad have wished to join forces with our side these past generations, but there are stories from the early days…the process for them was a test of loyalty, and that loyalty was proven only by endurance. It was survival of the fittest — for the empress only wanted the strong." Yelnirb's voice trailed off.

"What have I done?" I slumped into a nearby chair and covered my face with my hands.

Hairam had been right, and Nedys had surely known of these stories. I knew they were the stories of the tortured faces I had seen when I touched that knife. Nedys knew too, and yet he still came. I reached over and grabbed his hand, knowing he could feel my touch even though he could not respond. When my skin touched his, I felt another jolt, as if I'd been shocked at the touch. I quickly withdrew my hand, wondering if my interference would cause Nedys even more pain.

"It's best if you do," Yelnirb observed. I looked up at her in confusion.

"It's best if you touch him," she clarified. "The poison can sense that Nedys has a strong ally. Your presence can only help him."

"As long as I don't sing," I muttered. "Why would touching help him and singing hurt him?"

"It's not so much the singing. It's the particular song you were singing. You just can't sing that one — Siol, the tree spirit, claims it as her own. It was the song used by Empress Eneli to create her."

"Tree spirits can be created?"

"Not naturally, no," Yelnirb admitted. I shivered as a dark feeling crept over me. No wonder Siol was loyal to the empress. As her creator, Siol owed her existence to the dark powers of Eneli. I closed my eyes to listen for Siol's song. I wanted to hear what she had to say about my arrival, but Siol appeared to be giving me the silent treatment because I heard nothing but Nedys's staggered breathing. Did she see me as an intruder, or worse, a traitor? While there was probably nothing she could do to me, I knew Nedys was another matter altogether. I would have to try communicating later, maybe outside where I could put my hand to the bark of the tree.

"Here, Elli," Yelnirb said as she handed me a bowl. "You need to eat something."

I hadn't been paying attention to the hunger pains gnawing at my stomach. I couldn't remember the last time I had eaten. In fact, I could hardly believe that just last night Nedys had helped me escape. It seemed so long ago. In one day, I had not only been reunited with Leo, but I had also seen Lordess Nalla's face, been confronted by Idnim, and promised to return the orb to the forest. It had been a long day, a very long day. I finished the bowl of food Yelnirb had given me and laid my head on the arm of the chair, still holding Nedys's right hand. I turned his hand over and traced my finger over the knife wound. The brand of Eneli – I only hoped it would still be worth it when all was said and done.

Chapter Seventeen

Origins

"Elli," Yelnirb's voice woke me up. I forced my eyes open and tried to stretch the kink out of my neck. I immediately looked at Nedys, whose face was twisted into a grimace, though his body was still. His breathing was anything but slow and steady. I squeezed his hand and brushed the hair off his forehead. He was still on fire, the rash pulsating with his erratic heartbeat. Yelnirb handed me a cold rag, and I placed it on his forehead, knowing it would do little to bring him comfort or relief. I felt sick to my stomach at the sight of him suffering as he was.

"Siol must approve of the return of the empress," Yelnirb said.

"Why do you say that?" I wondered aloud.

"The palace has been put back to rights. What you saw last night was not what Yelnats and I saw when we entered last night. Siol restored the inner palace for you," Yelnirb explained, assuaging my fears from the night before.

"I had hoped she wouldn't view me as an intruder," I admitted. "You know what's odd, though? I can't hear Siol – not last night outside the tree and not now inside the tree."

"When she's ready to communicate with you, she will," Yelnirb assured me.

"Now, you need to get yourself cleaned up and eat some breakfast," Yelnirb instructed.

"But –" I started to protest.

"There'll be no resisting, Empress. He'll still be here when you're done, and Yelnats and I need to get him cleaned up as well. Between the two of you, it smells like a garbage dump in here," Yelnirb snickered as she wrinkled her nose.

"Do as your mother tells you," Yelnats directed as he entered the room. Yelnirb shot him a dirty look.

"I mean, you'd be wise to listen to Yelnirb, Empress," he quickly corrected.

"Please drop the pretenses," I urged. "If I need anything right now, I need my mom and dad. I know you don't look like you used to, but you're still the mom and dad I know and love."

"As you wish," they said in unison, both smiling.

"The bath water is ready in the chamber just through that door," Yelnirb told me as she pointed to a dark green door I hadn't noticed the night before. I looked down at Nedys one more time, reluctant to leave his side.

"We'll take care of the young fellow," Yelnats reassured me as he hefted a large bucket of water near the bed.

"His name is Nedys, dad, and you've got to let go of this grudge you're holding against him. He's not going anywhere, and I do owe him my life," I insisted.

"I'll see what I can do to convince myself he's worthy of the trust you've placed in him," Yelnats conceded rather grudgingly.

"He's risking his life through this branding process, so we can get the orb. Isn't that enough?" I asked.

"Yes, child. Yes, of course, it's enough," Yelnats put his arm on my shoulder and squeezed. It was as close to a hug as I ever received from him. I patted his hand.

"It's just that I'm supposed to be the protector," he admitted.

"You always will be," I assured him as I laid Nedys's hand by his side and opened the door.

The room I entered was much the same as the other two I had seen. Greenery and plant life abounded everywhere, from hanging on the ceiling to snaking along the stone tiles on the floor. I inhaled deeply, feeling surprisingly calm. I stepped into the large stone tub that had been built into the wall, allowing myself to be immersed in the steaming hot water. I quickly washed my hair and body with the coconut-scented soap Yelnirb had left by the tub, and then I allowed myself to relax as I tried to clear my head of its tangle of thoughts. By the time I emerged, my skin was pruned and wrinkly, but I felt refreshed. I wrapped myself in a long towel, noticing that Yelnirb must have come in for my clothes while my eyes were closed. She entered the room just as I sat down on a chair, holding my torn tunic in her hand.

"I've searched everywhere, but I cannot find any other clothes for you to wear," she said.

"Einnep has them," I told her.

"That doesn't surprise me, given the state this place was in. You'll have to put these back on." She handed me the tunic Lordess Nalla had given me. "I cleaned them the best I could, but I couldn't get the blood stain out, and the sleeve is missing so I can't sew it back on."

"That's okay," I told her as I quickly dressed and started to brush my hair.

"Let me help you with that, Elli," she offered, taking the brush from my hand. When she finished brushing my hair, she braided the black locks into a two-tiered spiral French braid. She turned me toward a mirror on the opposite wall, but I hardly recognized the face in the reflection.

"It's beautiful," I said, admiring her handiwork in the mirror. It felt so out of place on me.

"You look just like your mother," she whispered, almost inaudibly as she watched me in the mirror.

"What were my parents like? How did they meet?" I asked. Yelnirb sat down beside me.

"I knew the time would come when you'd want to know, and you have a right to know. Elli, your mother wasn't always evil. In her younger days I have heard tell that she was energetic enough, but also very jovial – just like Leo, I suppose. Tradition held that young empresses were expected to marry the strongest man in the army. The date for a marriage ceremony was set a year prior to the event – no groom named. Throughout that year a myriad of tests and competitions were held to determine the groom.

"Just prior to the announcement of her own marriage date, the young empress decided that she wanted to choose for herself the man she would marry. There was a soldier, much older than she was, who became the object of her fascination. His name was Ruhtra, and he was as handsome an Enelians as there was at the time. He warmed to her attentions, and a relationship developed. The empress, your grandmother, was not happy about the matchmaking her daughter had been about behind her back. She was determined to get rid of Ruhtra, so she sent him on dangerous tasks, into the fiercest battles, but he always seemed to come back stronger than before.

"She discovered that your mother was helping him, along with the Ancients. The Ancients felt that possibly a match made of true love might be enough to help the young empress harness her powers for good. Your grandmother was furious with her and ordered the execution of Ruhtra. The empress was too young to be a match against the power of her mother. Though she had been secretly training with the Ancients, she still had much to learn. Your mother begged the Ancients to intervene on behalf of Ruhtra, but they were frightened the empress would destroy them, leaving the forest folk completely unprotected. Their power had grown much weaker since the empresses of long ago had controlled the orb. They stayed their hands, and let the execution proceed."

"No!" I interrupted. "He didn't die, right? The story can't end that way."

"Elli, this is no fairytale. Your grandmother personally beheaded Ruhtra, forcing her daughter to watch the entire ceremony. It was your grandmother's way of keeping her people in check with her agenda. To justify his murder, your grandmother told many lies about Ruhtra being a traitor to the Enelians cause by trying to steal the orb, and no one had reason to disbelieve the lies. The young empress-to-be fell into a deep depression and began to nurture the anger in her heart rather than focusing on the love she had shared with Ruhtra. She fed the feelings and fueled the wrong fires until she had been consumed. The dark power took over, and she reigned with the same ruthlessness as every empress before her.

"She had been the first hope the Ancients had seen in many generations as previous empresses had been prone to dark mischievousness even in their tender years. That hope was quickly extinguished by their own inaction. The competitions and tests were held, and another was chosen to be the young empress's husband. She turned against the Ancients, her censure made clear when she had all but one of the Ancients rounded up and imprisoned inside the Siol Tree - left to wither and waste away. Their fear of extinction had been their own prison sentence."

"Idnim is the only remaining Ancient," I surmised.

"Idnim was the only one who was not captured. She withdrew into her own sanctuary," Yelnirb affirmed.

"What of the other Ancients?"

"No one knows what became of them. They may still be alive."

"And what of my father?"

"The empress's groom was meant to be nothing more than a means to an end. He was to provide an heiress, but he failed. The first child that your mother bore was Einnep, and then there were many years of barrenness. You see, the power within the queen takes its toll on her husband as well. Einnep's father weakened quickly, and then died. Never had the husband died before an heiress had been born. The empress forfeited the traditions of old and chose another to be her husband, a younger brother of Ruhtra. He willingly submitted to the task and quickly provided the heiress the empress sought, and to the surprise of all, a second child not long after – though he suffered much as a result."

"So Einnep is my half-brother?"

"Exactly so."

"And what turned him against my mother?"

"Child, I do not know such things. Yelnats and I were busy being your custodians. We were not afforded any opportunities outside of the Siol Tree, and any conversations held within the Siol tree were closely guarded."

"So how do you know this story?"

"Yelnats nursed Ruhtra's brother when he became too ill to care for himself, and it is from him he heard this tale. But I do believe it to be true."

"If you knew that the empresses were evil, then why did you lead me to believe the Annyadians were at fault for all the wars?"

"I believed it to be true, my child. I knew the empress was evil, but I was taught that the evil outside the forest was more barbaric. You see, we were told that the Annyadians tortured the forest folk. Quite often, friends and acquaintances would disappear, and that was the explanation. Why would we believe otherwise? We believed the death mark to be the product of the evil magic of the Annyadians. We never would have accused the empress of such atrocities against her own, and anyone with suspicions to the contrary, kept it to themselves. Like you, I had never heard an alternate telling of the tale until we returned. Elli, I lived in servitude. I did not have the choice to think or feel outside what I was told to think or feel. In fact, I didn't know I could until we were taken away when your parents were killed. That was the first taste of freedom we had ever had, and it was frightening. We had to learn to think for ourselves and care for ourselves with no one dictating to us what we must do. Many long nights we sat in council with Leo's custodians trying to chart our path the best we could in a foreign place."

"Where did you come from?" I asked.

"Elli dear, allow me to explain what is meant by *The Awakening*. You see, the resting place from which Empress Eneli took us was supposed to be our final resting place. We had lived our lives already in other places and other times. Empress Eneli awoke those new life forms like me for the sole purpose of serving her needs and wants. When we had surpassed our usefulness, the empresses simply returned us to our sleep until we were needed once again. We can only be awakened so many times before our sleep becomes permanent, however, and then we can no longer be awakened. We are no longer welcomed back to our final resting place, but left to wander in the realms between worlds, suffering in a wakeful imprisonment by no choice of our own.

"This is the first awakening for both Yelnats and I, as well as for Leo's custodians. We would have been put back to sleep as soon as you were sufficiently independent. Yelnats was the custodian to Master Einnep, so he has been here much longer than me. I want you to understand that I'm a much different being now than I was before I was taken from the forest. It was a difficult adjustment to say the least. It is a miracle we survived those first few days, let alone months in such a foreign place."

"How did you survive if you just showed up there like I showed up here? How did you find a place to stay and food to eat? How did you manage to learn how to make a living in a place so foreign to you?"

"Well, I must admit that your friend Mr. Martindale helped us along."

"But I thought you didn't like Mr. Martindale?"

"Rightfully so. Remember we were used to being told what to do and how to do it. In the beginning, we relied heavily on Mr. Martindale's expertise. At the time, we had no choice, but as we adjusted, we grew wary. We have a right to be suspicious of someone so generous to strangers, foreigners even."

"What do you mean?"

"The awful night when we found ourselves in the other realm, we were huddled in a wooded park, hearing strange sounds and noises, having no idea where we were to go. Mr. Martindale happened upon us and offered us assistance. It was he who gave us food and a place to stay. It was he who helped us learn the ways of that new world. He allowed us to live in his duplex at no charge until we could find a means to support ourselves and learn the ways of money and such."

"Well then, we're indebted to him for his generosity. Why not like him?"

"He kept a close watch – too close. We did not – could not – trust him."

"And now, after all these years when no harm has come to any of us – only good things?"

"There is something about him that makes me wary – some feeling I cannot explain." Chills ran up my spine as if Yelnirb had just told me a scary ghost story on a dark night amidst the crackling embers of a dying campfire as Leo used to do.

"You know, I did find that gumball in Mr. Martindale's shop. Do you suppose there was a reason – not just because Lordess Nalla dropped it into the pool at the same time I was getting my donut?" I asked, forgetting Yelnirb didn't know about my morning indulgences. She narrowed her eyes.

"Elli," she said, somewhat sternly. "Why would you go behind my back? Wasn't it enough that I let you keep your junk food stash and allowed you to work there during the summer?"

"You know about my stash?"

"Honestly, what kind of a custodian would I be if I didn't? It was against my better judgment to let you work in that bakery in the first place." Her words stung. I hadn't seen any harm in it.

"I'm sorry," I muttered.

"Such a trifle in the long scheme of things, I should think. If that's the worst that happened, I suppose I should count myself lucky."

"I am a pretty good kid, considering my genetic code has a predisposition toward evil."

"You're more than a pretty good kid, my child. I believe the Guardian saw in you the same traits the Ancients saw in your mother when they began her training."

"So you think the Guardian is the mastermind behind all this?"

"There is no one else it could be," she whispered with a tone of reluctance.

"You don't believe in the Guardian?" I asked, feeling somewhat deflated.

"We knew of no such being in our first existence, and I supposed it to be forest lore…until now. If there is no Guardian, there is no hope for you to reclaim the orb. I will believe in the Guardian to preserve the hope that you will come out of this whole affair unscathed," she rationalized.

Despite her professed doubts, I felt an odd sense of comfort in her words. I didn't realize until she revealed her own skepticism that I had come to believe in the Guardian. Whether it was Lordess Nalla's faith or Nedys's confidence or Einnep's conviction of the reality of the Guardian, I wasn't sure. In midst of all that had happened, I knew there was a being out there somewhere pulling on the strings in this marionette show.

Chapter Eighteen

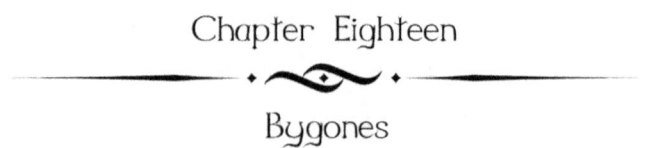

Bygones

I felt guilty indulging in my own comforts when Nedys was suffering on my account. I cut my conversation with my mom short, so I could get back to his side. Although his body didn't show it, I knew he was fully awake and aware. I sat down in the chair by the side of his bed. I gently grabbed his hand in mine, hoping the poison would sense my presence, so he could make it through this process as whole as possible. Silence permeated the space around us. I couldn't even hear Nedys breathing, though I watched carefully to make sure I could see the rise and fall of his chest.

His whole body was now covered in the flashing purple rash. He looked like a picture I had seen in my anatomy and physiology class of a map of the blood vessels in the human body. My knees went weak as I stared at his nearly lifeless body.

I decided that if he really could hear me, he might like to get his mind off the constant pain that was ravaging his body. The best way to do that would be to mentally remove him from his present situation, so I decided to tell him about my life. I started off by telling him how I met Mr. Martindale, since I hoped to soon be introducing the two of them.

My mom and dad grew delicious fruits and vegetables. They had been encouraged to sell them at the local farmer's market, but they hadn't acquired any social graces at that point in their learning process. The Parkin family offered to sell their produce for them at the farmer's market for a small cut of the revenue. When I was ten, I had been charged with helping out at the market in lieu of my parents. Mr. Martindale came to the stall one day, impressed with the quality of the produce I was selling. I was acquainted with Mr. Martindale since we rented our duplex from him, but I'd never really had much to do with him before. That day he bought all the fruits and vegetables I had brought to sell and stayed to chat for almost the entire afternoon. The Parkin family was well acquainted with Mr. Martindale and encouraged the association, knowing how backward my parents were. He came back every day, bought all the produce, and eventually began to teach me how to read and write. We had been friends ever since. I thought of Mr. Martindale as just another member of my family.

I next told Nedys about my parent's successful landscaping business. Neither of them could drive a car, and they were terrified of gas-powered lawn mowers. At least now I understood why. They didn't let that stop them, though. They had to find some way to make a living in the new, strange place they had come to call home. They acquired second hand bicycles and taught themselves how to ride. After a lot of pleading and begging, they eventually allowed me learn to ride a bike. I had been fifteen at the time and requested training in a secluded spot where no one could witness my foibles. They used hand mowers, which they carted around on a small trailer hitched to the back of their bikes. Though they weren't much for small talk, their work spoke for itself. Their reputation secured them plenty of work all year round as they put to use their natural abilities as Treefs.

As I related these memories, I was suddenly overwhelmed by the love I had for my parents. I wished Nedys could have grown up with something like that. His life might have turned out much differently. But then again, Yelnirb and Yelnats were not my biological parents either. Mine didn't sound much better than his.

I next described in detail our many camping excursions with Leo and his parents. My favorite camping was done near the beach, where I could hear the ocean waves crashing against the shore. It was often cold and windy, but I felt more at peace there than anywhere else, except for Mr. Martindale's garden. I described roasting tofu dogs over a crackling fire and popping popcorn. Later, Leo and I would sneak out of our tents and roast smuggled marshmallows over the last embers of the fire. My mouth started to water at the thought of the sticky sweetness.

I told him about working in Mr. Martindale's bakery every summer – a job I looked forward to as much as anything. I loved watching the dough rise from a flat dessert to a high mountain and turn from tan to golden brown in the heat of the fryers. I mostly loved taste-testing Mr. Martindale's newest creations and being charged with naming those he decided to add to the menu.

I talked about my favorite thinking spot. I could climb out of my second story bedroom window to sit on a small ledge. I snuck out there almost every night when the weather was good, just to stare up at the stars dotting the night sky. I closed my eyes as though I could smell the fresh night air and feel the slight chill raise goose bumps on my skin. I missed my nightly sojourns with the stars, but I assured Nedys he would love them.

I talked about Leo and the pranks we used to pull on each other. I told him about how smart he was and how he helped me with my homework even though I was older than he was. As I remembered all the stories I shared with Leo, I began to realize that I had been spending much more time alone and far less time with Leo as his circle of friends began to expand. Why did I feel like the tag-along all the time? Leo couldn't help it, of course. Leo was Leo, and I was glad he was not only my friend, but also my brother. As I vocally cataloged my memories, I realized how happy I had been, fully content despite my parents' oddities. How had I missed it before?

I spent three days talking to Nedys until my voice was hoarse, and I couldn't think of any more of my own stories to tell. I had started in my favorite fairytales, when I noticed the rash beginning to dissipate. At first, I was elated, thinking Nedys was on the road to recovery, until I noticed the bubbles of purple liquid appearing in rounded mounds all over his body.

"Mom," I called urgently. She came quickly with Yelnats at her heels. I watched as she exchanged a worried look with Yelnats. I felt sick to my stomach when she started wringing her hands.

"What is it?"

"Not good, I'm afraid," Yelnats said. "Not good at all."

"Can you help him?" I asked, my mouth suddenly dry.

"We'll have to lance each one," Yelnats explained as Yelnirb disappeared. "It won't be pretty, my dear."

Yelnirb reappeared with a mountain of white gauze and two small knives. They didn't waste any time. As they began to lance each blister, the thick purple liquid oozed out of the wound like hot lava freed from the confines of its barriers. I held tightly onto Nedys's hand, but I couldn't make myself watch the slow and painful torture he was enduring. When it was time to do his lower extremities, Yelnirb firmly dismissed me from the room.

"Go now," she said, her voice raised, after my second refusal. I had never before heard my mother get angry, so I didn't resist. I hadn't been anywhere besides the room in which I bathed and Nedys's infirmary, so I wandered somewhat aimlessly. I found myself in a wide, unlit hallway. I could hear a faint tinkling sound echoing through the hallway, drawing me further down the darkening corridor. Each step I took brought me further into the shadows, but I felt compelled to continue forward. The hallway twisted and curved, although I had no problem maneuvering in the dim light.

As I turned yet another corner, I suddenly found myself in a small open space. All was dark save the eerily beautiful glow from a seven-foot-wide waterfall cascading off the far wall. This had to be the Fountain of Glowing Waters. I maneuvered through the unruly bushes and climbing vines that were growing out of the walls and floor as I made my way to the back of the waterfall. I found my way blocked by more climbing vines, but as I approached, they parted to reveal another passageway behind the waterfall. At the end of the passageway, my eyes were drawn to a large flowering plant that seemed to hover in midair. The flowers were like nothing I had seen before, their colors deeper and more vibrant. As I approached, the flowers turned in my direction. A vine slithered out from underneath the plant with a scroll secured to its end. It slowly approached, stopping as if holding the scroll out for me. As I took the scroll from the vine, it immediately retracted to the bush.

With shaking hands, I unrolled the scroll and began to read the ancient script.

Dearest Enyala,

With a broken heart I must tell you that our path has been decided, and I was in the minority. The Ancients will not intervene on your behalf to save our beloved Ruhtra. They fear the risk would be too great to the forest and all within, and none would survive the empress's retaliation. Though your progress has been more than we could have imagined, you are not yet strong enough to give us the aid we would require to defend against your mother. Dearest Enyala, I know this news will be hard to bear. I know how much you love Ruhtra, but do not let his death be in vain, my child. Be strong, and do not succumb to the dark side of your power. I do not know

how you will bear it, but you must. To this end, I give you a gift — the seeds for
Flowers of Eternal Bloom. You spoke of the Fountain of Glowing Waters you
created with Ruhtra. Place these seeds in the dirt behind your fountain. They will
bloom and grow, and if you can endure it no longer, come to me. I will give you refuge
in my sanctuary, come what may. Only pluck the deep purple bloom, speak my name,
and a one-way portal will open to give you safe passage to me. Until we meet again,

Your faithful friend, Idnim

The paper fluttered to the ground as I tried to digest what I had just read. Tears sprang to my eyes as I thought about what Enyala had to endure. Any person would have been angry, but she wasn't just any person. Anger wasn't an emotion she could allow herself to experience even for a moment since it was a magnet for the dark power, yet she had planted the seeds. She hadn't been immediately consumed by anger at Idnim's missive, so she had mastered some constraint to which Idnim had alluded. Unfortunately, I knew the end of the story. Now I understood why Idnim was the only Ancient who remained, and I also knew the source of her coldness. Idnim had given my mother a way out. She had rested her spark of hope with Enyala, only to have it thoroughly extinguished.

The murmuring of the waterfall captured my attention as my thoughts turned to its origin. My mother had created it with Ruhtra, using her power for good, for love. This place was most likely their secret rendezvous before he was killed, but I knew it hadn't been a source of solace after his execution. I shuddered at the thought. It was more likely the source of her madness and fury. A wave of nausea crashed through me. I ran back through the twisting tunnel, away from the fountain and the flowers and the suffocating knowledge of what I could become. I couldn't let my mind travel down those dark paths for I might never return. I didn't stop until I had left the sanctuary of the Siol Tree altogether.

When I stepped out of the tree's entrance, the landscape was cloaked in darkness. I took several deep breaths as I tried to calm myself. I rested my hand on the bark of the Siol Tree for support as I searched the sky for the twin moons – the moons Leo had mistaken for eyes in his dreams. As I stared at them, however, I could have sworn a shadow not unlike a blink passed over both moons at the same time. A chill eerily snaked up my spine at the thought. At the same time, I felt warmth spreading through my hand that rested against the Siol Tree. I rubbed my hand up and down the smooth bark.

"Oh, Siol," I whispered. "How do I get myself out of this mess?" I half expected to sense a reply, but just as suddenly as it came, the warmth was gone – my hand cold.

"Elli?" Yelnirb poked her head out of the tree's entrance. I jumped at the sound of her voice. "Sorry, dear. I didn't mean to startle you. Is everything all right?" she asked.

"I'm okay," I said unconvincingly. "I just…" She waited patiently as I tried to compose my thoughts. "If Enyala, with of all Idnim's tutoring, could not fight against her own powers, then how can I?"

"You've discovered something, haven't you?" Yelnirb surmised. I nodded my head and launched into an explanation of my discovery. Yelnirb put her arm around my shoulders.

"You have a lifetime of experiences in a world so different from this one – a world untouched by the dark powers that reside here. In the end, your ignorance and innocence might just save you after all. And don't forget that you have the Guardian on your side, my child. Never before has he intervened. Put your trust in him," she told me with an assurance I had never felt from her before. She truly did believe I could do this.

"And Nedys?" I asked. "How is he?" She didn't immediately answer me, and her silence clearly told me that all was not well. She motioned for me to come inside, and I followed her back to Nedys's side.

Chapter Nineteen

Homeward Bound

For two more days, Yelnirb and Yelnats lanced the boils as the poison raged its war against Nedys. His skin was on fire, and I was certain his blood was literally boiling in his veins. On the fifth day of his torture, the boils began to dissipate. Unfortunately, a ghostly pallor blanketed his body. As the fever faded away, so did every ounce of his pigmentation. His hair turned a sickly white and his skin took on a milky hue. Then the chills started. His body would shake uncontrollably, despite the tonic Yelnirb administered to paralyze his movement. We had been feeding him a special liquefied diet with a syringe, but he could no longer swallow. His body temperature dropped so low, ice crystals were forming on his eyelashes even though the room was so hot I was almost sweating to death. As the day wore on, his milky skin became translucent, and he looked as if he were turning to ice.

"We've got to do something," I urged my parents.

"There's nothing left. I've exhausted all my knowledge and resources, Elli," my mother admitted.

"The vile. Idnim gave me a vile and told me to use it if his body started to reject the immunization. Where is it?" I began to look around frantically.

"Calm down," Yelnats cautioned. "It's here. It's always been here." He grabbed the small vile from the ornate table by Nedys's bed and placed it in my shaking hands. I carefully pulled out the stopper, placed a drop of the colorless liquid between Nedys's quivering lips, and waited.

Nothing seemed to happen. His body was still convulsing, his skin becoming more translucent. I held his hand in mine though it was ice cold and didn't warm as I rubbed it furiously. Every hour through the night I administered a drop of Idnim's remedy, and we would turn him from his back to his stomach or his stomach to his back. I found that I could not sleep or eat or do anything but watch and wait and worry. Trying to take my mind off his suffering, I recounted the newest information I had added to my arsenal about Enyala and Idnim. Unfortunately, my voice did nothing to soothe him or to quiet the poison inside him. After about eight hours, the convulsions abated, leaving him with only faint tremors, but that was the only improvement.

The following morning, I administered the last drop from Idnim's vile, and my parents turned Nedys onto his back before leaving the room. I held my breath as I watched. At first I thought I had imagined the glistening drop of water, but as I took a closer look I saw the frozen ice crystals slowly begin to melt - first into tiny droplets of water and then into narrow, twisting rivers. I sighed with relief as I grabbed a towel to absorb the small streams of water on back. This was a turning point – a good turning point. I paused as my eyes fixed on an eight-inch scar by Nedys's shoulder blade. I saw several more and drew back in alarm. The only scar I bore was on my hand; surely this couldn't have been from the immunization. I hadn't noticed the mutilations before, but if not from that, then what?

"Oh Nedys, what have I done to you?" I whispered as I reached out to trace the scars with my fingers, realizing that even if the scars weren't from the immunization, the blame still squarely lay on my side of the battlefield.

"You didn't." I barely heard his voice when he spoke, and I quickly drew my hand away. "That's me father's brand."

"Nedys?" I asked leaning closer to his face. He slowly opened his eyes, blinking in the brightly lit room. He struggled to turn over as I tried to help him. I urged him to take a drink of water as I supported his head, slowly bringing it to rest back down on the bed.

"How do you feel?" I asked as I moved his wet hair out of his eyes.

"Like a pack of reprahs took turns devouring me from the inside out without quite managing to kill me," he answered weakly with the hint of a smile on his lips.

"I'll get my mom. She may be able to give you something for the pain now," I told him as I got up to leave. He reached a trembling hand to my arm to stop me.

"Don't go," he mumbled as he drifted back to sleep, obviously still delirious with pain and exhaustion. I took his hand in mine again, knowing that when he was fully conscious, I wouldn't be able to that anymore. My mind returned to the scars and to his father. Those scars were no doubt a side effect of a war he was barely old enough to remember, if at all. What kind of a father would whip his only surviving son?

Nedys slept for the remainder of the day, only waking to take a few bites of food and a drink, before succumbing to sleep once again. My mom urged me to get some sleep that evening, so I retired to my own bed. I was so exhausted that I didn't stir until she woke me up as she brought in a tray filled with food.

"How is he?" I asked, hopefully.

"Go see for yourself!" she urged.

I quickly ate, bathed, and dressed before hesitantly returning to Nedys's room. He was standing beside the bed with his back to me when I entered. I felt more than a little awkward, as if I were an intruder. What could I say to the person to whom I had borne my soul while he appeared to be unconscious?

Would he remember? Did I want him to remember? I secretly hoped he did because I wanted him to know the real me. Then, my hope wavered. What if he didn't like the real me? What if he regretted volunteering to help me? I wanted to turn around and leave the room, but instead I cleared my throat to let him know I was there. I'd have to talk to him eventually, and I'd rather do it without an audience. As he turned his head around, a broad smile donned his face, accentuated by two small dimples I had never seen before. The smile seemed to be directed at me, but I was so taken back that I looked over my shoulder to make sure someone or something wasn't standing behind me. Maybe he was still delirious. When I saw no one, I turned back to look at him. The smile hadn't vanished, and my heart did a little flip-flop inside my chest.

"F-feeling better?" I stammered.

"Much improved, thanks to you I'm told," he answered with that irresistible smile. Did that mean he didn't remember anything? My hope skidded to an abrupt halt at the thought.

"Not me," I countered, feeling deflated. "It was Idnim's serum…and my parents."

"In the end, it may have been the serum that tipped the balance. That part gets a bit hazy, which is why Yelnats had to fill in the few blanks there at the end," he explained as he sat back down on the bed and started to tie his boot.

"Fill in the blanks…at the end?" I wondered out loud. He glanced up at me and winked. I felt a hot blush rise to my cheeks. How transparent I was! Yet, I couldn't prevent a small smile from spreading across my face. He remembered. Why was I suddenly embarrassed?

"Well…I'll just be going," I said awkwardly as I turned to leave the room.

"And where would you be going without me?" Nedys asked as he crossed the room to stand next to me, his close proximity causing me to blush yet again. "You do realize it's almost time for us to leave?"

"It is? I slept all day?" I hadn't thought to ask my mom what time it was.

"Watching after me for seven cycles of the moons takes its toll, I guess," he said with a shrug.

"Are you up for this?" It seemed too soon for him to be embarking on yet another adventure. He just smiled and gestured toward the door.

"After you," he whispered. My parents met us in the corridor outside his room. My mom was wringing her hands again, and my dad was patting her on the back.

"It's time," Yelnirb said, trying to make her voice sound hopeful.

"They'll be fine, my dear," Yelnats reassured her as he wiped a tear from her cheek.

"It's the first time she has ever gone anywhere without us to protect her," Yelnirb acknowledged. "I can't feel good about this."

"Nedys will look out for her, won't you, Nedys?" Yelnats looked at my companion. "And if you don't, boy, know that I've got bigger tricks up my sleeve than a mere sprinkle of sand! That I do! Just you remember that little bump to your head –"

"I don't need anyone to look out for me, okay?" I intervened before my dad could continue his tirade, although I was sure Nedys was trying very hard not to look amused at the string of threats that had just been leveled against him. I was more than capable of taking care of myself. I was eighteen after all. "This is my world I'm going back to, remember? I'm probably safer there than I am here, since no one has a death wish for me there. We'll be careful – I promise." Yelnirb grabbed my hands and squeezed them.

"I know. I know you will," she said, tears filling her eyes again. I felt my vision start to blur with unshed tears at my mom's unexpected display of emotion, but I blinked them back furiously.

"We better be off," I managed to say while maintaining my composure. Yelnirb let go of my hands and stepped back.

"We'll be here when you get back," Yelnats affirmed unnecessarily as he patted me on the shoulder. I led the way to the Fountain of Glowing Waters with Nedys at my heels. My parents didn't follow.

After navigating the twists and turns and bushes and vines, we finally came to hidden passageway that led to the Flowers of Eternal Bloom. The dark purple flower with the white center was leaning slightly forward from the center of the plant as if in anticipation of being plucked after all those years. I looked at Nedys.

"Ready?" I inquired.

"Ready," he affirmed.

I gently grabbed onto the stem of the flower with my right hand. Nedys followed, holding on just below my hand. We both drew in a deep breath. I smiled. He was as nervous as I was.

"Carry me plus one to the land apart, the land where I dwelt – the land of my heart," I repeated the words I had mulled over in my head a thousand times since Idnim had first told them to me. As I repeated the phrase a second time., the last word echoed as we stood behind the waterfall, holding expectantly onto the flower. I glanced at Nedys a split second before everything around me went black. There was a loud whooshing sound, and I felt as though I was on an elevator with a snapped cable, free falling several floors. I tried to focus on not crushing the flower in my hand. The sensation lasted for less than a minute, and though my eyes were closed, they squinted more tightly as they detected the presence of light. I blinked several times before my eyes adjusted.

I was standing by a tree near my high school, the same tree I had been sitting under before my unexpected journey to the Forest of Notxarb. I looked over to find Nedys staring in wonderment, his face slightly pale and clutching rather tightly to the flower. I gently unlatched his fingers from the stem and turned away to tuck the flower just inside the band of my pants. I figured it would be safer there.

"We made it," I finally broke the awkward silence.

"It's real," he whispered in disbelief.

"You thought I was lying to you?" I asked incredulously.

"Well…no…of course, not. It's just hard to believe that I'm really standing in a…in a…different world."

"Just wait. You haven't seen anything yet. That's just my high school," I smiled.

"Lead the way, Empress," he gestured toward me with a mocking bow. "Where you go, I follow." I knew he was teasing, but I felt a burden nestle itself squarely on my shoulders. I would have to find my way to the orb, somehow.

"I didn't mean anything by that," Nedys offered, noticing my downcast expression in response to his flippant comment.

"I know," I muttered under my breath. "I think we better head to my house first. It's not too far from here, and I think it's the best starting place." I started walking in the direction of home with Nedys by my side, trying to take in his new surroundings.

We had walked several blocks away from the school with Nedys pausing every few seconds to stare in amazement at every vehicle that passed on the street. I was a little surprised when I noticed dark clouds gathering in the sky. A chill sprinted down my spine. I hoped it wasn't a bad omen. I felt as if I was a cartoon character with a black cloud drawn above me, warning everyone to beware.

"Elli," I stopped in my tracks at the sound of my name and turned to see who was addressing me. Since school was out, I hadn't been expecting to see anyone.

"Hey, I haven't seen you around in a while." I tried not to roll my eyes at Kelsey Yardell and her posse. Kelsey was the leader of Leo's devoted fan club, and a girl for whom I didn't much care.

"I've been out of town," I said, watching as Kelsey eyed Nedys, her stare skewering him as fresh meat for her kabob of male followers.

"What on earth are you wearing?" In horror, I realized I still donned the blood stained, torn tunic of Annyad. I was sure my appearance was beyond description. I glanced at Nedys, whose tunic also looked out of place now.

"Oh this," I tried to laugh as I smoothed out my tunic. "It's dress rehearsal today for a little play re-enactment we're performing at the farmer's fair."

"It suits you," Kelsey smirked as my face flushed red at her insult. She had this uncanny ability to make me feel about two inches high with her cutting remarks. I would rather have felt invisible to the popular world than singled out by one of her kind.

"Have you seen Leo around? I haven't seen him since school got out, and he missed my party," she persisted. I knew the question was coming. It was the only reason anyone in her circle ever bothered to notice me.

"Family emergency, I think. He'll be out of town for a while," I answered, trying to shoo her away as fast as possible. I would never understand why Leo encouraged her advances by going to her stupid parties. That was the one thing

Leo and I never talked about – the elephant in the room so to speak – his obvious popularity and my obvious lack thereof. His other friends never spoke ill of me in front of him, but rather waited until he wasn't around to turn on me. I never told Leo how mean they really were – I was happy that at least he was accepted. I was also happy to know that he would never treat me that way, and I didn't want him to lose his friends on account of me. Not all of them were bad, but if he were to choose sides, he would only find me on my side of the line. I never asked him to choose.

"Bummer," she said, diverting her attention to Nedys. "I don't think I've seen you around before." Nedys looked at me, unsure of how to respond.

"Probably because he's new in town," I said curtly, but Kelsey didn't get the hint.

"Well, it's nice to meet you. I'm Kelsey, and these are my friends Paige, Cadence, and Isabelle," Kelsey said, holding out her hand for him to shake. Thankfully, he knew what to do and quickly shook her hand.

"And you are?" she persisted.

"Ned," I interjected. "He's a foreign exchange student."

"Oh, doesn't he speak English?" she asked, perturbed that I was interrupting her weak attempt at flirting.

"It was nice to meet you, Kelsey," Nedys spoke in his charming accent. The sound of it made the hair on my arms stand on end. I hoped he hadn't noticed. "But we've really got to be on our way…the rehearsal awaits." I smiled at his addendum.

"Oh," she muttered, offended. "Maybe we'll see you around." As we walked by them, I could feel her staring a hole in my back. Before they were out of ear shot, we heard her say, "Why do such cute guys always seem to be hanging around that Smelly Elli girl? Ew! I mean, seriously, she's weird. Did you see how she was dressed – in public, no less? I never have understood why Leo spends so much time with her. I just don't get it."

Although the biting words about me hurt, I knew they were true too. I was weird. I didn't fit in, and I never had. It had never really bothered me before, but it really bothered me that Kelsey would say those things loud enough for Nedys to hear. I didn't want Nedys to know how truly pathetic I was here. I had hinted as much before when I told him people didn't notice me, but I had failed to tell him the things people said when they did notice me – the whispered words behind my back whenever Leo wasn't around. I was no empress here. In fact, I was surprised Kelsey had even noted my absence. The only reason she did was because I was Leo's shadow, and she was looking for Leo. I felt a tear well up in my eye, and I blinked quickly to urge it back before it fell. I don't know why I was crying over something so stupid. I had been shot at with steel arrows, imprisoned, sentenced to execution, and discovered I was an evil empress. I had not managed to get through all of that only to crumble at a few harsh words spoken by a thoughtless peer. I wouldn't let it happen. I squared my shoulders and looked ahead.

Unexpectedly, Nedys's hand curled around mine as we walked. I felt of a shiver of pleasure run through my body at his touch. I only hoped that he didn't feel the shock that ran through me. He stopped walking long enough to lean over to place a quick kiss on my cheek. I felt a blush rise to my face, but Nedys didn't notice because he was looking over his shoulder at the gaggle of girls, who were gaping at us from behind. He gave them a little wave with the hand that wasn't holding mine, and then we commenced walking. I didn't look back, but I could clearly picture the look on Kelsey's face. A wave of satisfaction and gratitude washed over me.

"Thanks," I said, expecting him to let go of my hand as soon as we were out of sight. Again, I was pleasantly surprised when he didn't. He shrugged his shoulders at my offer of gratitude.

"Nothing to thank me for," he said as he squeezed my hand. I know Nedys had seen how the girls looked at him, and they were beautiful girls. As much as I wished they weren't, I couldn't lie about that. Any boy would have been flattered by the attentions of Kelsey and her friends, and yet Nedys held my hand. Nedys cared about my feelings, and he sensed that they had been trampled. I felt as though I needed to explain myself though. I wanted him to understand me.

"Sorry about that," I finally muttered, breaking the silence that had come between us as I had been ruminating.

"Why would you be apologizing? It seems to me that they owe you the apology," he countered. I smiled.

"That's not likely to happen. The only reason they stopped to talk to me at all was to find out about Leo."

"What makes Leo so sought after?"

"He's always been like that. People just seem drawn to his magnetic personality. He's easygoing, quick to make a person smile or laugh. Plus, he's smart. To Kelsey and her gang, he's a real piece of eye candy too. That always helps with the female population. He's the whole package, as they say."

"Eye candy?"

"He's attractive – tall, dark, and handsome. He's always got a bunch of girls after him, inviting him to parties and stuff."

"I see. Wouldn't you be considered part of his following?"

"Uh…no. He's my best friend. I guess I always thought of him as my brother, even before I knew he was." Although I had always been Leo's best friend, more recently I had only been his behind-the-scenes best friend. I tried to shrug off the unpleasant feeling that crept over me.

Certainly, Leo hadn't done it intentionally. I knew that for sure, but still, he had put me on the back burner a lot lately. I spent most of my Friday and Saturday nights by myself. How had I not noticed these subtle changes in our relationship before? Nedys seemed to sense my discomfort as he channeled our conversation into a different direction.

"And if you hadn't been taken away from here, what did you see yourself doing with your life?"

"Most people here would go to college, but I'm not really cut out for school. After I graduated from high school, I was going to help my parents with their fruit and vegetable business. They've been saving the money from their landscaping jobs, so they could buy a farm outside of town to expand. They are great at growing fruits and vegetables and making organic products from shampoo to toothpaste, but they don't interact well with people. I guess I saw myself as the face of the business. I've never seen myself doing anything but that. Until now…" My thoughts trailed off. That would not be happening now. My parents would never return, and I had no idea what would happen to me. I didn't want to dwell on it either, so I changed the subject.

"No more talk about me. What are you like when you aren't parading about the forest capturing evil empresses and then rescuing them?"

"I suppose I was a bit of loner," he admitted.

"What no gaggle of girls lolling after you?"

"Not any I was interested in at the time," he acknowledged with a mischievous grin. I was a little disappointed, but certainly not surprised. Nedys was a handsome Annyadian soldier who had been singled out by the much-feared Einnep as someone to be respected for his skills and potential. Of course, girls would be interested in him.

"I spent too much of me free time building me traveler," he continued when I didn't respond.

"You mean those aren't standard issue?"

"Oh no. If me father had ever discovered it, I would have been in a heap of trouble. It's a work of art, that traveler is – built with me own two hands with some help from Hairam, of course. He had a real knack for smuggling parts for me. There's nothing else like it anywhere in Annyad. I was feeling a bit too proud of meself too because it pales in comparison to the vehicles in this world."

"Even to the untrained eye, there's not anything like it here," I assured him.

"I very much doubt that!" he exclaimed as a Harley-Davidson drifted by. I had to admit I was beginning to see my life through new eyes – his eyes. Everything was a source of wonder and awe. It was a much different place than he knew. It was a good place, one that I should have never taken for granted. I supposed that was the human inclination – to never truly see until it was too late. The splat of a fat raindrop on my nose pulled me from my reverie. It was followed quickly by another and another until we found ourselves immersed in a heavy rain shower.

"We better run the rest of the way," I shouted over a loud clap of thunder. Nedys nodded, and I pulled him along the familiar route until we arrived breathless in front of my house. I tried the front door but found it locked. Reluctantly, I let go of Nedys's hand as I walked around to the gate at the side of the duplex only to find the gate locked as well.

"Wait here, and I'll climb over and get the spare key," I told Nedys. He looked wary but didn't argue. I noted that his face was pale and his breathing more labored than mine. I knew he wasn't fully recovered from his ordeal because he had been in tiptop shape when he had jogged the miles through the Forest of Notxarb with Sivart with relative ease.

"Wait a second," I turned around, suddenly remembering the flower tucked into my waistband. I pulled it out gently, trying to shield it from the pelting rain.

"You had better hold onto this, so it doesn't get crushed when I climb the fence," I said, handing him the flower. He tucked it into his tunic.

I quickly if not a little clumsily made my way over the fence, surprised to find the garden in perfect condition, weeded and growing as if my parents had never left. I made my way to the shed at the back of the property and lifted up a nearby brick border where we stored a spare key.

Unused to locking doors, my parents had learned early on to keep an extra key around. I let myself in the back door, surprised by the flood of relief that swept over me at the familiar smell of my house when I opened the door. I quickly went to the front door to let Nedys in. He was leaning against the fence, his chin tucked into his chest. My heart skipped a few beats at the thought of him not feeling well. After all he'd been through in the last week, I knew it was too soon for strenuous activity.

"Nedys," I called to him from the front porch. His head jerked up at the sound of his name, and he quickly walked toward me as I ushered him into the house. I grabbed a couple of towels from the bathroom and tossed one to him.

"You can dry off with this," I said as I toweled off my dripping hair.

"Thanks," he said, tossing the towel over his shoulder and removing the flower from the protection of his tunic. I filled a vase with water and put the flower inside, setting it on the kitchen table. I glanced at the clock, surprised to find that it was already half past seven.

"Are you hungry?" I asked as Nedys found his way to the kitchen after taking off his boots.

"Not really," he answered. "Yelnirb had just brought in dinner before we left."

"Who said anything about dinner?" I smiled. I darted up the stairs to my secret stash and extracted a bag of strawberry licorice. I inhaled deeply as I opened the bag when I got back to the kitchen table.

"Try this," I offered him a piece.

"Licorice?" he asked as he took a bite.

"How did you know?" I wondered aloud.

"Day four. You told me about how you and Leo wanted to build a tree house made entirely out of licorice. You also mentioned that the first thing you did when you opened a bag was 'breathe in the aroma of confectionary perfection' I believe were your exact words," he answered as he reached for a second piece.

"You remember all that?" I asked, slightly embarrassed at myself.

"That and more," he smiled. "It helped to keep me mind off...other things. You helped me to escape to an entirely new world."

"Speaking of that," I segued into my concerns. "How are you feeling, really?"

"I'm fine," he answered without hesitation, but I noticed he was suddenly concentrating very hard on the licorice he was twisting between his fingers.

"You're not a good liar, Nedys," I said, flicking him with my licorice. His eyes darted to mine as a slow smile spread across his face, revealing his dimples. My heart skipped a few beats.

"Seriously," I prodded, "is there anything I can do?"

"Since you've detected my deception, I'll amend me answer," he said with a twinkle in his eyes. "I will be fine. I just need some time – that's all. Don't worry about me."

"Promise to let me know if anything changes," I urged.

"You're as bad as Yelnirb," he teased. I leveled a glare in his direction, so he added, "But I promise."

I made some hot chocolate for both of us to take the chill off. That was the one indulgence my parents allowed, since my dad had been addicted to the stuff from his first swig. It had taken me an entire winter to convince one of them to try just a sip of the packets I was constantly smuggling into the house. Dad had finally given in, and that constituted my one and only victory in Operation Adopt Chocolate. My mom had put her foot down after that, but I didn't have to smuggle hot chocolate mix anymore. By the time Nedys and I had finished two cups each, I noticed the sky darkening outside as daylight bid its farewell.

"We need to get out of these wet clothes," I suggested. I got up to rummage through a drawer to find the spare key to Leo's house.

"Come with me," I instructed as I headed for the front door. We let ourselves into Leo's house, and I showed Nedys into Leo's Lair, as Leo called it. I went back to my house to change while he tried to find some of Leo's clothes that would fit. He agreed to meet me back at my house when he was done. I put on some comfortable pajama pants and a matching t-shirt, thankfully discarding the tunic. I brushed through my wet hair and pulled it back into a low braid. Nedys still hadn't returned, so I thought I'd take a few minutes in my favorite solitary spot – the ledge outside my bedroom window. The rain had subsided, and the cloud cover had dissipated, unveiling the canvas of stars of which I was so fond.

Chapter Twenty

Seeing Stars

"So many stars," I jumped as Nedys spoke from behind me. "Is there room for one more?"

"Sure," I said as I scooted over on the window ledge to make room for him as he crawled through the window.

"I've never seen stars before," he commented as he settled next to me.

"I noticed there weren't any in the sky the night you helped me escape," I noted, still looking at the thousands of twinkling lights in the night sky, unable to fathom their absence and realizing that the sky in Annyad had most likely once been populated by an equal number of stars that broke up the monotony of the blackness.

"And let me guess," I continued, "I have something to do with their disappearance, don't I?"

"Well, not you personally," he tried to reassure me.

"You might as well lay it on me. I'm sure everyone else is already holding me personally responsible, so I better add that to my list of infractions."

"Me mum once told me that the stars in the sky never held still. They were constantly shooting across the sky in spectacular show, and they were an assortment of colors. There were only a few left when she was a child. Of those, her favorite were the bright orange ones because they blinked to the rhythm of the Forest Lullaby," he explained.

"The Forest Lullaby?" I queried.

"You know it well – it's the song you sang me to sleep with the night you escaped. I should have known then that you were the long-lost empress because only she could work such magic with a song."

"But if it's a Forest Lullaby, how do you know it? Weren't you born in Annyad?"

"I was yes, but me mum was forest-born. Her parents were taken prisoner by the Annyadians during one of the many wars when she was just a babe. They denounced the empress and were set free to live their lives as Annyadians. She always had a bit of the forest in her, me mum did. She sang me that lullaby when me brothers and me father were off at war. I think it made her feel closer to them somehow, but she never sang it with me father around. He would have never permitted it," Nedys explained.

"I didn't mean to use it against you," I apologized, suddenly feeling guilty.

"I'm glad you did," he said softly. When I turned to look at him, I found he was already looking at me. My heart started to race, and I quickly looked away. No one had ever looked at me the way Nedys was looking at me now.

"About the stars," I prodded, trying to change the subject.

"The stars. They disappeared over the years as the empresses drained them of their energy. It's said they couldn't resist the draw of her power, and slowly each fell from the sky, succumbing to her call. And that's why I've never seen a star…until now," he finished.

"I wonder if there's a way to bring them back to the forest and to Annyad," I thought aloud.

"I suppose if there is, you'll find it," he surmised.

"I wish I could, but I don't seem to have much control over any power I have when I'm there. It's like little explosives that go off when I'm angry. I don't know where they come from or how to harness them to do anything useful," I confided.

"Empress," he began.

"Elli. It's just Elli," I quickly corrected him.

"Elli," he said with a smile, "I'm sorry all this has happened to you, and I'm sorry about how I treated you when we first met. I guess anger sets off little explosives in all of us." I laughed.

"I like to hear you laugh," he confessed.

"It's good to laugh. It's good to be home, no matter how short the visit." I stretched my legs out so they dangled over the ledge. "Thanks for helping me."

"I have to admit something to you, Elli. I thought you had used that lullaby to lure me – to make me take leave of me senses. After all, I had touched you. I've heard stories about the power of the empress's touch. After I dropped you off in the dungeon I went as far away from you as I could get and drank Orange Death Tea by the pitcher. It's said to weaken the pull of the dark magic.

"Nasty stuff that is. It's brewed with every dead bug you can find and special orange stones from the Black Caves of the South. Hairam had a hard time tracking those down for me. After talking to you the next night though, I realized you were telling the truth. I knew you were an innocent victim of circumstance. It wasn't dark magic that was drawing me to you after all. You are just like me in some ways. I was forced to be someone I didn't want to be – to play a role I detested. I knew I had to help – I wanted to help you."

"I don't blame you, Nedys. But do you realize that in helping me, you pretty much trampled all over your old life? You're probably on Einnep's most wanted list now."

"But I don't feel dead inside anymore, and I owe that to you," he countered. "I feel more alive than I've ever felt, and I've seen more than I could have dreamed of seeing – than I could have believed even existed outside Annyad and the forest. You've given me a whole new world."

"It won't last, Nedys. We have to go back."

"I know, but like you, I'm glad I'm here, no matter how short the visit. And we'll go back together. You and me." He reached over and grabbed my hand. I was so surprised by the sudden act of intimacy that I lost my concentration as well as my balance. In a split second, the only thing holding me from plummeting off the roof and to certain injury was Nedys's hand. I was dangling over the edge of the precipice as Nedys struggled to keep his balance while still holding onto me.

He put his other hand out, and I grabbed onto it as he pulled me back onto the roof, gripping me tightly in his arms. We were both panting for breath as the adrenaline rush of the experience began to retreat. I looked up into his face, his damp hair lifting slightly in the cool summer breeze. I couldn't make myself stop staring at his handsome features and his bright eyes. As he brought his face closer to mine, I felt the adrenaline in my veins take an abrupt U-turn, once again accelerating my heartbeat. My hands, which were now resting on his chest for balance, detected the same racing heartbeat in him. Before I even realized what was happening, I felt the softness of Nedys's lips upon my own. My eyes drew closed as he kissed me.

I had never kissed a boy before, and I was still struggling to believe that someone like Nedys would want to kiss me – not only as the evil empress of his world but as the ordinary, inconsequential girl of my world. It was hard to believe only a few short days before he had declared me his enemy as he aimed his arrow at my heart. Now he was shooting a different arrow at my heart – one that I feared would be more deadly than that of steel. I knew things between us would not – could not – work out in our favor. Good always conquers evil, and as much as I hated to admit it, my power was evil. I pushed these thoughts to the back recesses of my mind as I surrendered to the sweetness of the moment. I moved my arms up Nedys's chest and interlocked my hands around his neck, not only because I was driven by the basic human desire raging within me, but more so because of the raw emotion of love I felt for Nedys. For the first time in my life, I felt as if I mattered to someone other than members of my own family. Nedys had been able to see past all the lies he had been told about me to see the real me – the vulnerable, eighteen-year-old girl that I was. I kissed Nedys there on my rooftop, knowing that we could never be together. This would be our moment – most likely our only moment – but a moment I would cherish until the end of my days, however short they may be.

"No more near-death experiences for you, okay?" he whispered in my ear as he withdrew, although he continued to look at me. His gaze penetrated my very soul, but not in the discomfiting way as Idnim's fixed stare. He looked at me with admiration, longing, sadness, exhilaration, and joy. I'm not sure how one look can convey such a spectrum of emotion, but his did at that moment. I thought my heart might burst. I was grateful that he had not let go of me, since I'm sure my legs were as useful as jelly. Instead, he guided me back into my bedroom window.

"Well, I suppose we should get some sleep before morning comes," I said as I sat down on my bed. "You can have my parents' room."

"If you don't mind, Elli, I'd rather sleep on the floor here. I wouldn't want you wandering off on me and getting lost," he offered. I threw my pillow at him, and I was rewarded with his dimpled smile. I didn't want to admit to him that I felt safer with him near me, even if Einnep was a world away.

"If you think you can be trusted…" I said as I gathered some spare blankets out of my closet.

"If you can't trust me by now, then we have a problem," he answered back.

In all honesty, I was the one he probably should be wary of trusting because I didn't trust myself with the powers I now bore, however useless they were rendered in my world. We settled into our respective beds, and I was trying to will my mind to stop its hamster wheel of thoughts from its constant tumble, so I could at last welcome sleep.

"How can a person sleep here with all the noise?" Nedys asked as he stared up at the ceiling with his arms behind his head.

"What noise?" I asked, wondering for a second if he could somehow hear the gears in my head turning, as if my self-doubt was audible. I listened for a moment, deciphering the traffic on the street outside, police sirens in the distance, and the rather loud ticking of my wall clock.

"You really can't hear all of that?" he wondered.

"I guess you get used to it after a while," I replied, secretly wishing he would be afforded the time to get used to it.

"I suppose I won't have that luxury," he mumbled, as he turned onto his side. I didn't respond. I couldn't respond. A sense of dread was overcoming me as I thought of the hours to come – of our seemingly impossible quest – of my time with Nedys slipping far too quickly past.

Nedys tossed and turned a few more times in the darkness. He bore a big burden in me, and I wondered he was thinking. As my rescuer, he had essentially forfeited his life. His little adventure into my world and a night's sleep on a hard floor were hardly just recompense, but there was little else I had to offer. I saw the moonlight's bright arms stretch into my open window, and for a moment, seeing only one moon seemed strange to me. I remembered the nightmares of my youth: deep red strawberries crushed all over the floor, white bouncy balls being sliced with a sword, still silence with only red crayon scratches on the floor, pitch blackness with a haunting wailing amplifying the fright. I now realized that these were nightmares from my past life – a life my mind had somehow held onto and patched back together under the cover of darkness to remind me of where I had once been.

I remembered my mother's soothing voice, and the song that calmed my fears. Once again, I wished she was here to comfort me to the dawn of a new day in the way only she could. I understood that in gifting me the Forest Lullaby, she had also given me her calming assurance, even in her absence. I began to sing in the darkness of the night, the requiem of centuries past.

"Rise me moon, Rise me moon…" When I had finished, I noticed that Nedys had settled into a deep and more restful slumber. In that we shared our respite at least. Not long after, sleep also claimed me.

Chapter Twenty-One

Charade

"Where do we start?" Nedys asked eagerly over a blueberry breakfast smoothie.

"I suppose I'd like to talk to Mr. Martindale first. He was the first person to see my parents when they were transported here. He might be able to point me in the right direction. Perhaps the orb is still there."

"Sounds like a plan," Nedys said as he put his cup in the sink. I had to admit that Nedys looked very nice in Leo's clothes. I liked the looks of him before, but there was something about seeing him in jeans and a t-shirt. I was watching him with amusement as he turned the microwave on and off with curiosity. I would have been content to stare at him all day as he explored. He turned to look at me, and my face flushed to be caught staring at him. I was still trying to convince myself that the kiss last night on the window ledge had really happened. It seemed more like a dream, but Nedys's knowing smile was certainly real.

"Shall we?" Nedys held out his hand to me.

"We shall," I agreed as I took his hand without hesitation, feeling as if a hot air balloon of happiness was rising in my chest. I took the slow, scenic route to Mr. Martindale's shop as we walked hand in hand. We stopped frequently, whenever Nedys wanted to investigate something in more depth, which was most often parked cars or trucks or motorcycles or the occasional overhead airplane or military jet. Before long, we had made our way to the front of Mr. Martindale's bakery. The bell above the door jingled its familiar welcome as I opened the door.

"Elli, my girl!" Mr. Martindale exclaimed from behind the counter. "Where have you been?"

"It's kind of a long story," I replied.

"And who's this strapping young lad? He's not the usual riff-raff you hang around, eh?" Mr. Martindale's welcoming voice calmed my frazzled nerves.

"This is my friend, Ned," I introduced him. "Ned, this is Mr. Martindale."

"Ned, you say?" Mr. Martindale asked, holding his hand out for Nedys to shake. "Any friend of Elli's is always welcome here."

"It's a pleasure to meet you, sir," Nedys said as he grabbed the extended hand.

"Sir? A gentleman you have here. What brings you my way, Elli?" he asked as he handed each of us a maple donut. "I assume you've reconsidered your employment for the summer?"

"No…well…I'm not sure," I wasn't sure how to respond.

"Not sure? This is a story I must hear!" he laughed. "I figured something big must have happened for you to miss your first day of work. Why don't we go somewhere more comfortable, so you can tell me this long story?"

"Rebecca," he called out. A girl I recognized from my literature class poked her head out of the kitchen. "I'll be out back if you need me." He didn't wait for her response before escorting Nedys and me into his backyard.

"You hired someone else?" I asked in disbelief. I didn't expect Mr. Martindale of all people to cast me off so quickly.

"I can't wait around forever, my dear. I've got a business to run," he responded. "Don't be worrying yourself over something so trivial. It seems to me you've got bigger fish to fry. What about this story?"

"I doubt you'd believe my story," I muttered, suddenly wondering how to ask my questions without arousing a great deal of concern over my mental state. I only believed it myself because I had lived through it – so far, anyway.

"You might be surprised," he replied as he sat down in a generously cushioned patio chair. I sat down beside him, but Nedys remained standing, looking curiously out over the garden. I watched him for a moment before addressing Mr. Martindale again. There was something about the strange way Nedys was peering out over the garden and then eyeing Mr. Martindale.

Mr. Martindale cleared his throat, drawing my attention back to him. He was glancing between Nedys and me with an odd smile on his face. I was pretty sure I knew what he was thinking, and I was not about to broach that subject while Nedys was within earshot.

"Let me start with a question. Do you remember where you first met my parents?"

"I should hope so. I'm the one who brought them here," he chuckled. My jaw dropped open, and Nedys snapped his head in our direction.

"What?" Nedys and I asked in unison.

"You're the Guardian?" Nedys asked warily.

"Some call me that," he answered nonchalantly. "Others call me the Watcher, the Protector, the Keeper…I could go on and on."

"You're the Guardian?" I asked again, trying to make my mind register what he was saying. I was a little slow on the draw given the fact that I had known Mr. Martindale almost all my life and never suspected him as being anything more than a friendly baker.

"I'm pretty sure we've established that fact, Elli," he said with a touch of his familiar sarcasm.

"I just can't believe it! All this time, you've known who I am? You've known where I came from? And you never said a word – not even to my parents?" I raised my voice in anger. How could this be?

"Calm down, Elli," Mr. Martindale soothed.

"I don't understand why," I managed to whisper the words as my mind did a free fall.

"I was protecting you, Elli. Whether or not you ever went back to the forest was not up to me. Why bother you with an eventuality that may never have happened? As for your parents, I thought it best not to intervene too much. I kept an eye on them – made sure all was well as they adjusted. I had to keep my distance, you see," he explained calmly.

"No, I don't see. I wasn't prepared for any of this. I could have been killed when I ate that gumball, and you knew all about that since you gave Lordess Nalla the gumball to begin with," I seethed.

"You wouldn't have believed me if I had tried to tell you, my dear girl. You would have written me off as a crazed lunatic."

"But my parents knew. Why not talk to them?" I queried.

"They were charged to protect you as well, and they would have severed the connection I had with you. Need I remind you, until recently they didn't even believe in the mysterious Guardian? They needed time to acclimate – time to learn about life outside of the forest, outside of the confines of the empress's power. Besides, they have always been more than a little leery of me." I knew what he was saying was true. I think it took great pains for my mom to tell me to trust in a guardian she had only recently acknowledged might be a real being.

"The orb is here," Nedys spoke up, still looking out over the Mr. Martindale's garden, seemingly unfazed by the conversation.

"It is?" I blurted out. How could the orb have been here all along, and I have been completely oblivious? I followed Nedys's gaze, seeing, as if for the first time, the dozens of garden gazing balls. My eyes settled on a yellow one in the far corner of the garden by the waterfall fountain. I rose shakily to my feet and slowly walked toward it. The nearer I got, the warmer my wrist became where the cuff rested. It now emitted a faint yellow glow, visible even in the sunlight. I came to a stop in front of the orb I had seen at least a hundred times. I didn't feel a surge of power, but rather I felt content, as if I could stand in front of it forever and be perfectly happy. Was that the draw of Mr. Martindale's garden? I had a suspicion that each one of his gazing balls was an orb for a different land, sustaining life in a faraway place.

"You won't feel its full power here in my garden," Mr. Martindale observed from directly behind me.

"But I can feel it," I acknowledged.

"I know. You've felt its draw for some time now," he confirmed what I already supposed.

"But even in the Forest of Notxarb, I only feel little surges of power that I can't control. Is it because the orb was taken?" I asked.

"Because you are in the infancy of its stages, you have little ability to control your power. It is evoked with strong emotional response, such as anger. Having been raised away from the forest, it will take much longer for you to feel its full effect and learn to use it," he clarified.

"Or before it uses me," I contradicted. "Because it will, won't it?"

"I cannot foresee the future, Elli, my girl, but I would not have saved you if I didn't think there was a chance, not only for you but for Annyad and the forest as well," he explained as he rested his large palm on my shoulder. Instead of comfort, I felt a great weight settling on me.

"I suppose you won't tell me how I'm supposed to save everyone, will you?"

"Of that I cannot be sure, but I am confident that when the time is right, you, and you alone will know what you need to do."

"Where did this power come from anyway?" I inquired.

"The power has always existed, just as the orbs have always existed," he began. "It manifests itself at will, wreaking havoc wherever it goes. It is strong and powerful when it takes hold in a world, but the orb is stronger and more powerful. When the orb is threatened and its protectors compromised, I intervene. My role is to protect the orb at all costs. If I can do so while preserving the world in which it resides, I do. Otherwise, I help those who have fought valiantly against the power to escape, while the power destroys all those left behind," he explained with a distant look in his eyes.

"So, it's true then? You do watch over us?" Nedys had quietly joined us, though I hadn't noticed him standing on the other side of Mr. Martindale.

"You and many others," Mr. Martindale answered, gesturing with his hand at the large number of garden gazers sitting on pedestals throughout the garden. There had to be over fifty at least, each one different.

"Shall we check in on Leo?" Mr. Martindale asked as he lifted our yellow orb from its stand. He started walking up the path before suddenly turning around and tossing the orb in the air toward me as he shouted, "Catch!"

I shrieked as I lurched forward to catch the orb before it hit the brick path. Unfortunately, Nedys had the same idea, and our legs and arms got tangled as we rushed for the orb at the same time. I landed with a thud on the brick path, covering my ears so I wouldn't hear the shattering of Annyad's future. I waited, but no sound came until I heard the loud and familiar chuckle of Mr. Martindale. I took a chance and opened my eyes, only to find the orb floating in mid-air as it made its way back to Mr. Martindale's outstretched hands.

"That was not funny!" I shouted angrily as I took Nedys's offered hand. He pulled me to my feet as I waited for my heart to quit hammering in my chest.

"You don't think these are made to be destructible, do you?" Mr. Martindale asked as he continued walking up the path to an outbuilding by the side of the house, still chuckling and tossing the orb from one hand to the other.

"How would I know?" I muttered as I turned to look at Nedys.

"You have to admit, Elli, it was probably quite the spectacle from his perspective," Nedys offered. "In his line of work, I guess you have to take what you can get when it comes to comic relief."

"I still don't think it was funny," I fumed as we followed Mr. Martindale into the outbuilding.

We were greeted by a cozy little living room, complete with small kitchenette off to the side. A small table had been placed in the center of the room upon which sat a strange device that resembled a rather large microscope. Mr. Martindale was positioning the orb underneath the microscope. He stood still for a few moments, peering through the eye pieces. Everything started to fall into place. Leo had thought there were two eyes watching him in his dream, and I was sure I had seen something akin to a blink when I was staring at the twin moons that night by the Siol Tree. We were being watched, by none other than Mr. Martindale.

"This ought to be interesting," Mr. Martindale said as he pulled his face away. "Our timing couldn't be any better." He gestured for us to sit down on the couch, which we did. He turned out the lights and pushed several buttons. On the white wall across from us appeared the blurry images of what looked to be two men, squaring off against each other. My heart stopped momentarily as the projection focused, and the faces became recognizable. I reached a trembling hand toward Nedys, and blinked, hoping my eyes had deceived me. Unfortunately, I found myself still staring at the faces of my newly discovered brothers.

Chapter Twenty-Two

———— •~~• ————

The Guardian's Gazer

"Why? I don't understand why Einnep," Leo was saying. "You know why," Einnep answered.

"The power? You did all this for power?"

"Not for the power. No. I want to destroy the power, and the only way I can do that is to destroy the empress."

"But she's done nothing to you…She's not the evil person you've made everyone believe that she is. I've known her all of my life, Einnep."

"The power will change her, and she'll be just like the others."

"Like our mother?"

"Mother is not the term I'd use to describe that vile creature."

"Well, you made sure that we'd never have the chance to determine that for ourselves, didn't you?"

"I did you a favor, brother. After all that she made me do – after all she took from me…I was protecting everyone."

"Protecting everyone? By sending your own people to work in the quarries – to die in the quarries? That's how you protect people?"

"There was a high price to pay – to end the war."

"And you made sure you were excluded from paying that price, didn't you?"

"Not by choice."

"This I've got to hear."

"It was my reward for…"

"For betraying your people?"

"Don't interrupt! It was my reward for saving Lord Atrebor's life."

"Aren't you the one who endangered it in the first place, Imperator Einnep?"

"Do not ever call me that again," Einnep looked as if he might punch Leo right in the face. His fist was clenched at his side so tightly his hand was white, and I could see him exercising physical restraint as the muscles in his neck tensed. "That's what everyone believes. Yes. But that's not what really happened."

"Why should I believe this load of garbage –"

"Ah, but child, Einnep speaks the truth," Lord Atrebor appeared out of a darkened corner of the room, leaning heavily on a cane. He looked as if he'd aged another ten years, if that was possible. Leo seemed disconcerted.

"Elleon, may I present to you my father, Lord Atrebor. Father, this is Elleon, brother to Einnep." Lordess Nalla emerged from the shadows to offer the introductions.

"Young Elleon, I think it is time you heard the truth about your brother – the truth I daresay, he would never reveal to you himself."

"Lord Atrebor," Einnep tried to intervene.

"Einnep!" Lord Atrebor spoke in a commanding tone. "The time has come. This is your brother – your family. He needs to know the truth, and I shall tell the tale. The war had taken its toll on the Annyadian people…on me…on my family." Lord Atrebor settled himself into a large chair with Lordess Nalla's assistance before continuing.

"Elleon, back then it looked as if we would have to surrender for we had little chance of winning. Our last-ditch effort was to send in spies to infiltrate the Siol Tree – to find the orb. Those valiant men died during the branding ceremony, and with them, we buried our hope. We waited to see what the empress would do to force our hand. That is when I received the devastating news that my eldest daughter, Enna, had disappeared, and I feared all was lost," Lord Atrebor choked out the last words as tears began to stream down his sunken cheeks. Lordess Nalla left Leo's side to gather her grieving father in her embrace. Einnep stepped forward.

"What Lord Atrebor did not know at that time," Einnep picked up the storyline, "was that I had found Enna in the forest nearly a year before. I was patrolling the forest when I heard a muffled scream. I went in search of the noise, knowing there was a steep ravine nearby. I saw a young maiden clinging to a protruding root that was slowly giving way. I instinctively sent down a rope to aid her, though she barely had the strength to hold on. When she reached the top of the ravine, I immediately recognized that she was an Annyadian maiden.

"At first, I suspected an Annyadian trap. The maiden told me that she secretly ventured into the forest often to meet with her tutor, Idnim, the ancient tree spirit. I knew of no ancient tree spirits residing in the forest and demanded that she take me to see this tutor, for I thought it had to be a traitor to the empress. She told me I could only be admitted to Idnim's sanctuary if I secured permission from Idnim herself. She told me in exchange for her rescue she would petition the ancient tree spirit on my behalf. I had no reason to trust her, but as I questioned her, I saw no deception in her eyes, detected no lie in her voice. Duty called for me to take her before the empress, but my heart would not heed the call. I let her go, certain that I would never hear from her again.

"In the days that passed, however, I found myself frequently at the edge of the ravine. I was but a boy of no more than seventeen years with a boulder of responsibilities upon my back that a man at the prime of his maturity would have found hard to bear, let alone a boy at the cusp of his manhood. I commanded an army. I held life and death in my hands, and yet I found myself waiting for her return. In that, Enna did not disappoint.

"A week later, she appeared again, having secured passage for me to see Idnim. We traveled by magical means to ensure that Idnim's sanctuary remained hidden. In that place, I first learned that the empress was nothing more than a power-hungry liar who had robbed me of my childhood. The empress had told me that all the ancient tree spirits had fled this world when she had discovered that they were in league with Lord Atrebor, but Idnim's very existence proved her lie. Idnim would not go into detail about the story, but she told me that the empress had taken the tree spirits in her rage. Idnim alone had escaped and lived in her solitary confinement as her powers waned. Enna then enlightened me on the true state of affairs of the Annyadian people. Everything I had known to be true was nothing more than a web of twisted lies conjured up by the empress to align others with her quest for power.

"I was powerless against the empress, so I decided to bide my time until I found an opportunity to do something that would make a difference. Had I confronted the empress at that point, I would have been killed, which would have served no purpose in aiding Enna and her people. For a year I waited and continued my secret meetings with Enna in Idnim's sanctuary. By then, a full-scale attack had been launched against the Annyadian army – an attack I was in charge of executing. I tried to pass information to Enna to lessen the losses on the Annyadian side without revealing my betrayal, but I knew the time drew near that I must make my stand.

"Unfortunately, the empress had taken notice of the difference in my countenance. Unbeknownst to me, she had me watched. I should have known better. The tree spirits near the ravine where Enna and I would meet were loyal to Idnim, but there were others who were not. How was I to avoid detection when a forest of trees was watching my every move? On a day we were scheduled to meet, the empress insisted that I personally check a possible Annyadian breach. I had no choice but to obey. Enna understood the part I had to play, and I had told her to go on without me if ever I didn't come at the specified time. Unfortunately, she must have waited for me, and it was not I who came, but the empress herself. She kidnapped Enna, imprisoning her in a hollowed-out tree.

"As I was returning from my bogus mission, the empress met me before I reached the Siol Tree. I was surprised because she was great with child, and she held the orb in her hands, which was never taken from the confines of the Siol Tree. I knew something was terribly wrong. She bid me to follow her to the hollowed-out tree where Enna was held captive. I'm sure the look on my face when I saw Enna huddled in the small, cramped space seemingly asleep was all the additional proof the empress required to indict me. I'll never forget the words she spoke next to me: 'What a disappointment you are – a pathetic excuse for a son. Thankfully, I have my darling Ellinnet to whom I can entrust my legacy.' She then told me that if I ever wanted to see Enna alive again that I would have to negotiate a complete surrender with Lord Atrebor, execute all prisoners, and claim the city of Annyad in her name. To ensure my compliance, she then somehow transported Enna from the hollowed-out log to the inside of the orb. As the empress held the orb out, I clearly saw Enna inside the ball for just a moment before the yellow shell returned, obscuring my view. No one would know where she was unless I complied.

"I was escorted by an armed guard to Lord Atrebor's encampment to convey the news of Enna's capture to force him into surrender. I was trying to formulate a plan of escape for all of us, and my attention was focused on that purpose alone. As we approached the Annyadian camp, there was a clash. It all happened so fast. I can't be sure of exactly what actually occurred. I only know that as I was shaken out of my contemplation by the commotion, I saw one of my guards detonate a light ball inside Lord Atrebor's tent, igniting it with fire. I reacted instinctively, jumping into the tent to try to save anyone inside. I was able to pull Lord Atrebor from the flames before the tent collapsed, but then everything went black as I lost consciousness.

"I woke up some time later in Idnim's sanctuary. I had been badly burned on my back, upper arms, and legs. Idnim had rescued me and healed me as best she could, but she could do nothing for Lord Atrebor's eyesight. The light ball had blinded him. I recounted to Lord Atrebor all that had happened to Enna, and we formulated a plan to rescue Enna and destroy the empress. We set up several diversions to distract the tree spirits as I took Lord Atrebor, acting as my prisoner, and several Annyadian soldiers, posing as Enelians, to the Siol Tree. Since Lord Atrebor could not enter the Siol Tree, I summoned the empress out of its protection. In her gloating, she brought her ailing husband as well, so they could witness Annyad's disgrace together.

"She didn't have time to defend herself against the swiftness of the Annyadian soldiers' deadly blades. She had mistaken me for yet another pawn in her twisted games, thinking she could control me as easily as she always had. My time with Enna had changed me. My thoughts had not gone beyond the empress until I noticed two wide eyes staring out of the entrance of the Siol Tree. In those eyes, I did not see childish fear; I saw only the childlike eyes of the empress staring back at me. I started for the Siol Tree, but the girl ran away from me. As I darted inside, I saw the orb hovering near the entrance. I paused to pick it up, wondering how long it would take for Enna to reappear since the empress was now dead.

"Then it occurred to me that she would not be freed for the new empress was alive and well. In that moment, I knew what I had to do. I reached Ellinnet's chamber just in time to see her custodians hovering over her, and then they were gone. They vanished into thin air, and I found my hands strangely empty as the orb vanished with them," Einnep finished his story without the slightest show of emotion other than the usual aura of hatred he carried about him.

"Though Enna was lost," Lord Atrebor interjected, "I do not blame Master Einnep. He has a brilliant mind, and he risked his life to save me – a man he was raised to hate above all others."

"Why did you let everyone believe the lie?" Leo asked, his confusion evident from his facial expressions.

"To lure the empress out of hiding, so the power can be destroyed once and for all," Einnep answered matter-of-factly.

"And what of Nalla in all of this?" Leo wondered aloud. "Your supposed betrothal is all part of the ruse?" Einnep's silence answered Leo's question.

"Einnep," Lordess Nalla stepped forward, touching Einnep gently on the arm. "I cannot hide myself anymore. Though I don't remember my sister, I know you have told me that we look so much alike. I'm sorry that my face causes you such pain, but I'm not Enna. I won't stand aside any longer and let the Enelians suffer in the quarries. Elleon and I have met with them these past days, and they have agreed not to retaliate – not to raise weapons against us after they are given their freedom under one condition...you recuse yourself from your position of power," Lordess Nalla explained as she removed her veil to reveal her beautiful face and golden hair. Einnep didn't seem shocked or angry. He suddenly looked very tired.

"Will they renounce the empress?" he asked calmly.

"They will swear their allegiance to another…Elleon," Nalla answered.

"Where is the empress, anyway? With Idnim?" Einnep asked as Nalla's eyes danced with surprise. The fire of anger in his eyes faded into embers of deep sadness.

"Yes, I know about you and Idnim, Nalla…so like your sister, you are," he said quietly as if he were in another time and place. He reached out his hand as if to touch her cheek, but quickly withdrew it and turned away.

"Do not be angry with me, Einnep, but I'm the one who brought her here. The forest is dying, and I…I thought she could help. That's why my father forbade you from searching for her when she escaped. I needed time to talk with her away from your presence. I thought she'd have the orb with her…maybe hidden in the forest," Nalla's rationalized. Einnep sucked a deep breath, never turning to look at her.

"And did she have the orb?" his voice quavered as he asked the question, his body tense with anticipation of the answer.

"No," Nalla almost whispered the answer as her eyes filled with tears. "We believe the Guardian still has it in his possession in the world from which she came. She's gone back to retrieve it."

"And you trust her to return?" Einnep spat the words in disbelief.

"Of course, she'll return," Leo defended. "How many times do I have to tell you that Elli is not the monster you've created in your warped head? Now, what of the Enelians?"

"I repeat my question: Will they renounce the empress?" Einnep turned an icy glare on Leo, careful to avoid Nalla's face.

"They will if I ask them to," Leo replied stiffly.

"And will you ask them, brother?" Einnep persisted. Leo rubbed his forehead with his hands as he turned his back to Einnep. Lordess Nalla appeared at his side, resting her arm around his waist as if to buoy him up.

"Elli would never allow any blood to be spilled on her behalf. I won't have to ask," he spoke confidently as he turned to face Einnep again.

"The blood will be on your head, little brother. What are you, about seventeen? Not much older than I was. We'll see how high you hold your head after innocent blood has been spilled because of you. Will you stand so tall under the strain of that weight? The stains may easily be washed from your hands, but they will scar your soul. Mark my words, brother. You underestimate the empress," Einnep snapped.

"No," Leo defended. "I believe it is you who underestimates her. Enna convinced you that the lies you had been told and believed all of your life were untrue. Elli – I mean Empress Ellinnet knows the truth as well. She's the one who convinced me to believe it, which is one of the reasons I'm here. There's a saying where I come from that your actions speak louder than your words. Empress Ellinnet has done nothing to hurt anyone since she's been here. You, on the other hand, don't have such a spotless record, do you? I am only beginning to unravel all the pieces to this twisted tale I've been sucked into. I don't profess to understand how hard your life has been, but no one is forcing your hand now, and you're still bent on murder. You can say what you want Einnep, but I'm not sure I can hear what you're saying over what you're doing."

"We have nothing further to discuss," Einnep seethed as he turned to leave.

"Let me ask you again: What of the Enelians? Will you recuse yourself?" Leo demanded.

"I suppose that depends on your sister, doesn't it?" Einnep hissed.

"You mean our sister," Leo corrected as Einnep walked away in a huff. Lord

Atrebor's hand searched the air until it came in contact with Leo's shoulder.

"The Enelians should have never been put in the quarries," Lord Atrebor's voice was barely a whisper. "That is my fault, and no apologies will turn back time to reclaim them from that awful fate imposed upon them by one who was not only blinded by a light ball, but also by hatred. I acknowledge that I am a weakened leader. I was once strong, but I've lost much – my beloved wife – who died after birthing Nalla while I was away at war, my eldest daughter, my people who lie buried in shallow graves from the war, those who returned from the war ghosts of their former selves, my eyesight... I hated the Enelians, and I allowed that hatred to harden into my heart. I am but a broken man with only my dearest Nalla to hold the pieces together. I think it is past time that I abdicate my leadership to someone who is worthy to hold the office – someone not tainted by the hatred of loss and betrayal – someone like you, Nalla. You will rule our people. You and Elleon will forge a new future for this place."

"But father," Lordess Nalla exclaimed.

"Be still, child, and do not argue with me. This is who you were meant to be," Lord Atrebor chided.

"And what of Einnep?" she asked.

"Einnep. Einnep, my wayward son," Lord Atrebor murmured. "Time will tell, will it not? Now, I grow tired. Please escort me back to my rooms." Lordess Nalla did as he asked. She took his hand in hers and began to guide her father back to the stone castle with Leo at his other side, poised to catch the old man if his cane gave way.

Chapter Twenty-Three

Tours and Tremors

Mr. Martindale moved toward his gazer and removed the orb, leaving the wall blank once again. I sat in shocked silence as the scene replayed itself repeatedly in my mind, a spinning tilt-a-whirl that I could not control or stop.

"So, Einnep only wants Enna. He doesn't care about the orb," I surmised, baffled that I had so completely misread him.

"Unfortunately for Einnep, he doesn't know as much as he thinks he does. In seeking your life, he will be sacrificing Enna's life," Mr. Martindale expounded as he ran his fingers down his long goatee.

"What do you mean?" Nedys queried, his hand still entwined with mine.

"Enna is indeed trapped in the orb, preserved in an eternal sleep in which she has not aged. Though the empress thought her ploy to turn Einnep back to her favor would work, she acknowledged that there was a small chance that he may not bend so easily to her will. She sought to protect herself and you, so she added a failsafe to her curse on Enna. If her heiress was killed by Einnep, then Enna, too, would die. Your mother didn't have a chance to play her cards. She didn't expect the Annyadian ambush because she didn't suspect how deeply rooted Einnep's hatred of her had become in the year he had known Enna and Idnim. Elli, Enna can only be freed by the empress, which is now you. Your lives have been tied together all these years, unbeknownst to anyone but me."

"She was a sly one, wasn't she?" Nedys ventured. When I looked into his eyes, I noticed that they flickered with a shade of hope. I had to admit, Mr. Martindale's newest revelation had embedded a small seed of hope into my own heart as well. I wasn't ready to water it by entertaining thoughts of a possible future where the Enelians were free, the forest and Annyad were restored to their proper order, and Nedys was at my side. I did, however, plant that little seed in my heart, inviting the possibility that one day it might even sprout into that very future I had just tucked away.

"Well, I've got a business to run," Mr. Martindale proclaimed. "My star employee didn't show this year, so I'm training a new upstart and don't want to leave her alone for too long. I think it best if you leave the orb with me, and don't worry. Each orb has its twin, so I'll still be able to keep an eye on everything when this one has been returned. Meet me back here tomorrow morning at 7:00 am sharp. The forest can wait until then. Help yourself to a bite of lunch and anything else you want." He left us in the outbuilding as he walked back to the garden to replace the orb.

"Einnep did this all because he loved someone," I spoke my thoughts of disbelief aloud.

"You say that as if you have a hard time believing a person capable of such a love," Nedys inferred.

"To murder, to enslave people…isn't it a bit of a contradiction…more of a selfish motivation?" I asked, thinking that Einnep was more like his mother than he knew.

"I suppose that depends on how you look at it, Elli," he responded.

"You're siding with him?" I felt my heart thump awkwardly in my chest at my angry tone as I let go of his hand and stood up.

"I'm asking you to view the past from a different perspective. In killing the empress, he saved the Annyadian people, who would have surely been annihilated. He saved an entire civilization. He saved me, Elli. And I don't think he only did it in an effort to save Enna either. He did it in honor of Enna – for the sacrifice she made for her people and for him. He shouldn't have enslaved the Enelians. I grant you that. Some of them were his closest friends – the people he had grown up with, but in not renouncing the empress, he must have felt that they, too, would betray him as she did," Nedys countered, remaining seated.

"How can you say that?" I demanded.

"I suppose in recent days, I've come to understand how powerful love really is and the value of looking beneath the surface. We were wrong about Einnep's motivations and much of what he did was for the better," Nedys defended himself with pleading eyes.

"What are you saying, Nedys? You agree with Einnep now?" I could hardly believe we were having this conversation.

"No. I'm merely saying that I can perhaps begin to understand why he acted as he did," Nedys replied calmly.

"As he did, not as he does. Let's keep in the present for now. He wants to kill me, and he'll stop at nothing until he's accomplished that," I reminded him.

"He'll not kill you when he finds out that in doing so, he'll also kill Enna," Nedys said as he rose to stand by my side. Unease crouched silently in the shadows of my mind, waiting to pounce. Not only was my life at stake anymore. I did not know how to free Enna once the orb had been returned.

"I'm to be saved by his warped sense of love? That's assuming I even get a chance to reveal the fact that his dastardly plans for me will end up killing his beloved." I turned my back to him as I spoke.

"We cannot undo what has been done, but we must see passed all this long-held hatred. What would have become of you if I had not stopped to see you as the person you really are? Does not everyone deserve that? Do we not all have our weaknesses, our regrets?" Nedys asked as he turned me around to face him. My anger cooled when I saw the look on his face, his eyebrows knit with concern.

"I wish I could be more like you, Nedys, but I'm afraid I'm not there yet. And I certainly don't trust Einnep, especially with my life." Nedys's words, however, burrowed their way into my thoughts and nestled snuggly there. They would not be leaving me alone anytime soon because I knew that Nedys spoke the truth. I knew it would be up to me to put aside the hatred and anger, but I wasn't ready to relinquish my hold just yet or maybe it wasn't ready to relinquish its hold on me. Either way, it didn't seem fair. Whether I forgave Einnep or not, he would still harbor hatred for me as he always had. Then again, I knew this journey wasn't about Einnep, and I would have to decide once and for all what kind of person I was. I would have to choose whether or not I wanted to feed my power with the same hatred with which Empress Enyala had. I had already declared to everyone that I wasn't that person, and I would have to prove it to myself sooner or later.

Unfortunately, that was harder than I had thought it would be. The problem was that I wasn't sure how to move past it. I didn't know if I was strong enough to fight it. I didn't know how to let go. That's what scared me the most.

"Elli, I don't want to spend the little time we have left here arguing with you about Einnep," he uttered softly as he moved some stray hair out of my eyes. He wrapped his arms around me and pulled me close to his chest in a tight hug as he rested his chin on the top of my head. A swell of emotion rose in my chest at the tenderness of his actions. Even after I had yelled at him, he still comforted me. He remained by my side. Maybe I could draw the strength I needed from the small moments like these – the moments when I wasn't afraid or lonely.

"I'm sorry," I declared as I pulled out of his embrace. "It just seems like every fork in the road brings some new surprise, and it's not so easy to digest – you know? Before I ate that gumball my life was pretty straightforward – mundane even. I didn't have to deal with hardly any changes – life was predictable. Now there's change at every step, and I feel like I'm just stumbling my way along as I'm pushed this way or that way."

"Change isn't always bad, is it?" Nedys quirked his eyebrow at the question, and I knew he was referring to his presence in my life. I shook my head and smiled.

No, some changes weren't bad at all, I thought.

"Besides, I'd like to experience this mundane life of yours. Shall we?" Nedys offered me his arm and escorted me through the door of the outbuilding. We made our way up the stairs to Mr. Martindale's house above the bakery. He had already prepared a lunch of club sandwiches on his homemade parmesan rosemary bagels, fresh garden salad, fresh lemonade, and apple turnovers for dessert. Nedys seemed to savor every bite. I had to admit that Mr. Martindale's food had never tasted so good.

After we finished every crumb, we walked back to my house, where I taught Nedys how to ride Leo's bike. Unlike me, he proved to be a natural. I took him on some of my favorite bike trails and showed him my favorite spots. I knew a bicycle was hardly comparable to the automobiles Nedys so admired, and certainly not as exciting as his traveler. Unfortunately, I didn't know how to drive nor did my parents. I decided the next best thing would be the light rail train. I grabbed some money I had been saving, and we caught a bus to the train station.

I didn't usually venture downtown. Leo's parents manned the downtown farmer's market, and I only helped at that location on occasion with one of my parents as a chaperone. My parents thought there were too many strange people milling around for their liking. I had gone downtown once or twice with Leo and his friends, but my parents never knew that – at least I hoped they didn't. Nedys was as fascinated by the train ride as he was by all the people who boarded with their various technological gadgets.

"What do you think?" I leaned closer to ask him.

"I've never seen anything like it," he proclaimed. "It's almost as if everyone is absorbed in their own little bubble though." I looked around and saw a couple of teenagers with ear buds in their ears, a man talking on the phone with his Bluetooth, a woman perusing the internet on her phone, a young woman texting on her phone, and another woman reading on her e-reader. There were very few conversations amongst the many passengers.

"I've never really noticed that before," I commented. While I didn't have any of the devices these people were using, I realized that I, too, kept myself in my own little bubble, rarely venturing out to meet new people.

"Just like you can sleep with all that noise in your house?" Nedys smiled as he averted his eyes to the buildings whizzing outside his window. I hadn't noticed that before either. There was so much I had been blind to until my little excursion to the Forest of Notxarb. I had to admit that I was in some ways grateful that my eyes were opening.

We explored downtown well into the early evening hours, admiring the buildings and checking out all the shops and stores lining the streets. We opted to buy dinner at one of the many food carts – another wonder for Nedys to see so much food in one place. When we boarded the train to go home, I watched the setting sun out the window with a sinking feeling of my own. The day had gone by far too fast.

There was one last thing I wanted Nedys to experience before we had to leave. When we returned to my house, we went over to Leo's house to watch a movie. I didn't think Leo or his parents would mind if I helped myself. My parents did not approve of the fact that Leo's parents had allowed him to get a TV, but that had never stopped me from enjoying it before. I popped some popcorn and put in one of my favorite movies before curling up next to Nedys on the couch.

I spent more time watching Nedys than I did watching the movie. He was so fascinated and mesmerized by the movements on the screen and touched the TV screen several times to make sure the actors weren't really in the room. I watched his facial expressions as his eyes widened in amazement or narrowed in concentration or crinkled with laughter. For that short time, I forgot about the next day. When the movie was over, we went back to my house and got ready for bed. Nedys again insisted on sleeping on the floor of my room, though I knew how uncomfortable it must have been for him.

That night, I awoke out of a dead sleep. My heart was pounding, my body shaking uncontrollably. I couldn't breathe. I was disoriented, unsure of where I was. I looked around the darkened room. My room. I was in my own bedroom. I glanced at the floor. I didn't see the outline of Nedys's sleeping figure. There was no one there. Had the entire thing been a nightmare? I needed air, but I couldn't seem to make myself move.

"Mom!" I yelled. "Mom!" I did not hear her familiar footsteps running down the hall, but I was surprised when a head suddenly appeared in my window. I let out a blood curdling scream, completely paralyzed by fear. The figure deftly hopped through the window, coming to rest at my side. I tried to back away.

"Elli," I recognized the voice that spoke to me. "Elli. It's okay. You're okay.

It's me, Nedys." He put his arm on my shoulder, and I melted into him.

"Everything is going to be okay. Was it a nightmare?"

"No, it wasn't. I just woke up out of a dead sleep and couldn't breathe," I explained as my breathing started to return to normal, and my shaking became less pronounced.

"Night tremors, then? Me mum had them frequently."

"After your brothers died?" I surmised, grateful for the distraction.

"I wasn't much more than a pebble then, but me guess would be that they started as soon as me brothers left. Her night tremors were always a part of me life as far back as I can remember, but they got worse near the end. Me father was none too understanding, but I'd sneak in to try to comfort her when he was on night patrols. The Forest Lullaby usually did the trick."

"How old were you when she died?"

"I was but ten. Sometimes it seems like just yesterday, but she's been gone for eleven years."

"I'm sorry, Nedys," I didn't know what else to say. He shifted next to me, and I raised my head off his shoulder. He pulled the cord from around his neck to reveal the smooth, blue stone I had seen when he was recovering from the branding ceremony. He held it in his hand, a slight tremble in his fingers.

"She gave me this the day before she killed herself," he revealed. I looked at his face, but he was staring intently at the rock. "No one knows but me. I never even told me father."

"Oh Nedys…" I couldn't finish the thought. How could a ten-year-old boy bear such a burden?

"She always wore this around her neck – never took it off. She found it one day when she was foraging for food in the north lands just before I was born.

She often told me that the stone was her strength – that it had once been large and rough but the waters had worn it down into a smooth, polished gem – just as life was doing with her. I guess she stopped believing it after a while," he finished softly, quickly wiping away a stray tear.

"Me father started whipping me after that. He'd be out after late patrols, drinking his grog with soldier buddies. He'd come home in a drunken rage, and I was too young to protect meself. In the years since I've wondered if he did the same to me mother. She hid it well if he did, but in the end, it was too much for her to bear. Maybe she didn't realize she was protecting me. She might have thought he'd treat me better because I was his only son – the only son left anyway. No point speculating about it though," he dismissed his thought as he turned the rock over and over in his hands.

"I had no idea…I'm…I'm so sorry," I managed to say despite my shock.

"I'm glad someone else knows – I'm glad that someone else is you. It's good to remember those I've lost because it makes me grateful for those I've found. If it hadn't been for that, I never would have met Hairam. After a few months, I smarted up and started sneaking out of the house before he got home. I took to sleeping in a cave that was near enough I could make it home before he woke up. One night I heard a ruckus on the ledge and went to check it out. I saw this little ragamuffin of a boy not more than five or six, clinging for dear life. He had been scavenging for food and chased a critter onto the ledge before he realized where he was. I scooped him up and gave him a bite to eat. He rarely left me side after that. He told me he ran away from a large family of twelve kids who lived in a nomadic clan that roamed about, but I suspected he somehow managed to escape from the quarry." As he talked, my gaze settled on the purple scar on the palm of his hand – a scar I had inflicted upon him. I knew then that his reaction to the pain the night the knife sliced through his skin had been learned over years of his father's abuse. He had taught himself not to flinch, not to cry out, not to show weakness, thus not giving his father the upper hand. In that fierce defiance, however, he had also taught himself not to feel. Not only had he sought refuge in a cave, but he also had built himself his own personal cave that sheltered him from the pain around him. I knew I needed to tread very carefully because he had allowed me into his protective barrier.

"Didn't they miss him in the quarry?" I asked.

"Not at that age. One less child underfoot wasn't going to set off any alarms, especially if he was an orphan. When I first became a soldier, I was guarding the quarry, and I tried to find his family. Because I was the Annyadian oppressor, no one would talk to me. They thought I had an ulterior motive in trying to find the boy's family. Besides that, it had been seven years since he had disappeared, so it took me a while to find anyone who had even known he existed. Eventually, I did find an old woman who had tried to care for a boy who called himself Hairam. She told me that his father had been killed in a rock slide, and his mother had been too sick to care for him and died not long after he disappeared. I never did tell Hairam though. He lived in the cave, and I took care of him.

"We figured out how to dye his hair, so he looked a bit more like an Annyadian. Because everyone saw us together all the time, they simply assumed he was me cousin. When he was old enough, he applied for service as a soldier. I tried to talk him out of it, but he wouldn't listen to me. Being a soldier gave him clothes, food, and a place to stay." I very much doubted that Hairam's decision had little to do with his physical needs being met and much more to do with the fact that Nedys was his anchor. I wasn't so sure myself that I wouldn't follow Nedys wherever he went at this point, and I had known him for much less time than Hairam.

"Is life so bad in the quarries then?" I wasn't sure I really wanted to know the answer.

"It's much improved since Lordess Nalla took an interest in the workers," he acknowledged.

"She did? But how?"

"Most of her guards are more loyal to her than they are to your brother. How do you think she gets out all the time? We help her get in and out whenever and wherever she wants. That's how I knew about the passage that I helped you escaped through. Einnep lost interest in the quarries not long after he sent all his people there. Lordess Nalla was too young then to do anything, but as she got older, the quarry became a pet project of hers. Hairam would have been well cared for if he had born much later. His mother may still have been alive to take care of him herself. But as it was, he had me. I suppose I was better than nothing, and he was good for me as well."

"And your father? He never questioned your friend's origins?"

"Nah. He was too preoccupied to care about any of me friends. As long as I followed his prescribed path, he let me be. I just hope Hairam stays out of me father's way until I get back. Border patrol duty isn't the worst me father could do to him," Nedys said quietly as he slipped the cord back around his neck, tucking the blue stone away inside his t-shirt.

"I shouldn't have said anything to him about the branding ceremony and the orb. I didn't realize –" I started to say, but he didn't let me finish.

"I told him what I was about before I rescued you. He knew there were risks to be had for both of us, but he agreed with me scheme. He has me traveler if he needs to escape in a hurry, and we came up with a contingency plan if he needs to lay low for a while. I'm sure he'll be fine. I just let me worries get the best of me at night, I guess. It's probably time we both get some sleep," he suggested as he put his arm back around me and leaned against the wall. We sat there in silence, not needing to speak, but rather relishing the comfort we felt in each other's arms.

I must have fallen asleep not long afterward because the next thing I knew, the sun was streaking through the window announcing the arrival of a new day. I was lying in my bed with the covers tucked up around my chin, and Nedys was nowhere in sight.

Chapter Twenty-Four

Excursions

I looked at my clock, which read 6:30 am. I was used to getting up before 5:00 to work at the bakery, so I was surprised I had slept in so long. There wasn't a sound in the house, and I wondered where Nedys was. Surely, he should have been exhausted enough to sleep in, especially after last night. Nedys knew more about me than anyone, and I had a feeling I knew more about him than anyone else as well. Where did that leave us? Not liking the direction of my thoughts, I got out of bed, showered, and dressed for the day. Nedys was sitting on my bed when I returned to my room. He was also dressed and ready for the day.

"Where have you been?" I asked nonchalantly.

"I couldn't sleep, so I decided I might as well get up."

"Is that why you were on the roof last night?" I probed. Nedys nodded his head in response. "By the way, I'm sorry about last night."

"Do you know you're always apologizing for things you shouldn't?" he said, smiling. I knew he didn't regret the opportunity to share the burden he had carried for so long alone.

"Are you ready to go? If we leave now, we'll be right on time. I'm sure Mr. Martindale will have some fresh donuts we can eat for breakfast."

"May I offer you a flower?" Nedys asked as my heart began to flutter. He pulled Idnim's flower from behind his back, and my face fell. Nothing could have brought me to reality more quickly. Nedys noticed my reaction.

"Did I do something wrong?" he wondered with a bewildered expression on his face. "I just thought we ought to bring it with us when we retrieve the orb."

I realized that Nedys didn't know that bringing flowers to a young woman was a romantic gesture in my world. Flowers didn't even grow in Annyad. I immediately dismissed the notion of a romance. Nedys had done nothing more than hold my hand since our first kiss, and I knew there could be nothing between us. I had a really hard time getting my heart to understand the logic. It seemed to be set on securely attaching itself to Nedys, despite my objections. I decided not to enlighten Nedys on the topic of flowers and romance. There was no reason to further complicate an already complicated relationship.

"You're right," I answered. "We ought to bring it with us." I pasted a fake smile on my face, but Nedys looked at me skeptically as though I was completely transparent. He looked as if he might say something but seemed to reconsider. Instead, he got to his feet.

"We better get going then," he urged as he handed me the flower. I tucked it carefully in the front pouch of my backpack. I wistfully looked around my surroundings, trying to memorize my little house, unsure of whether or not I would ever see it again.

The walk to Mr. Martindale's was relatively quiet. We both felt the burden of our impending return weighing us down like an anchor, slowly drowning the contentment we had found in each other's company with each step we took. I smelled fresh donuts as we walked into Mr. Martindale's bakery. Despite my uncertain future, a sense of peace settled over me as I inhaled the familiar aroma, perhaps for the last time.

"Right on time. Right on time," Mr. Martindale clapped his hands together when we opened the door. He held a sack in one hand and a large cooler in the other as he approached from behind the counter. I wondered if the orb had to be chilled during transport.

"Ready?" he asked, a little too cheerfully given the gravity of the task ahead.

"As ready as we'll ever be," I stated unenthusiastically. The time had gone by too quickly.

"Don't sound so excited. Rebecca, I'm headed out now," he called to the kitchen. Rebecca poked her head out and smiled.

"I'll try to hold the fort down while you're gone," she waved as we exited through the side door. He didn't turn to the left to go to the garden; however. He turned toward his garage, where his Toyota Prius was parked.

"Hop in," he said as he opened the rear door for me.

"What?" I asked in confusion.

"All is well for now in Annyad. The quarry workers have been given leave of their duties until your return," he told us, as if that explained everything.

"I don't understand," I responded.

"You'll understand this: If you don't get in, I won't let you take the orb back," he threatened, trying to look stern but failing miserably.

"I think he means it, Elli," Nedys whispered, trying to conceal the smile lurking in his eyes.

How could I refuse even if I had wanted to? I felt my body relax at my unexpected reprieve as I sank into the leather seat behind the driver's seat. Nedys slid into the passenger seat as Mr. Martindale passed around donuts and juice from one of the sacks he had brought. For the next hour and half, we weaved along forested roads on our way to the coast. I dozed off as Mr. Martindale and Nedys fell into easy conversation about mechanics and cars and a myriad of other topics in which I found little, if any, interest.

We spent the entire day at the beach, courtesy of Mr. Martindale. We ate a picnic lunch from the cooler Mr. Martindale had thoughtfully packed, flew a kite, built an incredible sandcastle that bore an eerie resemblance to the stone castle of Annyad, waded in the cold ocean water, and forgot about everything else. For a few hours, it was just Nedys and I, since Mr. Martindale had conveniently disappeared not long after we got settled on the beach. My heart trilled with the excitement in Nedys's eyes at each new discovery from the rotted crab leg he found to the slimy tubular plant that washed in with the waves from somewhere in the ocean's depths. He looked at me the same way – with a glint of amazement. I wasn't sure why he found me so intriguing, and I found myself reaching for his hand on occasion, just to make sure he was real. I had to admit that I didn't have the imagination to dream up someone as wonderful as Nedys.

I watched as he reveled in his liberation, perhaps for the first time in his life. Nedys was free from his father and the burdens he had foisted upon him. He was free to be himself, free to leave his cave with no fear of being hurt, free to indulge in his passion for life. He trusted me fully and completely, which no one had ever done before, not even Leo. Leo had his secrets, I was sure. Besides, the feelings I had for Leo were of sisterly affection, even before I knew he was my brother. Those certainly were not the feelings vying for my attention in Nedys's presence.

Before we left, Mr. Martindale treated us to a delicious seafood dinner. He even pulled onto a back road and gave Nedys a few driving lessons. I politely declined the invitation, not wanting to make a fool of myself and feeling a little bit guilty about having so much fun while my parents were consumed with worry. I could safely say it was one of the best days of my life. When we returned to Mr. Martindale's house, the sun wasn't quite setting. My stomach soured in anticipation of our return to the Forest of Notxarb.

"Thank you so much, Mr. Martindale," I said as he led us into the garden.

"Yes, thank you for a most wonderful day, sir," Nedys echoed.

"Not at all. Not at all. After all you two have been through and have yet to face, you deserve it," Mr. Martindale stated with a hint of melancholy in his tone. He led us to the orb and took it off the pedestal.

"I'll be watching," he assured us as he handed the orb to me. I gently slipped it into my backpack.

"I have a little something else for you," he added with a wink as he handed me a small yellow box. "Tuck it away until you get back, and remember, Elli: Gifts can be very powerful." His were eyes more serious than I had ever seen them. I knew he was sharing with me some great secret, but I didn't understand. I tucked the box safely into the pouch of my backpack, hoping the secret would be revealed when I opened it.

"Sir, it was a pleasure to meet you in person," Nedys stepped forward with an extended hand. "This whole experience has been beyond belief." Mr. Martindale heartily shook Nedys's hand.

"The pleasure was all mine – all mine indeed! You are more than a worthy companion for Elli," Mr. Martindale replied. I felt a blush rise to my cheeks as Mr. Martindale winked at me again. Nedys had the decency to try to hide his obvious amusement, but I still caught a glimpse of his dimpled smile.

"Take care of yourselves," Mr. Martindale advised as I took the wilting flower out of my backpack.

"Do you remember the words?" I asked as Nedys gently grabbed onto the flower, his fingers brushing mine.

"Sometimes I wish I didn't," he admitted, his voice quiet and serious. My eyes locked on his. He had the same look in them the night he had kissed me on my rooftop. As much as I enjoyed my extra day with Nedys, I knew it would only make our eventual separation all the harder. My heart confirmed its betrayal as it started to pound a pleasant staccato beat in my chest as Nedys launched into his recitation of the required rhyme in his deep, accented voice, "Carry me plus one back again – the land of my birth – to the ancient den." He paused and took a deep breath before repeating the words again, his eyes never leaving mine.

Chapter Twenty-Five

Homecoming

When our eyes adjusted to lighting, we found ourselves back in the Siol Tree, where our journey had begun. The flower withered and vanished into thin air as we watched, finding ourselves holding onto nothing. I felt a surge of energy course through my body as my backpack started to lift me off the ground. Nedys, grabbed onto my hands to keep me from floating away as he reached for the backpack, somehow managing to get it off of me. I fell to my feet with a thud.

"What was that?" he asked as he gripped the backpack in his arms in an effort to keep it grounded.

"I...I don't know," I stammered, trying to catch my breath. I reached over to unzip my backpack, and the orb floated out. We followed as it weaved around the twisting corners of the passageway, into the main foyer, and onto the pedestal. I saw my dad peek his head around the corner as the orb settled into place.

"You brought her back unscathed, I presume?" Yelnats inquired.

"As you see, sir," Nedys responded.

"If anything, Nedys is the worse for wear. He couldn't seem to sleep with all the noise," I interjected.

"Ah...that adjustment I remember well," Yelnats commented with a knowing smile. "Did she make you some hot chocolate?"

"That she did, and it almost made the sleepless night worth it," Nedys smiled in return. "She also made a delicious blueberry smoothie, and I must commend you on your growing skills in such a foreign place." My dad beamed at the unexpected compliment. It seemed Nedys had finally won him over.

My mom came out of the doorway, stepping into the entryway. I saw the relief in my mother's eyes. Interestingly enough, I was having a hard time remembering what she had looked like before – so familiar had her Treef features become. I knew she would not hug me, and for that I was grateful because she would never know about Nedys's kiss, our excursion downtown, or our voyage to the beach. She would have been none too pleased with any of it. Her eyes drifted from me to the orb and back again, a smile upon her face.

"You found it!" she exclaimed. "But where? Surely, I should have known where it was." I led her into a sitting area, where she sat forward on her seat, eager to hear my tale. I launched into the story, or at least the part of the story I cared to divulge that wouldn't leave her wary of Nedys.

"Mr. Martindale?" she queried. "I always knew there was something about him."

"But it wasn't bad after all," I confirmed.

"I feel like I should have known he was the Guardian, but I never suspected he would be among us. Mr. Martindale – the Guardian?" She was shaking her head as she tried to let the information sink in.

"That will take some getting used to, won't it?" my dad chimed in.

"I shouldn't even ask given all you've been through, but how's the garden?" My mom unexpectedly changed the subject, and I could detect a surprising sense of longing in her voice.

"Perfect," I reported happily. "It seems Mr. Martindale has been looking after it in our absence." Both of my parents clapped their hands in delighted relief before their expressions grew somber once again.

"Now what?" my dad finally asked.

"I turn over the orb," I answered with more confidence than I felt, "to Idnim, as I promised."

"You mean to say that we will turn over the orb," Nedys stepped to my side. "We're all on the same team, you know."

"I'm afraid we're not on the winning team though," I countered, "and we don't know what losing entails. It may mean our lives, and I can't let you do that."

"You may not have a choice, Elli," Nedys's jaw set stubbornly as he shot a hard stare in my direction. I knew there was no point in arguing with him, so I didn't attempt it.

"How do we contact Idnim to let her know we've returned with the orb?" I asked, shifting my gaze in the direction my parents to avoid Nedys's disapproving look.

"I daresay she already knows," my mom surmised, "but we can send a message to her through the tree spirits."

"I suppose we ought to arrange a neutral meeting place," I ventured. "Any ideas?"

"Yelnats and I have conferred, and we believe the most ideal place to meet would be at the Stone Pedestal," my mom suggested, and seeing the question in my eyes, launched into an explanation. "The Stone Pedestal was the orb's original place of honor when it was bestowed upon the people of Annyad by the Guardian. Because there was no division among the people in the ancient days, the pedestal was built in the middle of the forest. Since the forest retreated with Eneli, the stone pedestal now resides at the edge of the forest. While you were away, Yelnats and I were able to locate the Stone Pedestal and clear out the overgrowth in the area, restoring it to its natural beauty. I hope you don't mind us taking such liberties."

"Mind?" I whispered, choking back unexpected tears. A sense of foreboding shimmied its way into my stomach as I thought about what would happen to my parents in the days to come. "Why on earth would I mind?"

"On earth, you never did mind – when it came to following the rules, that is," Yelnats stifled a chuckle, and I was able to maintain my composure as he lightened the mood.

"It's settled then. We'll send the message right away," my parents stood as my dad spoke. "And Elli, I would suspect that Einnep will get word as well. I daresay he'll show up, so we'd best be prepared. Elleon will most likely accompany him with Lordess Nalla. Nitsud and Necap have been keeping in regular contact with him as they have been encamped at the Stone Pedestal these last few days, which is as near as they can get to Annyad and their young charge without leaving the borders of the forest."

"You both look exhausted. We've kept you up long enough with this chatter. Now, off to bed with you," my mom said, ushering me away from Nedys to the room I had been sleeping in before I left, without allowing either of us so much as a goodnight glance.

I was exhausted, more exhausted than I had ever been in my life. I snuggled underneath a layer of blankets and surrendered myself to the sleep that never came to claim me prisoner. I tossed, and I turned. I strained to hear the hint of a sound in the silence, but there was nothing. The night suddenly seemed to be suffocating me, trapping me in its fingers of darkness. I quietly climbed out of bed, attempting to escape the invisible creature that would not let me sink into the depths of a dreamless sleep. It stalked me until I stepped out of the entrance of the Siol Tree.

Before releasing my grasp on the tree's bark, I commanded her to stay put. There would be no disappearing acts tonight. I would not spend my last night evading Sivart's arrows. The Siol Tree's leaves rustled in response, and I felt her compliance to my request.

I took several deep breaths of the fresh night air, filling my lungs fully and expelling my breath slowly. I glanced up at the starless sky, my gaze settling on the twin moons. Was Mr. Martindale even now watching and waiting? I blanketed my restless thoughts with some measure of comfort from the knowledge that he was the silent sentry of this war-torn land, as well as my advocate.

Lying down on the ground, I stared at the beautiful iridescence of the dark leaves of the tree as they shimmered in the moonlight. This place was almost peaceful. I closed my eyes as I listened to the nighttime sounds of the forest as the nocturnal animals began foraging for their midnight snacks. I could feel the tree spirits celebrating the return of the orb, and I found myself smiling. No matter what happened to me, I was glad they could once again draw strength from the long-lost orb. I was so deeply immersed in their festivities and rejoicing that I almost didn't hear the snap of the twig too near to me.

My eyes flew open as my heart thudded painfully in my chest with the sudden increase in adrenaline. I scanned the area quickly, but nothing seemed out of place. Maybe my nerves were making me a little jumpy. At any rate, I decided it was probably better for me to go back inside the Siol Tree, since the last time I took an unauthorized excursion from its interior, I didn't fare so well. I admittedly wished to delay my inevitable reunion with my older brother as long as possible.

"Can't sleep?" a voice called from a nearby tree. I jumped at the unexpected question, but immediately recognized Nedys's calming voice. "I didn't mean to sneak up on you."

"What are you doing out here?" I asked, regretting that I sounded like my mother.

"Same things as you, I suspect," he answered, not moving from his perch against the tree.

"Sorry. You just startled me. I didn't expect anyone else to be out here," I explained as I sat up.

"Sleep has been a bit fleeting for me since I met you." I could tell he was smiling, though I couldn't make out his facial features even with the moonlight.

"I just went for a short stroll. I wanted to get a message to Hairam to let him know I was back, alive and well."

"I suppose he would be worried," I conceded, "but how did you give him a message if you don't even know where we are in the forest?"

"When we were just lads, we rescued a rare Lladnek bird. It was just a babe and had somehow managed to get trapped in a rock crevice near our cave. Lladnek birds are beautiful with speckled gray feathers that have a shimmering silver sheen to them. They are the only birds in our lands with eyes of purest blue that allow them to see in the dark. They are loyal to those with whom they bond, though bonding with a Lladnek bird is most uncommon. Hairam and I nursed this particular Lladnek chick back to health, and Oj has been our constant companion ever since. 'Tis a wonderful creature, he is. Hairam, the silly lad, came up with his name. We signal Oj with a special call when we need to communicate with each other. Oj carries our messages back and forth when we're on different patrols. Good thing too – I wouldn't have dared venture too far from this ever-shifting tree. I wouldn't want to get lost in this forest with bow-yielding, grudge-holding Annyadian soldiers on the prowl," he had sauntered closer now, and I could see his dimple in the pale moonlight as he approached my side.

"You did make a great first impression," I rallied.

"It turned out well in the end, despite the rocky start," he surmised as he sat down by me. He stretched out his long legs and lay down on the grass opposite me, twining his hands behind his head. I smiled as Leo's borrowed shoes came to rest next to mine. Nedys's position afforded me the opportunity to observe his every feature as he sprawled on the ground. He was quiet for a while as he stared up at the moons. I watched his face in the moonlight as he studied the night sky.

"Curious," he muttered after a while.

"What?" I queried as I plucked at the dark blades of grass by me.

"I miss the stars already," he whispered with a tone of reverence that made me feel guilty for all the little things I had always taken for granted. He chuckled lightly under his breath.

"Why are you laughing?" I asked, wondering how anyone could find anything to laugh about given our schedule of events for the coming day.

"I never imagined that one day I'd be sitting under the most feared, poisonous tree among all Annyadians chatting with the vanished and very powerful empress of the Forest of Notxarb. This has truly been an adventure." I couldn't disagree with him on that point, but I also couldn't help being disappointed at his description of the moment. "Why are you so quiet, Elli?"

"Just thinking, I guess – thinking about how differently people can see the same event," I answered as Nedys sat up in curiosity. When I looked up from the blade of grass I had been aimlessly twirling between my fingers, I was surprised to find Nedys directly in front of me, staring at me rather intently.

"What do you mean?" he prodded.

"I never imaged myself sitting under a tree across from anyone but Leo. Up until now, he was my closest friend, and yet here I am." I meant what I said. Of all the improbable and fantastical transformations that I had been thrust through since I ate that gumball, I almost thought that was the hardest to believe. There was someone else out there who knew everything about me besides Leo or my parents and hadn't been repelled. Nedys leaned closer, reaching for my hand. My heart started to beat faster as I thought about the last time I had seen that look in his eye, illuminated by the moonlight. The moment he touched my hand, a spark coursed through my fingers, shocking him. I pulled my hand away in horror.

"I'm...I didn't mean...I'm so sorry," I stammered, getting to my feet in embarrassment and walking toward the entrance to the Siol Tree.

"Elli, stop," Nedys called after me. I didn't listen. I couldn't listen. I had honestly thought to myself that I didn't repel Nedys, yet in the next moment, my powers flared up, and I literally zapped him away. The irony was too much to bear. I brushed the tears from my face as I raced to my room, careful not to wake my parents. I didn't look back to see if Nedys followed. I shut my door and covered my face with my blankets. I let the rivers run from eyes, not attempting to dam them with false courage. This was a disaster. I didn't ask to be in this predicament. I didn't want to be in this nightmare. I had to admit, however, that some of my most cherished memories originated from this warped reality, and I couldn't honestly conclude that I should have never eaten that gumball. As my mind was aimlessly twisting and turning through this labyrinth of worry and unrest, I attempted to settle myself into a deep breathing routine to quell my nerves and queasy stomach. I heard a soft rapping at my door. I froze as my pulse quickened. I was lying on my side with my back to the door, but I didn't turn toward the noise. I knew who it was before the door creaked open. Although I didn't hear any footsteps, I sensed Nedys was standing by my bedside.

"Elli?" he whispered. I held my breath and pretended to be asleep. "Elli, I know you're not asleep." Still, I pretended. Nedys sat down on my bed and placed his hand on my shoulder. My body tensed instinctively as if to avoid hurting him again.

"Would you like to talk about it?" he gently urged.

"I'm scared, Nedys," my voice cracked. I didn't dare turn toward him to look in his eyes. "I'm so scared. I can't seem to stop hurting people whether I intend to or not. I'm scared of what tomorrow will bring. I'm scared of what might happen – of what I might do…" I attempted to explain. Admitting my fear didn't make me feel any better. Instead, I only felt more desperate, more alone than I had ever felt in my life. Nedys had not removed his hand from my shoulder as I spoke.

"Fear is but a part of the battle, Elli," he tried to console me. On that one point he was right: I was in a battle, but I wasn't sure who the enemy was. Was it Annyad with its war-torn lands and losses? Was it Einnep with his seemingly unquenchable thirst for my blood? Was it Idnim with her guilt-ridden conscience at what her young protégé, my mother, had become? Was it myself with this uncontrollable power bubbling inside me at unexpected moments?

"Me mum used to tell me that fear comes from dwelling on the unknown. 'In moments of fear,' she would say, 'you must focus on what you do know.' Being so young as I was, I never quite understood what she meant, but I think I'm beginning to understand a bit more now. You don't know what tomorrow will bring, but you must think instead upon what you do know. You know you've done as you were asked and seek only to return the orb to the forest. You know Leo and Lordess Nalla are on your side and will hold Einnep at bay if it comes to that. You know Idnim cares only about the orb. You know Lord Atrebor cares not for any more war or bloodshed. You know that the Guardian has a keen interest in your welfare and has intervened once before. You know Yelnirb and Yelnats will be watching out for you, and you know I won't leave you alone. In that light, the fear begins to dissipate a bit, wouldn't you say? Now, you've had a long day, and you need to get to sleep. If you don't mind, I think I'll lie on the floor here for a bit." He squeezed my arm once before getting off my bed.

As my mind began to sift through his soliloquy, I felt the fear loosen its hold on me. Once again, Nedys proved to be a fount of wisdom. As soon as he settled himself on what I could only imagine to be a very uncomfortable floor, he began softly humming the Forest Lullaby just loud enough for my ears to latch onto to the sound and carry its necromantic tune throughout my body like a sedative. Exhaustion, more emotional than physical, overcame me then, and I somehow managed to close my eyes in sleep.

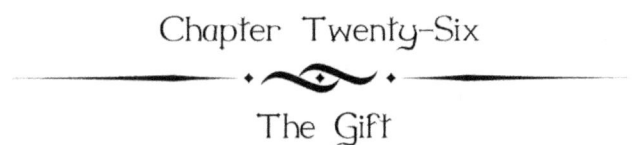

Chapter Twenty-Six

The Gift

When I awoke the next morning, I was not surprised to find the floor empty of Nedys. He had a way of disappearing before I could thank him for his consolation. I was greeted by my mom, who was doing her best to act as though all was well. She failed miserably. I could see the dark rings of worry under her eyes that had clearly robbed her of a good night's rest as well. She set down a tray of food.

"Try to eat something, dear," she urged as she pressed a cup of some kind of juice into my hand. "This will give you just the boost of energy you need to face today's events." I reluctantly took a sip and instinctively puckered my lips at its sour taste. I nibbled at the rest of the food she had set before me, but I found myself too nervous to eat much of anything.

"I only wish I had some finer clothes for you today. Jeans and a t-shirt won't make much of an impression on anyone here, and regardless of how anyone feels about it, you are the empress," she said as she began rifling through my backpack as if she might magically pull something out of it.

"What's this?" she asked as she withdrew the small yellow box Mr. Martindale had given me. I had completely forgotten about it.

"A gift Mr. Martindale gave me before I left. He told me to open it when I got back," I answered.

"Well, if it came from the Guardian, Elli, don't you think you ought to open it as he said?" she prodded, handing me the small box. I reached out my hand as she pressed the small box into my open palm. I wasn't sure what to expect as I hesitantly untied the delicate ribbon and opened the lid. There was a flash of blinding light followed by a faint popping sound. I managed to keep a hold of the box despite the surprise. When my eyes finally adjusted to the dim lighting of the room, they settled on a beautiful gown laid out on my bed.

"Oh Elli! It's magnificent!" my mother exclaimed as she gingerly fingered the deep purple material. I couldn't disagree, though I had never worn anything as elegant before.

"I know just what needs to be done, my dear," my mom assured me as she held the dress up for closer inspection. The shimmering satin fabric was overlaid with an intricate black lace that snaked over one shoulder of the gown and crisscrossed along the bodice and waist, coming to a dramatic A-line point on the opposite thigh. With its high neckline and long sleeves, the formfitting gown gradually flared just above the knee. Surprisingly, my mom danced about with it in her arms. I was more intrigued with her reaction to the dress than the dress itself. She seemed to come to her senses after a few moments in her imaginary ballroom.

"Oh, Elli! This is how you were meant to dress as the empress," she exclaimed as she held the dress up in front of me admiringly. "All these years, I encouraged you to dress in disguise to blend in with your peers, not to draw attention to yourself, but now…now you can embrace your true identity."

Suddenly, my life seemed to make a lot more sense. To my recollection, I had never owned a dress, and my parents always discouraged my efforts to make myself more attractive with make-up. I had always assumed that my parents were simply naturalists, so they didn't approve of such worldly indulgences, but that was just another ruse they used to protect me. Admittedly, I would have much rather stuck to my au-naturel look than adopt the persona of the empress.

Detecting my opposing somberness to her gaiety, my mom hung the dress over the chair.

"Forgive my indulgence," she took several steps in my direction before checking herself. She still wouldn't risk touching me, although I wasn't sure what harm it could do at that point.

"I'm glad someone can find a silver lining to this day, even if it is just a dress," I replied.

"A dress that symbolizes that great and uncertain burden you have been called to bear. May I say that I am honored to have you as my empress, Elli! As much as it weighs on you, I would have no other don this apparel," she voiced.

"Thanks for your vote of confidence because I'm not really feeling up to the task," I admitted.

"You will. You will. Your mother used to say that there was a certain power that accompanied a woman's dress, and I know you will use that power for good. Now, let me help you into this. the Guardian no doubt intended for you to wear it, and that, if nothing else, should assure you that there is something special about it."

I didn't argue with her as she helped me into the folds of fabric. I tucked the small box Mr. Martindale had given me into a nearly invisible pocket. My mom directed me to a chair where she set herself to the task of winding my long hair into an intricate, circling braid, woven with the beautiful leaves of the Siol Tree. I did not argue when she produced a make-up pallet and proceeded to apply the cosmetics to my face. Today, more than ever, I needed to feel like someone different.

When I looked in the mirror after my mom had worked her magic, I had to admit that the beautiful face staring back at me seemed to possess a regal and powerful bearing. Perhaps my biological mother had been correct in one thing: There was a certain element of confidence that emerged with adornment.

"My work here is finished, Elli," my mom said a little tearfully. "You are certainly no longer a little girl," she blinked her eyes rapidly, "that I can say for sure. I had better go check on Yelnats." She rushed from the room, so I wouldn't see her cry, but I knew how she felt.

Not long after she left, I heard a faint tapping at my door. My heart started to race because I knew to whom that tap belonged. I watched Nedys closely as he entered the room, and I was not disappointed by the expression that lit up his face. I had never felt more beautiful in my life, and it had little to do with my dress and hair, and everything to do with Nedys. Prior to eating that gumball, I had been just another ordinary and often overlooked teenage girl. On the few occasions I had tried to impress Leo's friends, they hadn't even noticed me. I seemed to be invisible. That all changed when Nedys was around me. For some reason, he made me feel beautiful, and he had believed me to be beautiful even at my worst – physically and emotionally. Somehow, he had seen past all that. He had even seen past my own self-doubt and insecurity. To this definition of beauty, I desperately tried to anchor my beating heart. Nedys walked quickly toward me, his eyes never leaving mine. He took my face in his hands as he leaned close to me.

"Whatever happens..." he whispered as I felt his lips touch mine for an instant. I was awash with the tremor of anticipation and happiness that swept through me like a hurricane.

Unfortunately, it was to be short lived. I felt an explosion rip us apart, and when I opened my eyes, I saw Nedys crumbled against the opposite wall. I looked around to see if someone had penetrated the Siol Tree with a bomb, but there was only Nedys and me. Realization struck me with the force of an aluminum bat aimed right at my chest. I heard Mr. Martindale's words echoing in my head: "Because you are in the infancy of its stages, you have little ability to control your power. It is evoked with strong emotional response, such as anger."

He had said anger, not love, and I never thought for a minute I could harm someone I loved. I stood motionless as my tear-filled eyes drifted to the ornate mirror that adorned the wall to my right. It was the first time I saw the face of the monster I was, so beautifully disguised and innocent. I was at the mercy of this power that coursed through my veins, and there wouldn't be enough time to learn to control it. From what I understood, the desire to do so would also dwindle. I was losing the battle.

I had thought that Nedys had been knocked unconscious, but as I turned to look at him again, I saw that he was fully awake and aware of everything that had just happened. He got to his feet somewhat wobbly and approached me just as a tear escaped down my cheek. I backed away from him, not wanting to hurt him again. Step by step, he came closer, saying nothing at all, and step by step, I backed away, until I hit the wall behind me. As he stood in front of me, he raised his hand to my face and wiped the tear from my cheek. I was staring at his boots to avoid eye contact because I was afraid of the emotions that would be betrayed in his eyes. He raised my trembling chin, forcing me to look him in the eye. I braced myself for the disgust, regret, and pain I would see, but I only saw the same look of love, defying the very power that could destroy him. He pulled me into his arms, and I crumpled against his strong chest.

"Whatever happens," he whispered in my ear, "I'll always be here for you." I gave him a tight squeeze as I gained my composure and pulled away.

"It will be the death of us both," I acknowledged glumly.

"I don't know about that," he said smiling down at me. "A little bit shocking maybe, but not deadly." I laughed at his joke even though it seemed to hang about my neck – the anchor dragging me under the current.

"This time, anyway," I acceded.

"So, you're telling me there will be another time," he said, a mischievous gleam in his eye.

"Nedys, I could have killed you," I said forcefully. "Please don't."

"Elli, what just happened only confirms in me mind what I had hoped was true."

"What are you talking about?" I wondered.

"Strong emotional response, isn't that what Mr. Martindale said might trigger these little surges of power?" He asked as my face flushed. There would certainly be no disguising my feelings from Nedys from now on.

"I thought he was referring to anger," I tried to deflect.

"Love is far more powerful than anger," he asserted.

"And pain is pain and death is death, and that is what my power brings." I broke free from his embrace and turned toward the door, my heart ready to break.

"If that's what it brings, then so be it, but we can love each other while we have the chance," he said quietly.

"You can't even kiss me," I admitted.

"Surely love is more than that, Elli," he countered.

"This," I said as I gestured all around us, "this is far greater than you and me, Nedys. This is my duty. This is the burden for which I was born – to free your world of me – of this darkness that's inside me. We can't be together. You've got your whole life ahead of you. Don't waste it on me."

"I might not once me father and your brother discover what I've been about lately," he refuted.

"I'll make your safety a condition of my surrender," I assured him.

"I'm not worried about me own safety, Elli. I've said it once already, and I'll keep saying it as many times more until you believe me. This has been worth whatever the price. If I wanted to be safe, I would have never rescued you, but I did rescue you, and I have no regrets." He clearly wasn't going to take no for an answer.

He intertwined his fingers in mine, only receiving a slight jolt when he did. I quickly glanced at him apologetically, but he only shook his head, a broad grin on his face. I couldn't help but return the smile. I only hoped one day maybe I would gain control of my emotions where Nedys was concerned. I only hoped I was given the chance. As we emerged from the room, Yelnirb eyed us warily. I don't think she was particularly amenable to the idea of Nedys and me – ever the protector she was.

"What was all that racket in there?" Yelnats asked, looking up from his carving. "I refrained from coming to your rescue Empress on account I didn't want to hurt young Nedys again."

"I tripped and fell," Nedys lied. "No Yelnats necessary."

"Oh really? Is that why your hair is practically standing on end?" Yelnats ribbed him good-naturedly, a sly smile on his face. Nedys actually blushed, immediately trying to smooth down his hair with his free hand.

"Quite a spectacle, I'd say, seeing as Elli is beaming from ear to ear," Yelnats continued. This time it was my turn to blush.

"Yelnats, drop it," Yelnirb warned, clearly not as encouraging as her companion. "I hope you know what you're doing, Empress," she scolded. My confidence wavered, and I loosened my grip on Nedys's hand. He would not, however, allow me to retreat. With a quick squeeze, he tightened his hand around mine. I tried to ignore the hornet's nest that Yelnirb's comment had disturbed in my head. I didn't know what I was doing, and that's precisely why I needed Nedys. But at what cost?

Chapter Twenty–Seven

At the Stone Pedestal

Nestled in a small grove of trees, the gray Stone Pedestal stood in stark contrast to the vibrancy of life surrounding it. The custodians had been hard at work by the looks of the well-groomed vegetation in the area. Surely before I had returned to the forest, the derelict stand had been overtaken by an unruly outgrowth of vines and weeds – a reminder of all that had been lost in the previous two decades.

We were the first of the parties to arrive. Walking toward the pedestal, I carefully placed the orb atop the smooth, dark stone. It immediately rose from the surface, floating up six inches into the air, where it hovered as though it had never been gone. At this magnificent site, I felt the relief of the entire forest in the slight breeze of their united exhale as the orb was returned to its rightful place. I, too, breathed a sigh of relief. If nothing else came of this, at least the forest would be whole again. As I backed away from the Stone Pedestal, I caught a glimpse of Idnim, who was fluttering just behind a copse of trees. As we made eye contact, she nodded her head and then disappeared.

"Did you see that?" I whispered to my parents and Nedys.

"Surely we did, Empress," Yelnats confirmed.

"Do you suppose that's it then? It can't be that easy," I mused warily.

"I'm afraid that was the easy part, Elli," Nedys answered as I followed his gaze to the opposite edge of the clearing, where Einnep, Sivart, Lordess Nalla, Leo, and a small number of Annyadian soldiers were emerging. Einnep's gaze settled on the orb, eyeing it almost hungrily. He narrowed his eyes as they locked on mine. Nedys was right – returning the orb was definitely going to be the easy part. We still had to negotiate the Enelian release. Scanning the rest of the area, I spotted Hairam peeking out from behind a tree. He looked me over and gave me an approving thumbs up. Apparently, he liked my new regal look. I gave a hint of a smile before he disappeared again behind the tree. I glanced at Nedys, whose smile also indicated he had seen his friend.

Einnep and his group did not venture very far into the clearing, positioning themselves so the orb was directly in the center of the gathering. I made eye contact with Leo, who did a quick double-take and mouthed the words, "Who are you?" At least he hadn't changed, although I was surprised that he didn't cross over to stand by my side. We were on the same side, weren't we?

"Nice work, Nedys," Sivart spoke first. "Come here, my boy – the charade is up." Nedys didn't move a muscle.

"Son, come here," Sivart insisted more sternly. It took a moment for his words to register in my mind. I glanced at Nedys, the surprise reflecting on my face. Sivart was Nedys's father – the father from whom he was trying to escape. I could hardly believe my ears. Nothing in Sivart's interaction with Nedys when I was being taken to Annyad gave the slightest hint the two were related, let alone father and son. In fact, Nedys only ever referred to Sivart as the Admiral. Still, Nedys stood his ground, his eyes fixed on his father with an icy glare.

"Son, you will obey an order!" Sivart shouted. Nedys didn't flinch, though I had to admit that I did. Instead, he coolly reached over to take hold of my hand – a final act of defiance severing any remaining ties that held him to his father, if there had been any ties to begin with. I must have been improving in my ability to steel my emotions because Nedys didn't get a jolt when he touched my hand, though I know my emotions were broiling. Sivart took a step forward, but

Einnep's arm shot out, preventing him from making any further progress toward us.

"You had such potential, young Nedys. Are you sure you've chosen the correct side with which to align your allegiance?" Einnep asked, though I doubt he was really offering Nedys a second chance free from any punishment.

"Perhaps it is you who ought to reconsider your stance, Einnep," Nedys replied with confidence.

"I see she has drawn you into her web of lies – her power was too much to resist. I should have known. Be warned, young Nedys. She will be your demise," Einnep cautioned.

"Nedys," I whispered. "He's right. Go. This is your last chance." Nedys finally turned to look at me, his eyes filled with so much pain I wished I could retract my words.

"My last chance at what exactly?" he whispered back. I didn't have an answer.

"Nedys, I don't know how this will end, and I don't want anything to happen to you," I admitted.

"Elli, I still choose you. There's no turning back," he answered with a determined look in his eye.

I turned my eyes back to Sivart. He had the look of murderous rage in his countenance as he fixed his gaze squarely upon me. Nedys noticed as well and squeezed my hand in reassurance.

"You have what you want, now let her go," Nedys demanded.

"How do I know it's the genuine article?" Einnep inquired. Releasing my hand, Nedys stepped away from me. He walked toward the orb, the center of the cuff on his wrist glowing brighter and brighter yellow the closer he got.

"Is this proof enough? The cuff came from Idnim herself. Lordess Nalla can attest to its authenticity. She has no reason to lie," Nedys stated.

"He speaks the truth, Einnep," Lordess Nalla affirmed.

"Now, let her go," Nedys repeated his demand, placing emphasis on each word.

"It's not that easy, Nedys," Einnep seethed. "You don't know what you're dealing with here."

"I want my people freed," I interrupted before he launched into his soliloquy.

"Your people?" Einnep challenged. "Since when have you taken an interest in anyone but yourself, Empress?"

"Since I found out I was the empress. The Enelian people will be set free if the orb is to remain here," I demanded as my heart began to pound in my chest. I took a deep breath in an effort to calm myself. I didn't want my emotions revealing my inability to control my powers.

"I see no reason why they should be kept prisoners any longer as long as you turn yourself over to me," Einnep bargained, his voice solid and sure.

"They will be given provisions, housing, and whatever assistance they require to begin their new lives in freedom," I stated, surprised at the commanding tone that resounded in the clearing. "Leo...I mean Elleon and Nedys will be appointed as their guardians." Einnep bowed his head slightly in agreement, although Leo quirked his eyebrows in surprise while Nedys stiffened at my side.

"Then, I will exchange myself for their freedom as long as the orb stays here at the Stone Pedestal, where it can be of use to both of our people as they embark on this transitory journey. You must assure me of the safety of the Enelian people and their guardians," I offered, straining to keep the uncertainty out of my voice as my stomach wobbled nauseously with my pronouncement.

"Elli," Nedys began to protest. "You can't trust him."

"He's right, Einnep. I cannot trust you with so great a task; therefore, I will not trust you. I happen to know that Lordess Nalla has been named as the leader of the Annyadian people since Lord Atrebor has stepped down. Lordess Nalla, I do trust you," I directed my gaze toward her, watching as her eyes widened with surprise that I had known of her recent appointment.

A sudden movement out of the corner of my eye caught my attention before a reply was made. Before I realized what was happening, an arrow was hurtling in the air. At first it looked as if it would come for me, but another blurry movement caused it to deviate from its intended target. The arrow crashed into the orb. Upon impact, the arrow ricocheted off the orb and began racing with an amazing trail of glowing, colorful light and sparks, courtesy of its contact with the orb. Unfortunately, the deflection righted the arrow's course, so it was once again on the path to meet me, its intended target. Nedys, calculating the trajectory of the arrow, jumped in front of me, seconds before impact, only to be hit in the chest by the now flaming arrow. Nedys fell hard to the ground. No one dared move as the flame inched its way from the end of the arrow toward Nedys, whose chest lay still. I had never known death until this moment. I found my breathing increase rapidly as if I could breathe for him – as if somehow, I could breathe his life back into him.

When the flame reached the arrow's tip, which was lodged deep in Nedys's chest, his entire body was engulfed in a brilliant green fire. Hairam leaped from his hiding place in the forest, hurling himself at Nedys's body just a moment before the steel arrow exploded into a thousand bright sparklers, blinding us onlookers. When I could see again, Nedys's dead body was gone, completely consumed by the orb's fire, as was Hairam. I stood frozen in place, numb.

He was…gone. I sank to my knees as the realization hit me. Nedys was dead. I felt my security freefall inside of me, plummeting through my insides and landing in a crumpled heap of confusion and fear in the pit of my stomach. My breathing slowed as I tried to come to grips with what had happened. One minute…all of this had happened in less than one minute. My mind raced back through the events. Sivart raised his bow. He had raised his bow at me, but just before he released it, Leo had pushed him, so the aim was off. Instead of hitting me, the arrow hit the indestructible orb and bounced off. The orb's deflection put the arrow back on course to hit me only this time Nedys jumped in front of it, but Nedys wasn't indestructible.

Falling to my knees, I stared at the ground where his body should have been. Not even a skeleton remained of the brief love I had known, and my only hope had vanished with it. I traced my hand over the smoldering grass, which was still hot to the touch. Nedys was dead. Sivart had killed his own son. For the first time, I raised my eyes to look at those around me. For them everything was happening in real time, but for me, the world had suddenly stopped – time suspended – as I saw everyone's reactions in slow motion. The only sound I heard was my own inhaling and exhaling as my breath forced me to keep living. The sound was amplified and echoing in my own ears.

I looked at Einnep. His eyes were trained on me – cold and unfeeling – his hand gripping the hilt of his sword. His hateful stare burned my soul, igniting a spark somewhere inside me. Leo's worried gaze was also on me, until he was distracted by Lordess Nalla's weeping. He broke eye contact to go to her side. He wrapped his arms around her, pressing his face into the golden hair on top of her head. That tender embrace turned my spark into flames of anger. I loved Nedys. I loved him! Now my heart could never be whole again because Nedys had been murdered.

My gaze shifted to the killer. Sivart was lying on his stomach on the ground, his eyes staring blankly at the smoldering grass where Nedys should have been. The flames inside me exploded, and I did not try to extinguish them. My breaths now came in quick succession as my heart pulsed the fire of anger throughout my body. My eyes widened, and I felt my hands leave my sides. I couldn't contain the fire within anymore. It longed to be free. It needed to be free. I heard a shout, but I released that internal energy in all its fury. In an instant Sivart was engulfed in flames – not colorful flames like those from the orb that had consumed Nedys, but red-hot flames of vengeance. I felt such relief as the fire burned out inside me that I must have blacked out for a minute.

When I opened my eyes, there was a pain at my neck. As my eyes focused, I saw Einnep hovering above me, the point of his sword pinning me to the ground at my throat. Leo was at his side, his hand gripping Einnep's arm. My hearing returned.

"She must die now!" Einnep snarled.

"You saw what he did. She was defending herself," I heard Leo's voice tremble as he tried to justify my actions. Even he did not believe what he said. Sivart posed no threat to me lying on the ground with his bow and arrows out of reach.

"Do not deceive yourself, young brother. You saw what she did. She is a murderer! She is a monster! This must end now!" I felt the sharp blade pierce my skin. I closed my eyes, waiting for this nightmare to end...finally. I didn't care whether Einnep knew my death would also mark the death of his beloved Enna, but I felt a tinge of satisfaction that he would have no one to blame but himself. Why had I fought so hard against this fate? I knew I could not stay in

Annyad or the Forest of Noxtarb. I was a monster. I could not deny that Sivart was dead because of me, though I had not intended to kill him. Honestly, I wasn't sure if I had consciously done anything at all. My body reacted on auto-pilot – almost as if I was watching from a distance rather than willingly participating. That thought scared me. What if that anger had been directed at Leo or Nalla or Yelnirb?

"Stop it!" Leo's pleading was frantic as I felt blood drip down my neck from the sword point puncturing my skin.

"Leo," I finally managed to say. He dropped to his knees and smoothed the hair back from my face. I felt a tear trickle down my cheek, but I wanted Leo to know...the truth.

"I didn't mean to...to hurt him," I stammered. "I don't know what happened...I couldn't...I couldn't stop it." I knew that was not quite true either, which was probably why I stammered so much when I lied those words. I could have tried to stop it, but I hadn't wanted to. I chose not to. Nedys would have been so disappointed in me – so ashamed. I had told him all along that I wasn't the person he had been taught to hate – that I wasn't an evil empress – and at my first major chance to prove it, I faltered. I failed him. He had believed in me, and I had failed him. I killed his father. I could have shown his father who I really was. I could have proven Einnep and him to be the liars, but I only gave them more evidence confirming their strongly held judgments against me.

Nedys gave his life in vain. I wasn't worth saving. Oh, Nedys. The tears came freely, and I did not mask them. I was weak. I could have doused those raging flames with the droplets of love I had been clinging to – love for Nedys, for Leo, for Yelnirb, for Yelnats, for Mr. Martindale, for Nalla, for the forest. It may not have been enough, but now I would never know. Realization donned on me that

Mr. Martindale had delayed my return to give me more time to make the memories that would be necessary to fight this power – memories with Nedys.

"I know, Elli. I know," Leo attempted to console me. He looked up at Einnep.

"She has to die," Einnep reiterated, as if we weren't already painfully aware of his position on the matter. Leo stood up to his full six-foot height and looked Einnep in the eye.

"Not here. Not now," he pronounced as if he were the commander of the world. Einnep snapped his sword away from my throat as Lordess Nalla rushed toward me, tearing a piece of fabric from her underskirt, and pressing it to my throat.

"But she will die," Einnep affirmed as he started to walk away. I struggled to sit up, holding the makeshift bandage to my own throat.

"Einnep," I called after him.

"Elli, don't," Leo grabbed my arm, his eyes pleading with me to stop. Einnep halted his angry retreat, his back toward me.

"There's something you ought to know before you carry out your plans," I said coolly.

"Elli, shut your mouth. What on earth do you think you're doing?" Leo asked, more forcefully this time.

"Be quiet, Leo. I know what I'm doing," I rebuffed.

"What exactly would that be? Sealing your own death?" Leo quizzed.

"I'm trying to save a life," I said loudly.

"What?" Leo asked.

"I'm trying to save a life – a life Einnep has a very intimate and personal interest in," I answered. Einnep snapped his head around, but he didn't take a step in my direction.

"I think you know who I'm talking about, don't you?" I asked, enjoying the fact that for the first time the ball seemed to be in my court. Einnep was standing inches from my face within a millisecond. I had never seen anyone move so quickly.

"What do you know about it?" he seethed.

"Everything," I replied, "and more."

"What do you know?" he demanded.

"First, I want to tell you a little story. There once was a boy, who fell in love with a girl. Theirs was not a happily ever after story, however, because this boy was forbidden to love this girl. She wasn't good for him. Worlds seemed to separate them, and yet, the boy still loved the girl, and the girl loved the boy with all her heart. They decided that they would be together, no matter who or what stood in their way, but they couldn't have foreseen the intervention that would come at the hand of one of their parents. The boy was taken from the girl, and the girl was taken from the boy. What does the boy do, Einnep? Does he vow to kill the parent and anyone else who stands in his way? Does he not only vow to kill the parent, but also carry out that vow by murdering the parent in cold blood? Is that how the story ends?"

"Don't play games with me!" Einnep shouted.

"It's a funny thing, Einnep, how you see the world so differently through your own eyes. Are you a murderer? Are you a monster? Aren't those the honorary titles you just bestowed upon me not five minutes ago? What did I do differently than you? I just followed in my big brother's footsteps." The thought had come to me just moments before – how eerily, similar both of our stories were. As much as Einnep hated me, I now understood that he hated himself just as much.

"You thought I was telling your story, but really, I was telling mine. You see, Einnep, the boy in my story is not you, and the girl is not Enna. The boy was Nedys, and the girl was me. I loved Nedys, Einnep, just as you love Enna. I knew in the end, we couldn't be together because of what I am, but I had hoped…well, that doesn't matter now, does it? Sivart, a parent – albeit a poor one – intervened, and now Nedys is gone. And yes, I am responsible for the death of Sivart, but I fail to see how that is any different than your story. You fell in love with Enna, which displeased your mother greatly, so she took Enna away, using her as a pawn to control you. You thought when your mother was dead that Enna would come back, but that didn't happen, did it? And you don't know why, but I do."

"Where is she?" Einnep demanded.

"Why should I tell you?"

For the first time since I had been talking, Einnep broke eye contact with me. He had given me no reason to tell him. He had given me no reason to show him mercy, and he knew it.

"I'll tell you why," I continued when he didn't answer. "Because I am not the person you think I am. I am not evil. I deserve to live just as much as you do – just as much as Enna does – just as much as Nedys did. I will not let my love be turned into the same hatred that consumes you – the same hatred that consumed your mother. I realize that the power within me can and probably will eventually change me, but you have no excuse – no excuse at all. You are a monster because you choose to be a monster. Now, because one of us deserves a happy ending, I will tell you that Enna is trapped in the orb. When I was rescued by the Guardian, he took the orb and Enna with it. As much as you think you knew your mother, you apparently didn't know her well enough. She, however, certainly knew you very well. When she imprisoned Enna in the orb, she built her own failsafe into the curse."

"A failsafe?" Leo repeated.

"If I, the heiress, was killed by Einnep's own hand, then Enna, too, would die. And the only way she can be freed is by the empress herself, which is now me." I watched as Einnep's eyes widened and drifted to my neck, where I still held the piece of cloth. He staggered for a moment – Lordess Nalla coming to his aid. I watched with surprise as Einnep's eyes filled with tears.

"I…I…You mean I almost killed her?" I heard him whisper, as Nalla led him to a nearby rock to sit down until he could gain his composure.

"You almost killed me – your sister – your own flesh and blood, even after I had done all that was asked of me," I countered. I walked toward him with my arms raised as if in surrender. "I leave the choice to you, brother. Will it be Enna or me?"

"I've only always wanted Enna," he muttered, his hands covering his face as he leaned on his knees.

"Then meet me here tomorrow morning at first light. This time, no entourage," I managed to say without my voice betraying my emotions. I turned my back to him as I began to walk swiftly away. Leo reached out to grab my arm.

"Elli," he began, turning me toward him. I tried to blink back my tears, but my lower lip was still trembling. Unaccustomed to seeing my emotional display, Leo let go of my arm and averted his eyes.

"I have to go now," I croaked, "but thank you for standing up for me back there."

"But Elli–"

"Leo, you can't be around me right now. I don't know what I'm capable of, and I couldn't bear it if something happened to you, too," I insisted. "I'm sure I'll figure something out, but right now, you're safer with Nalla and Einnep." I ran away before he could protest further. I ran straight into the waiting arms of my parents, who had been watching the entire scene unfold, too stunned to move until now. At their unexpected embrace, the floodgates opened, and I cried like I had never cried before.

Chapter Twenty-Eight

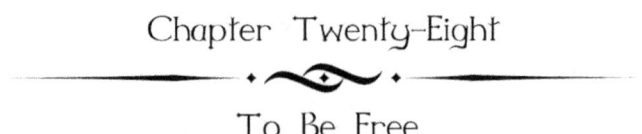

To Be Free

My parents led me back to the confines of the Siol Tree, though I don't recall much of the journey. I couldn't pull myself out of the trance I had been drawn into. I was exhausted from the day's events, but I could not seem to get my eyes to close. I simply stared at the wall, seeing nothing.

"Drink this, dear," my mom offered me a mug of steaming liquid. Although I didn't have much of an appetite, I raised the cup to my lips to appease her worry. The liquid was sweet to the taste, and I soon found my eyes drooping. I was sure my mother had added a sedative to her offering, but I did not object. Instead, I drank the rest of the cup, hoping to find a respite from my woes. I managed to scramble to my bed before I sank into a dark, dreamless unconsciousness. I was awakened the next morning by the gentle nudging of my father.

"Elli," he whispered, while smoothing back my hair. "It's time, my dear. The suns will be rising soon."

I blinked my eyes several times to get my bearings. I felt groggy and unrested, but it only took a moment before I remembered where I was and what had happened the day before. I closed the door on that mental meandering; it was a dark corridor of a painful maze I would never be able to escape once I started. This was no longer about me. I knew I had to force myself to focus on undoing the damage of the centuries of my predecessors' misused power. Enna was merely a beginning, and I still wasn't sure how to free her. I took a few bites of food from the tray Yelnats offered me, before slipping into a hot bath that had been prepared for me. I noticed my dress had been washed, pressed, and set out for me, and I decided to wear it again. I still had a few more official acts to take care of as empress before I could put that part of my life behind me.

"How can I help?" My mom came into view as I sat drying my hair. "Work your magic again, would you?"

"Of course," my mother agreed. To anyone else, I probably looked much the same as I had yesterday. When I looked in the mirror; however, I saw only vacant eyes staring back at me as if they belonged to someone else who no longer existed. Perhaps this is how the last empress felt before her fall. I seemed to have more and more in common with my biological mother each day, and the thought was not the least bit reassuring.

Because I wasn't sure exactly how to free Enna, I decided to go to the orb to see if any inspiration struck. As I placed my hands on its smooth surface, I closed my eyes to focus on finding Enna amidst the energy I was feeling. There seemed to be too much chaos, too many pleas for freedom. I concentrated on one of the voices, straining to understand its weak whispers.

"We have been trapped for years, Empress. We acknowledge that mistakes were made, but we sought only to protect the forest. We must be released soon, or we will be no more. We depend upon your mercy to reunite us with Idnim," the voice pleaded. My mother had in fact captured the other ancients, trapping them inside the orb all this time.

"Be free," I thought, but nothing happened. My heart sank, as the pleas became more desperate.

"You must command the orb to release them," I heard Mr. Martindale's voice echo from the orb. At least, he had not entirely abandoned me, although I found little comfort in that thought. I pushed my melancholy aside, focusing once more on the voice inside the orb.

"As the Empress of the Forest of Notxarb, I command the ancient tree spirits to be released immediately," I demanded as I felt a rush of electricity leave my hands and enter the orb.

Instantaneously, the ancient tree spirits emerged from the orb, each looking much like Idnim. Without uttering a word, the nine figures bowed simultaneously before disappearing in a gust of wind. I felt the forest rejoice at their release, and I couldn't help but smile.

I returned my attention to the orb, placing my hands once again upon its surface. There, I saw in its center the beautiful face of a young sleeping girl who looked so much like her sister that I had no doubt I had found Enna. She didn't appear to be much older than me as she lay in the midst of the orb resting peacefully as if no time had passed at all. At that moment, the twin suns lit the sky with a brilliant light as they emerged from their nightly slumber. I withdrew my hands from the orb and stepped several feet away from the orb as I watched the bright sentinels rise to their appointed post in the sky – the silent witnesses to the great tragedies of yesterday. My thoughts inadvertently turned to Nedys. He would never see another sunrise because of me. I blinked back the threatening tears, not wanting to appear weak when Einnep arrived. I started to walk toward the orb once again, but a hand reached out, grabbing me roughly. Only one person would grab me like that. I swung around, ready to defend myself.

"Wait," Einnep released my arm when he saw my face and immediately backed away with his hands up. "Sorry…I didn't mean to grab you so forcefully." As I studied his face, I was surprised by the emotion his eyes revealed: fear. He was afraid, but of what I wasn't sure.

"You've waited for sixteen years, Einnep," I observed.

"Sixteen years is a long time, sister. I…I've changed…and not for the better. I have accused the former empress of being a monster. I had her killed for it, but I…I am no better. I, too, allowed my hatred to turn me into a monster, just as you said. Enna doesn't deserve that. I don't deserve her." Einnep's arrogant, foreboding façade crumbled before my eyes. After all his waiting and plotting to get her back, he was afraid of her rejection.

"Enna deserves to be released, Einnep, whether she accepts you or not. That is her decision, just as your actions were your decisions. You cannot escape the consequences now." He didn't meet my gaze.

"Einnep," I continued in his silence, "I will never understand all that you have endured, nor will I judge you for how you've acted – not anymore – not after having lost so much myself. I wish I could say I would have chosen a different course had I been in your stead, but I can't. I wasn't there. I've made my own mistakes. I have my own regrets. I know that everything you have done, you have done for her, and she will know that as well."

"I was but eighteen when she was taken, and she but twenty," Einnep spoke softly. I had all but forgotten that Einnep had been my age when his life too had been turned upside down.

"Einnep, she'll still be twenty. You know that right?" By the expression on his face, he hadn't thought she would not age.

"But…" Einnep didn't finish his thought, so I jumped in to explain.

"She's been frozen inside the orb, Einnep. Her body has not aged, and when she is revived, she will be just as she was when she was frozen. She will remember everything up until that moment, but no more."

"This cannot be," he muttered as he raked his hands through his hair. "I'll be an old man to her."

"Not old. More mature yes, but not old. She might appreciate that," I tried to lighten the situation. He didn't crack a smile.

"Einnep, I can't delay any longer. She needs to be freed," I urged as I stepped uninhibited toward the orb once more as Einnep retreated to the perimeter of the clearing.

"As the Empress of the Forest of Notxarb, I command the release of Enna, daughter of Lord Atrebor, sister to Lordess Nalla of Annyad." Another shock of electricity raced from my fingers as a figure emerged several yards away from me. She stood there, a vision of beauty just like her sister. She looked dazed, and I watched as her eyes eventually focused on me.

"Who...who are you?" she stammered as she scanned the rest of the glen. When her eyes lit upon Einnep, who was still standing in the distance, I saw recognition flash across her face with a radiant smile. She ran toward him and threw herself in his arms. He tentatively returned the embrace, his arm wrapping around her petite frame. Enna pulled away and looked up into his eyes.

"Einnep? What's wrong? You...you look so different," she said as she traced her hand along his face. I'm not so sure it was his more mature appearance as much as it was the shadow that still cast itself across his features. "You're wearing an Annyadian tunic."

"Enna, you've been trapped inside the orb for sixteen years," he explained softly, his eyes betraying his sadness.

"But I was just on my way to see Idnim in the forest," she said as she looked over her shoulder at me. He turned her face gently back toward him.

"Enna, listen to me. You were on your way to see Idnim in the forest sixteen years ago. The empress...she found out about us...and she put you to sleep inside the orb when she found you in the forest. She thought she could use you to control me...to get your father to surrender the city of Annyad into her possession."

"My father! Is he –"

"He's well," Einnep interrupted her worry. "He was blinded in a fire, but he's alive and well, as is your sister. Your father did not surrender, and the empress, my mother, is dead."

"Dead? You didn't..." she studied his face without finishing her statement. "Oh, Einnep. You didn't kill her, did you?"

"I had no choice. It was the only way to end the war without more bloodshed. It was the only way to get you back, but the Guardian intervened and took the orb and you with it. For sixteen years, I searched. I waited," his voice broke off as he struggled to control his emotions.

"Who is she?" Enna asked, nodding in my direction.

"That..." he hesitated, his long-held emotions of hatred warring with his newfound humanity toward me, "is my sister." Enna gasped at the revelation and clung more closely to Einnep. The look on her face was a perfect cocktail of fear and revulsion, almost causing me to peek over my shoulder to see what hideous creature loomed behind me – until I realized that she had her eyes now locked on mine. A wave of nausea washed over me as I tried to keep my demeanor from shirking at her unwanted scrutiny. Attempting to quell my urge to scream at her to stop staring at me as if I were a beast ready to prey upon her happiness, I inhaled deeply and swallowed once instead.

"She rescued you, Enna," Einnep intervened, perhaps sensing my distress. "If it hadn't been for her, you would be dead right now...because of me." Einnep lost his composure as his voice cracked, and I saw several tears escape their imprisonment. Enna smoothed away the tears.

"I'll leave you two to get reacquainted," I muttered as I turned my back on the reunion I couldn't bear to watch anymore, disappearing into the Forest of Notxarb, alone once again.

I wandered aimlessly for hours before I found myself drawn back to the orb. Einnep and Enna had long since departed. My mind ran the obstacle course of the events that had just transpired, trying to navigate to an acceptable finish line. I wasn't sure what my future held. I knew I did not belong in this place. I could not belong in this place and not be changed. It was a battle I could not win because I didn't have the weapons I needed to fight it. I was eighteen years short on time – on training. I drew in a deep breath for I also knew I had no way to return to my home.

My eyes settled on the blackened patch of grass that had been Nedys's temporary grave. As I sank to my knees, the grief oozed out of my eyes in tiny rivulets of sorrow at the loss I felt inside. How long would it take before my memories of Nedys slipped through the cracks of forgetfulness? How long could I peruse the photo albums of time before the images became too faded to recall clearly? All I once had was lost for people I had never even met. I caught a glimpse of a winged figure hovering in the air above me, the silver wings glinting in the waning light. Slowly, it descended until it came to rest by my side.

"Oj," I muttered to the most beautiful bird I had ever seen. Its blue eyes turned to stare straight into mine, imploring me for answers. Nedys had the same blue eyes. I reached my hand tentatively to stroke him. He did not move, instead allowing me to offer what little comfort I could.

"I'm so sorry, but they're both gone, Oj," I whispered in a sob. He bowed his head low, placing a talon on my leg. A single, glistening teardrop wet my dress, and then he was gone, just as quickly as Nedys and Hairam had been snuffed away from me. There, I wept. The painful prickles of retreating numbness broke my heart into a thousand tiny, piercing shards.

I felt a hand on my shoulder and a little squeeze. I didn't have to see his face to know the hand of attempted comfort belonged to Leo. I looked up, wiping my eyes, only to have them fill with a fresh reservoir of tears as I saw Leo's eyes glossed over with tears of his own. He pulled me into a tight bear hug, and I buried my head against him, clinging to him as if he could rescue me from this raging river of grief that threatened to drown me.

"I wish things had turned out differently, Elli," he spoke softly in my ear. "You were a much better person than I could have been to Einnep, that's for sure."

"At some point there has to be an end to the suffering, right?" I said, pulling away to look into his eyes. "Was it worth it?"

"Oh, Elli. You should see the celebrations in Annyad right now as the Enelians are welcomed by the Annyadians, as the Annyadians celebrate the return of Enna, as they unite to triumph in a new beginning. It's a spectacular sight. They all honor you as well, Elli. There is to be a feast tonight in your honor, and in honor of Nedys, of course. If not for you, none of this would have ever happened. You must come to meet the Enelians. I've met so many of them over the past few days, and I know you would love them," he urged, excitement lighting his features.

"I'm afraid I don't feel much like celebrating right now, Leo," I muttered. "I'm happy for them though – truly happy."

"What happens next, Elli?" he asked, his eyebrows quirked with worry.

"I'm afraid I honestly don't know Leo. That seems to be my lot in life lately.

I find myself in these situations, and I don't know what I'm supposed to do. I do think the reign of the empress is about to come to an end though," I answered.

"What are you talking about? Elli, don't do anything drastic, okay?" Leo grabbed my shoulders as if to shake some sense into me.

"Leo, don't let your imagination run away with you. You've watched way too many movies. I merely meant that I can't stay here," I reassured him.

"But where will you go?"

"I wish I knew. I wish I knew," I whispered more to myself than to him. "What about you?"

Leo did not look at me. The thought of life without Leo hadn't crossed my mind amidst everything else that had happened. There was no way I could have prepared myself to be separated from the one friend I had ever had in my world. No, it was better this way – more like the sudden pain of ripping a Band-Aid off rather than the slow, drawn-out pain of tugging at it little by little.

"So, you're leaving me for another girl, huh?" I saw his smile break the tension between us. I tried to memorize it.

As if on cue, Nalla walked into the clearing toward us. As much as I didn't want to admit it, I knew Leo belonged here – unlike me. He was accepted and loved, maybe even revered. He was Leo. How could anyone not love Leo? I knew the people needed Leo here to balance Einnep – to contrast Einnep. The people of Eneli needed Leo most of all. He was their hope like I should have been. My power had brought them nothing but heartache. They needed me to leave so they could heal, and Leo (and Nalla) were just what the doctor ordered.

I knew all these things, and yet I couldn't help but feel angry that I had to sacrifice myself. It wasn't fair. I hadn't asked for this curse, for this life. I was innocent, and yet I was to be banished – cast out – alone. At least I would know that Leo was happy. I watched as he grabbed Nalla's hand. There was no doubt in my mind that Leo would be happy.

"Are we off then?" Nalla asked rather solemnly as her gazed shifted to the burnt patch of grass. Leo shook his head and gave Nalla a look I couldn't interpret. Already things were changing. I thought I knew every look of Leo's. Apparently, they had previously discussed this possibility. Unexpectedly, Nalla rushed forward and embraced me in a tight hug.

"Thank you! Thank you so much!" she exclaimed softly with tears in her eyes. "You will never know how much you have impacted my life. It has been a privilege and an honor to call you my friend." There was such a finality to her words that I knew this was goodbye.

"The privilege was mine," I acknowledged. "I've only ever had one friend, but it's nice to know I don't repel everyone – I just have to be transported into a different world." I tried to lighten the tone for all our sakes. Emotions were too charged right now, and I had cried far too much in the last day as it was. Both Leo and Nalla laughed. Nalla hugged me once more.

"I'm sure we'll see you later, Elli," Leo said without conviction as he turned to leave with Nalla. I merely nodded my head as I watched them leave the meadow, hand in hand.

My gaze was drawn to the orb once again– its yellow sheen luring me closer to it. As I stared at the orb with its swirling colors, I heard Mr. Martindale's voice, or maybe it was just the memory of his words: "Gifts are very powerful." I replayed the moment over in my head, noting the twinkle in Mr. Martindale's eye as he spoke those words. After opening his gift I thought I knew what that twinkle met. I had felt powerful in that gown, but now I was second guessing myself.

Perhaps there was more behind his words, and it had nothing to do with his gift to me. 'His gift to me' – I mulled the words over in my mind.

For an instant, I saw Mr. Martindale's face appear within the orb, and I clearly heard his words, "Elli, I have given you a future. That is why I saved you. I watched innocent young girl after innocent young girl corrupted by this power with not so much as a choice in the matter. I could not stand back and watch any longer. This is the gift I wish to bestow on you: the gift of choice."

There was only one thing I wanted – to be just me again. No power. No title. Just plain, old, ordinary me. A gift was a powerful thing, and I was going to do exactly that – give away my power. Mr. Martindale had given me a way out. I was going to give the gift of my power back to the forest. As soon as I had made up my mind, I did not hesitate to place my hands once more upon the orb.

This time, however, I focused my energy on all the musical sounds of the forest, trying to summon Idnim to me. She materialized almost instantaneously, a look of curiosity burrowing into me as I removed my hands from the orb.

"Why have you called for me?" she asked, her words unexpectedly clipped and cold.

"I wish to give you a gift," I calmly replied. She eyed me warily. I motioned for her to grasp my hands over the orb. She hesitated.

"Have I not done all that you asked of me and more? The orb has been returned. The other ancients have been freed. Yet still you do not trust me?" I implored, my voice sounding depleted.

Idnim did not answer; instead, she reached her own hands forward, gripping mine in hers. Her hands were smooth and warm, and I immediately felt at ease in her presence. Words began forming unbidden in my head, and I heard myself speak:

> "Upon the receiver of this gift I bestow,
>
> All the powers that in me flow –
>
> Save those I return to those laid low:
>
> To the stars return their glow,
>
> To those awakened who choose to go –
>
> Send them back to the homes they know.
>
> Let the plants and trees in Annyad grow,
>
> Heal the rift caused by my power's woe,
>
> For I no longer claim a foe,
>
> All my powers I shall forego."

I kept my eyes locked on hers as the words swirled out of my mouth. They widened with surprise as a jolt of energy surged from my hands into hers, causing us both to float several feet off the ground. I did not feel any exhilaration at the prospect of flying; however, I did feel incredibly tired, as if all my energy was being drained from within me. I did not resist. I closed my eyes and welcomed the darkness that embraced me.

I think it was the silence that woke me. I had become so accustomed to the hum of the forest conversation that I felt its absence keenly. In giving away my power, I had lost my connection to the life forces that still surrounded me. I knew I could no longer draw from their strength either, since my body felt frail and weak.

"Elli, what have you done?" Yelnirb's whisper broke the silence. My heart plummeted. I had no idea how my decision to give up my power might affect the Treefs that had been forced into servitude. My mind raced through the blurry chant that I had spoken as I transferred my powers to Idnim.

"To those awakened who choose to go…" the words echoed eerily in my head. They all had a choice, but I hadn't considered what my parents would choose. It was bad enough without Nedys and Leo, but without my parents…the thought made me shutter.

"What have I done?" I repeated her question in a raspy voice I hardly recognized as my own.

"You've done what no empress has had the courage to do in the past, my girl. That's what you've done. You are the true heroine in this sordid world, as we well knew you would be," Yelnats beamed as he offered his hand to help me up.

"But what will happen to both of you? To Leo's guardians?" I inquired.

"Necap and Nitsud have already offered their farewells to your brother and returned to their true home," Yelnirb reported solemnly. "As for us…"

"We are where we want to be," Yelnats interrupted. It was Yelnirb's arms that wrapped around me, however. She pulled me into a tight hug, and I felt her tears fall like plump raindrops on my head.

"The only question that remains is where we are to go," Yelnats observed. Of that I wasn't sure. I looked around the familiar meadow in which we still stood. I did not know where to go. As my eyes rested on the orb, I remembered the small gift box Mr. Martindale had given. Even now, my fingers fumbled with the box as it rested in my pocket. As I drew it out of my gown, I heard a sound from within. Curious, I opened the lid to peek inside. My eyes widened with surprise for rolling about in the box was a black gumball streaked with color - the same gumball that had been the catalyst for this little misadventure. I had a choice. Mr. Martindale had given me a way out. He was still watching out for me.

"How would you feel if we went home?" I asked nervously. Both my parents let out an unexpected sigh of relief.

"We wouldn't feel right staying here in the forest after all that has happened, but we didn't know if there was a way we could go back home. I've surely missed my blueberries and my nice, soft bed these few weeks," Yelnirb admitted with a laugh.

"And I've had about enough of all this excitement for a lifetime. I'd like to go back to the mundane world of gardening and landscaping. It tends to be less life and death work," Yelnats chimed in.

"I've only ever just wanted to be regular, ordinary me," I conceded as well.

"And Elleon?" Yelnats questioned.

"Won't be returning," I answered. I bit my lower lip and started to blink furiously to stave off the unwanted tears this pronouncement forced upon me. I would miss him and all our adventures, but in my heart, I knew this was his place. Our last encounter truly was our final farewell.

"I trust Idnim will relay my whereabouts to both Leo and Nalla, so they won't worry when they can't find me," I said. An answering wind confirmed her agreement.

"Shall we, then?" Yelnirb linked her arms through mine. I cast one more look about the meadow, surprised to see the Siol Tree so close to the edge. My parents must have brought it.

"I have one more thing to do," I said as I approached the beautiful tree.

I ran my hands over the smooth bark. I had felt the fierce loyalty the tree spirit had for the empress, and the sacrifices the she had made to protect the underground world Eneli had created. Her life had been unnaturally prolonged by the power of Eneli, and in my long absence she had been experiencing painful exhaustion. She was suffering. I was ashamed that I had been too preoccupied to notice before.

"Siol," I called to her. "You have been a good and faithful friend for such a long time. You have endured much and given more, and I release you." I hated not to be able to communicate with her – to feel what she was feeling.

I realized that I was offering her the freedom to die. Anyone would probably hesitate to accept an offer to step into the great unknown. Perhaps I should have freed her before I gave my power away. Maybe she was trapped.

"You're free," I urge, "and thank you." As I backed away the Siol Tree was consumed in fire and reduced to a pile of purple ash – the underground palace, gone forever. She had merely been waiting for me to withdraw, so I wouldn't be harmed. I walked back to my parents, linking my arms with theirs.

"Let's go home," I said as I plopped the gumball into my mouth and braced myself, but not before I glimpsed the first star of the night – a bright orange one, blinking to the rhythm of the Forest Lullaby. My last thoughts as I left the Forest of Notxarb on the border of Annyad were of Nedys.

Chapter Twenty-Nine

Home at Last

I walked by Mr. Martindale's shop, surprised to find it locked with a sign posted on the door that read, "Closed for Remodeling." Mr. Martindale had never mentioned remodeling the shop this summer. I desperately needed to start work this week. Working at the bakery was the one thing I had left. It was the one thing upon which my hope hinged, and now it seemed, it was gone too. I suddenly felt my mood darken as nausea overtook my stomach. Had he been punished for intervening? Had my return somehow banished him to a different world? I stood on my tiptoes at the side fence, trying to get a glimpse of the garden, but the fence was too high, and the gate was locked up tight. I kicked a wooden fence post hard with my sandaled foot, only to feel a searing pain on my big toe.

"Stupid fence," I muttered under my breath as I headed in the direction of home, brooding over this new development in my already shattered life. As I rounded the corner that led to my street, I lifted my eyes just in time to see Kelsey Yardell coming down the sidewalk toward me. I lowered my head and quickened my pace, careful not to make eye contact. If I was lucky, she wouldn't see me because I was not in the mood for her today. Luck was not on my side. I suppose I shouldn't have been surprised.

"Elli," she called after me as soon as I had passed by her. I spun on my heels.

"Leo has moved. He's not coming back, so you can quit talking to me now, okay? In fact, I would prefer if you never spoke to me again!" I said sharply, anticipating her question and the next one hundred that would surely follow. She stared at me in stunned silence, and I didn't wait for a reply. I carried on toward home. Nedys at least would have been proud that I had finally stood up for myself – if Nedys had still been alive. Tears pricked my eyes as I walked in the door, slamming it behind me.

Mom poked her head around the corner, took one look at me, and rushed to my side, enveloping me in a big hug. I hugged her tightly. At least some things had changed for the better. She was no longer constrained by her oath.

"Mr. Martindale's shop is all closed up with a sign that says he's remodeling," I told her as I wiped my tears. "I think he's gone…for good."

"I'm so sorry, Elli," she whispered as she stroked my hair. "This won't be easy, but we'll get through somehow. We'll get through together."

"I know," I conceded. We had no choice but to move on…somehow.

"I do have some good news," she offered as she returned to the kitchen. I followed her, smiling at the blueberry pie she was slipping into the oven. She had missed her blueberries, but in a pie? This was very atypical, and I entertained a small hope at that moment that my sugar ban would be lifted.

"Oh?"

"I finally got a hold of someone at the school," she said.

"The school? You called the school?" I asked, not masking my surprise. Mom had never called the school before. She had never been proactive about my education. That burden had always fallen upon my shoulders.

"Well, you've got to finish high school, don't you? The man I spoke with said that you passed your classes, even with the missed finals. I think the exact words he used were 'she passed by the skin of her teeth.'" She chuckled to herself. "If he only knew…"

I let out a sigh of relief. I had passed. I was a little bummed because this had been my best trimester yet. I was on course to get all Bs for the first time in my life, but I'd take a passing grade if I didn't have to repeat the courses. After all I had been through, I wasn't about to complain. It really didn't seem to matter as much to me anymore.

"And so you made me a pie?" I queried with a smile on my face. I had never thought I would smile again, and yet here I was, smiling over blueberry pie.

"Don't be getting any ideas, Elli. Special occasions only," she retorted.

"Thanks," I said. "Thanks for coming back with me."

That night, I found myself staring out my window, unable to sleep. I crawled onto the roof to stare at the stars, but something glinted in the moonlight as I unlatched the window. A piece of paper was tied to the lock with a piece of leather cording. I carefully unwound the cord, only to find the bright, blue stone of Nedys's necklace secured within the rolled paper. How could this be? I quickly unrolled the paper to read the unfamiliar handwriting.

> *Ellinnet,*
>
> *As I cannot sleep with all the unusual noises interrupting me, I find meself drawn to the stars. It's such an amazing sight to watch those small, twinkling lights brighten up a dark sky. Just so, you are me star, Elli. You brought light into me life when I thought I would suffocate in the darkness. I need you to know that. I knew me luck would come to an end sooner or later. Since you're reading this, it must have come much sooner than I wanted. I need you to understand what you mean to me. I need you to see yourself as I do, so you can become who you were meant to become.*
>
> *I give you this small token of meself, not to remember me by but as a reminder of who you are. You are an empress with infinite power to change lives for the better, just as you have done for me, just as you are doing for people you don't even know. You are the reason I have lived my dream of freedom from military life and me father's*

oppression. You gave me the courage to be meself, and now I hope to do the same for you in return.

You know there are reprahs even in your world. We came across some not long after entering your world. They parade about in regular clothing with false smiles. They may not look as fearsome, but they are just as deadly if you let them get you down. Protect yourself from them just as I would if I were there. You may not shoot arrows of steel, but you can certainly shoot arrows of your own self-worth in their direction. They can't push you down if you don't let them, and I've seen first-hand your strength - not the strength you draw from the forest, mind you, but the strength of your inner character.

That's what I love about you, Elli. In the face of fear and uncertainty, you trudge onward in pursuit of the good that counters all evil. You show kindness to unknown enemies that bind you and revile you. (I can never apologize enough for me actions on our first encounter.) You bargain with ancient beings to save the life of someone you barely know. You sit at the bedside of said stranger to ease his pain in constant vigil, sharing with him intimate details of your own life to draw his attention away from his ordeal. Can you begin to see what I see? How about you let others see that same you? Your life should not be wasted in loneliness.

Don't let the sky of your life be dark as it is in Annyad. You be the star that lights the way, not only for yourself, but for everyone around you. You have come back to an amazing world - embrace it! While I wish I could be by your side watching the night sky every evening, I know you'll live life to the fullest for both us. Be happy — you deserve nothing less.

With all my love,

Nedys

I placed the blue stone necklace around my neck. As I fingered its smooth surface, I realized that I had a purpose larger than myself. I could make my mark in this world. There could be no better memorial for Nedys than to do as he asked. I smiled at the thought of comparing Kelsey Yardell with a reprah, but I saw Nedys's wisdom as well. Even from the grave, he was going to make sure I made something of myself. I watched a cloud drift over the moon, hiding its light temporarily. I determined that I would not let this cloud of grief do the same to me. I owed it to Nedys, to myself, and to my parents. When I finally retired to my bed, I slept soundly.

The next morning, I set off once more to the bakery. I noticed Rebecca sitting on the bench outside the front door. Normally, I would have headed in a different direction to avoid any awkward conversation, but this time, I stayed my course.

"Hey there, Rebecca," I greeted her, a little hesitantly. I hadn't realized how much I kept to myself at school. She looked up in surprise. "How was that English final?"

"Okay, I guess. It wasn't that hard if you studied the notes. I don't recall seeing you the last week of school – just that once in the bakery," she answered.

"I had a family emergency and had to leave town unexpectedly," I replied.

"I hope everything is alright."

"It will be…with time," I averted my eyes as I spoke.

"So you missed all of your finals?" she queried.

"Yep. My GPA took quite a hit, but at least I passed all of my classes. So, um, how do you like working with Mr. Martindale?" I decided to broach the inevitable subject.

"He was a great boss," she affirmed. "I really needed the job, but he left so suddenly."

"He didn't say where he was going?" I asked hopefully.

"Nah. He walked in one morning as I was icing some donuts and said he'd been called away on business for one of his other shops in a different state. He handed me my paycheck and told me to close for him after my shift was over. He gave me the sign to hang on the door that said there were renovations being made, and then he left. He was in a big hurry and seemed a little unsettled. I didn't look at the paycheck until later, so I didn't realize he had paid me my whole summer's wages. I come here every day just to see if he's back…to thank him."

"That is strange," I said, absently rubbing Nedys's blue stone with my fingers just as the bus pulled up to the bus stop.

"Well, that's my ride," Rebecca excused herself from the bench and headed for the opened door.

"Maybe I'll see you around," I offered. She looked at me quizzically then smiled as she boarded the bus. I took that as a good sign. I decided to head back home. There was no point wasting my time milling about the bakery waiting for Mr. Martindale to show up. I was on my own, and I had a lot of work to do if I was going to get myself back on track.

For so long, I had lived in my self-contained little bubble – too afraid to leave its comfort and security, but I realized that I was in fact hovering in fear and hiding in Leo's shadow. I wasn't going to be the background singer in my own life. I was making a mental list of things I needed to change when I bumped into someone.

"Sorry," I mumbled as I looked up to see whom I had hit. There stood James McKean, the very guy I had a crush on for as long as I could remember.

"It's okay…Elli, isn't it? Aren't you Leo's friend?" he asked uncertainly. I nodded, surprised he even knew my name. "You look like you're a little preoccupied. Big plans for the day?"

"Not really, no," I managed to say, and then quickly added, "You do know that Leo moved, right?"

"Now that you mention it, Kelsey said something about it. Bummer. I hope everything is okay with his family," he replied. James wasn't in Leo's core group of friends, but they had hung out a few times.

"They're fine. The move was for the best," I assured him.

"Well, uh…see you around," he said.

"Yeah," I replied awkwardly.

Before I had learned of my ill-fated destiny as an evil empress, I would have obsessed over that snippet of conversation for days as starved as I was for attention. Not now, though. Now, I knew my happiness didn't depend on anyone else but me. It didn't seem to matter anymore what James McKean thought of me. I didn't find myself swooning over our short exchange like I might have done a mere month ago. It was a liberating feeling.

When I got home, I went over to Leo's duplex to gather his old school books and notes. I figured I better get a head start on studying for next year, so I could get into college to get a business degree to help with the family business.

Three weeks slipped by rather painlessly. Since I wasn't working at the bakery anymore, my dad put me to work in his landscaping business. Thankfully, his loyal customers were more than understanding when he informed them of his family emergency. Then, there was the farmer's market. My mom's fruit had begun to ripen, so I was off to sell our goods at the fruit and vegetable stand. I had even found Rebecca's phone number in the student directory, and we'd gone to a movie. She had offered to help out at the farmer's market as well, so a friendship was already beginning to develop. I was surprised by how easy it had been.

We had just finished dinner one night when I heard the doorbell ring. I figured it must be a door-to-door salesman since those were pretty much the only people who ever dropped by unannounced. I debated about just not answering it, when my mom banged the dishes a little too loudly for us not to be home. I didn't want to leave the poor guy loitering on our doorstep.

I opened the door only to find Mr. Martindale staring back at me. When I recovered my senses, I lunged forward to give him the biggest hug I could. Oh, how I had missed him! If only Leo had been by his side. When I finally let him go, he cleared his throat in embarrassment, unaccustomed to such open displays of affection. I found myself suddenly overcome with emotion. I couldn't express my joy at his unexpected return.

"Good to see you too, Elli," his voice boomed with laughter. "I just wanted to stop by to tell you I'm back in business, and I wondered if you were still looking for a summer job."

"That depends on the pay," I joked.

"Well…before we negotiate terms, you might want to know that I've taken on an additional hand in the form of a foreign exchange student so to speak," I cocked my head quizzically as he spoke. A foreign exchange student? What was he rambling about?

"His name is Ned, and I was hoping you'd show him the ropes." My eyebrows shot up in surprise, and I'm sure my mouth dropped to the ground. Mr. Martindale chuckled jovially as he stepped to the side. I could barely believe my eyes when Nedys poked his head from behind him. Thankfully, I had the fortitude not to pass out. Instead, I ran into Nedys arms, hugging him tightly, just to make sure he was real. He groaned, and I immediately released him.

"You're still hurt?" I asked, gently placing my hand on his chest. I could feel bandages beneath his shirt. Tears pricked my eyes. I couldn't bear to lose him again.

"Easy now," he said, touching my face with his hand. "No need for tears. I'll be fine. Coming back to life takes a bit of time. That's all." He withdrew his hand from my face, wrapping his fingers around my hand, which still lay on his chest.

"I might have healed faster if you'd been by me side to nurse me back to health," he smiled, and I remembered his time in the Siol tree. I reached up with my free hand to touch his face, his hair.

"You're really here," I whispered, still struggling to believe it. He bent down and kissed my lips as if to prove his existence to me. I felt my knees almost buckle and give way as a tremble raced through my body at his touch. He wrapped his arms around my waist to shore me up.

"Looks like I'm the one with the power now. You better watch out, Empress. You're in for quite a shock," he smiled again, and I thought my heart would burst as he kissed me once more.

"But how?" I asked, unable to contain my curiosity.

"Shall we say, someone intervened on me behalf," he answered, turning me toward Mr. Martindale, who was intently studying a nearby bush.

"You?"

"Guilty as charged, Elli," he admitted, returning his stare to our direction. "I was watching the whole thing unfold in my Gazer. A nasty business that. Young Nedys didn't deserve to die any more than you did."

"The flames? That was you! But Nedys was dead. His chest wasn't moving."

"He was as close to death as a person can come without actually dying. I snatched him up and transported him to a friend...er...a fellow guardian who owed me a favor. He patched him up well enough, and here we are."

"How can I ever thank you?" I asked, leaving Nedys's side to give Mr. Martindale another hug.

"I think you've thanked me enough, Elli," he replied, trying to cover a deep blush that was racing up his neck and onto his face. "The plan didn't work quite as I was expecting though. We had a stowaway."

"Stowaway?" I echoed.

"Harry." He answered simply.

"Harry?" My mind was reeling, but understanding slowly dawned on me as I watched a grin spread on Nedys's face: Hairam.

"Hairam is here?"

"He probably has my entire house disassembled by now," Mr. Martindale mumbled, "which is why I need to talk to your parents. I'd like to discuss with them the possibly of new neighbors in Leo's duplex. I'll be leaving you two alone now. I'll let myself in," he said as he disappeared into the house.

I led Nedys through the gate to the backyard, where we could have more privacy. As happy as I was to see him, I was also overcome with guilt. Nedys seemed to sense my tension.

"What's wrong, Elli?" he asked, turning my face toward his.

"Nedys, I killed your father," I blurted out.

"No, Elli. You didn't. Mr. Martindale told me all that happened after I was shot. You must realize that me father died in the war. That man was a skeleton – a ghost – but not me father."

"But I killed him. Well, I let my power kill him. I didn't fight it when I could have."

"Ellinnet, had our positions been reversed and it was you who had been hit by that arrow, which it almost was, and if I had been left behind thinking you had died – I can't say I wouldn't have killed him meself," he assured me.

The thought of his father reminded me of the necklace I wore around my neck. I pulled it out from under my shirt, tracing my fingers along the smooth, blue stone.

"Why did you leave this behind?" she asked. "It might have saved you, you know?"

"I figured if you stayed in Annyad or the forest, I'd have you, and wouldn't need it anymore. But if you came back here alone, you'd need it more than me."

"Thank you," I said, grabbing his hand. We didn't have time for more conversation because the bushes by the gate started rustling fiercely. Before we could investigate, Hairam's head appeared around the corner. My parents must have heard the racket as well because they, along with Mr. Martindale, rushed out of the house onto the back porch.

"How did you know how to find us?" Mr. Martindale asked with exasperation.

"This little guy," Hairam answered with a broad smile as he held up a GPS.

"You're like a little kid with his hand in a candy jar," Mr. Martindale said, shaking his head.

"Candy? I'd like to get me hands on some more of that," Hairam responded with a mischievous twinkle in his eye. I almost felt sorry for Mr. Martindale.

"I don't know if I can ask you to take on this kind of a burden after all you've been through," Mr. Martindale said as he turned to my parents.

"They'll have nothing to worry about, sir. I'll take care of him, just as I always have," Nedys offered with a disarming smile.

"That's my only solace, young man. I do trust you, and I trust you'll enroll him in high school for the fall. That ought to channel some of his energy, and maybe Elli can keep him out of trouble," Mr. Martindale instructed. My future was looking better and better. I had an inkling Rebecca and Hairam would get along quite well.

"It would be my pleasure, Harry," I laughed as I watched Hairam tinkering with my dad's lawnmower. Mr. Martindale shook his head with a half-hearted scowl. A person couldn't help but like Hairam.

"We'd best be off, boys. It's been a long day, and it'll be an even longer one tomorrow if we're to get you all settled into your new place," Mr. Martindale remarked. Nedys gave my hand a squeeze before letting go. He grabbed Hairam by the arm, escorting him to the gate.

"Until tomorrow, Elli," Nedys said with a smile.

"Until tomorrow," I whispered after him.

That night I was once again gazing at the stars from my ledge. I thought about all that had happened this summer, and I knew that one gumball had changed my life forever. I knew who I was. I was Ellinnet Clay, daughter of Ann and Ed Clay. I had a choice about what I would do, and who I would become. That choice gave me greater purpose in life than I ever could have imagined possible. I had been granted a second chance, and I didn't intend to squander it. I would not look at each day as though I had a thousand tomorrows ahead of me. I would live each day as though it were all my tomorrows. I was the empress of my own destiny. And I was head over heels in love with Nedys Martindale...

Author's Note

Naming characters in a work of fiction requires a certain element of creativity. Because this story flipped a fairy tale upside down by transforming the heroine into a villain rather than a princess, I decided to use that twist as my inspiration. The names of the characters and places in Elli's alternate reality are the names of members of my immediate and extended family spelled backwards. You never know what might spark your imagination!

Check out the playlist for this book on Spotify.

About the Author

Tennille Jo Mortensen grew up in rural Idaho where she developed a passion for writing as she began composing poetry and short stories at a young age. After graduating with an MBA from Idaho State University, she became a full-time mother to two daughters. While focusing on her faith and family, she draws inspiration for writing from her everyday life. She enjoys hiking, photographing waterfalls, transforming socks into unique monkeys with needle and thread, and creating memories with her husband, children, and two dogs in Portland, Oregon.